The Cuban Sanction

By J. Thomas Stovall

Keys Publishing

Franklin, NC

This is a work of fiction. The events described here are imaginary. The settings and characters are fictitious and not intended to represent specific places or living people.

Copyright © 2014 by J. Thomas Stovall
Library of Congress Cataloging-in-Publication Data
ISBN: 978-0-578-14891-5

Acknowledgments

My idea for this book began thirty years ago and was handwritten on a legal pad. Over the years, I pulled it out of my desk drawer and added a chapter or two. Finally, a year ago, I decided it was time to finish it. I hope you will find it entertaining.

I want to acknowledge and thank those who were an integral part of this process:

Diane Strickland, the love of my life, provided support, encouragement, and advice and spent unremitting hours editing, without which this book would not have been possible.

My brother, Gary Stovall, offered valuable advice and undertook the huge job of transferring the written manuscript to digital format.

My sister-in-law, Phyllis, a published author of "The Root Cellar," gave constructive advice and undying support.

I would also like to thank Neil TS Flanders, graphic artist extraordinaire, for his creativity in designing the Cuban Sanction book cover.

Tom

If you can read, you can do anything.

J. Thomas Stovall

The Cuban Sanction

Chapter One

Dark, cumulonimbus clouds had built over the Everglades and were moving toward the East Coast at about fifty miles an hour. It would be one hell of a storm. During the summertime, this was not at all unusual in South Florida. At forty thousand feet, the clouds created a premature dusk. A wide band of wind moved in front of the storm. As it moved closer, the warm breeze transformed into gusts from twenty up to seventy miles an hour. The southern half of Miami would be drenched with rain in less than ten minutes.

Two blocks down the street from the Jansen's residence, a limb extending from the trunk of a giant Banyan tree scraped against the resident's bedroom window. There was a shrill squeaking and scratching noise, then the shattering of glass, all of which went unheard throughout the empty house. The owners had been in New York for over two weeks, where they anxiously awaited the birth of their first grandchild. The shattering glass triggered a silent message from the Rollins burglar alarm to the Dade County Sheriff's sub-station on Southwest 117th Avenue.

Five-year-old Jeffrey Jansen sat in a neighbor's living room playing chess with his inseparable companion, six-year-old Dennis Strickland, a sandy-haired, blue-eyed, mischievous little boy, three months older than Jeffrey. "It's your turn," Jeffrey laughed, looking down at the board. He had all but won the game. For some reason, the closer he got to the board, the more he increased his chances of winning. He stretched out on the worn, rust-colored carpet, rolled over on his stomach, and tucked his strong but small hands under his chin. Maria, his mother, had often said that Jeffrey looked like his father, Michael, because of his fair complexion and sandy brown, sun-streaked hair. Michael had disagreed because Jeffrey possessed Maria's beautiful, warm, nugget brown eyes. They were both correct. In deep concentration, Dennis crossed his legs taking a Chief Sitting Bull position as he made his move, hoping for a chance at finally beating Jeffrey.

Jeffrey studied the board just like a Master chessman. For him, solving problems was easy. He was an exceptionally smart boy. At his kindergarten graduation, the principal presented him with the highest academic award in his school. Maria and Michael had smiled with pride at the accomplishments of their brilliant little boy. Though trying not to show it, Jeffrey was ecstatic too, even jumping around and grinning shyly through his embarrassment.

Paige Strickland, Dennis' mother, hung up the phone. A tall, slender, but not particularly attractive woman, Paige walked into the living room wearing an apron over her well-tailored, beige, light-weight pantsuit. A divorced working mother, she had just gotten home from work before the wind had started to blow. Still in her work clothes, she had rushed into the kitchen to start supper before she changed into a pair of faded denim shorts and her favorite blue Gator tee shirt.

"Jeffrey, your mom just called," Mrs. Strickland told Jeffrey. "You have to run along now before it starts to rain. Dennis, pick up the board and put it away."

Not happy about having to leave before the game was finished, Jeffrey reluctantly looked up at her and said, "Oh, Mrs. Strickland, just a few more minutes, please?" he begged.

Large drops of rain began hitting the window awnings.

"Your mother said now, honey. You better hurry, or you will get soaked!" she warned.

"Okay," he said, showing his obvious disappointment. "I'll see you later, Dennis," Jeffrey said, rushing out of the house and slamming the front door behind him.

Officer James Callahan of the Dade County Sheriff's office received a 2-11 call while parked in a 7-Eleven store parking lot about twelve blocks away from the alarm site. He had just finished writing a minor traffic accident report that involved two cars parked at the store.

Though she was at fault, Officer Callahan did not give the plump, elderly Jewish woman from New York a citation because the accident occurred on private property. He did, however, give her a harsh warning. She left the scene in her slightly dented Sedan de Ville, flustered and crying.

Callahan threw his clipboard down on the front floorboard of the passenger side and jammed the gears of the 1976 Mercury Marquis into reverse. In his haste to back out and turn around, he barely missed an ancient, blue pickup truck entering the overcrowded parking lot. With an impatient scowl on his face and an exaggerated motion of his arm, he waved the driver aside. Confused, the driver hesitated and stalled the truck. Callahan whipped the cruiser around the disabled vehicle and fishtailed it out on the street. The car quivered as it straightened up on the pavement. It began to rain.

As Callahan switched on the wipers, a grayish film streaked the windshield, impairing his vision. A few swipes later, it improved slightly. The cruiser moved through a middle-class residential area on Southwest 104th Street. Callahan momentarily removed his eyes from the wet pavement to glance down at the speedometer. The needle swept past sixty. He was approaching 97th Avenue and would have to make a right turn, so he released his pressure on the accelerator. The rain fell harder.

After Jeffrey had slammed the door, he stopped on the Strickland's porch and hesitated before running into the rainstorm. Across the street, he saw his mother open the front door and step out onto the small porch. Looking down the street and through the downpour, she shouted something to Jeffrey. In the heavy rainstorm, Jeffery failed to hear his mother's warning to be careful crossing the street.

"I'm coming, Mommy!" he yelled. Lowering his head, he dashed out into the pounding rain toward his mother.

A mother's intuition made Maria glance both ways again. To her right, she saw the fast-moving cruiser, lights off, speeding up the street. Jeffrey ran blindly across the neighbor's yard, nearing the road. A helpless terror filled Maria's stomach. Fighting back the bile, she ran with outstretched arms, palms up and flat, trying to push her son back. Jeffrey kept running, not seeing the danger of the speeding car in the pouring rain.

In that instant, Officer Callahan saw a tiny blur at his right front fender and simultaneously heard a thump. *It's probably a dog*, he thought, *without braking.*

Maria's horror-stricken eyes watched the cruiser as it knocked her son fifteen feet through the air, landing on his face.

Mrs. Strickland heard Maria's frantic screams and ran to a picture window overlooking the front yard. Maria was bent over Jeffrey in the downpour.

"Oh my God!" gasped Paige Strickland, tears filling her eyes. She rushed to the phone, and with shaking hands she dialed 911.

As Maria leaned over her son's lifeless body, water and dirt splattered into his mouth and nose. "Jeffrey! Oh my God, Jeffrey," she moaned in unbearable pain.

The vacant stare in Jeffrey's blue eyes told her that his pain was gone forever. "No! Oh no!" she sobbed uncontrollably. She sat down on the lawn in the growing puddles of water, pulling Jeffrey's head and shoulders to her lap as she began rocking him back and forth, trying to bring him back to life. Tiny groans welled up from deep within her throat, quietly at first, and then growing into animal-like screams.

Michael Jansen, Maria's husband arrived home just a few moments after the ambulance attendants had put Jeffrey and Maria in the ambulance for transport to Baptist Hospital.

In a dreamlike haze, Michael vaguely remembered being in the emergency room. Maria lay on a gurney in an austere cubicle being attended by a nurse, with Michael at her side tightly holding her hand. The emergency room staff would not let him see his son. He watched as doctors and nurses quickly rushed in and out of Jeffery's cubicle. He strained to hear the hushed whispering.

Maria fought the strong sedative a nurse had given her. Sleepily, she tried to raise herself from the stretcher, but Michael gently pushed her back, murmuring comforting words that she didn't seem to understand. Minutes seemed like hours, and an eternity later a tall, unsmiling doctor in his late twenties walked into Maria's cubicle and said, "I'm so sorry. Your son has a broken neck. There is nothing we can do."

Maria fainted. Michael supported himself on the rail of the gurney. An orderly came in and wheeled Maria off to a more private room to rest.

As Michael leaned against the door frame collecting his emotions, a sturdy hand gently touched his shoulder. He heard a stranger softly say, "I'm so sorry." Michael turned to see a medium-built, light-haired, compassionate-looking man in his mid-forties wearing a Dade County policeman's uniform. It was his first time meeting Sonny Mitchell; the officer called to the scene to investigate the accident. Looking into Sonny's somber green eyes, Michael knew that Sonny understood the depth of his pain.

There was something surreal about their first meeting. It was like father-son magnetism. Michael had never fully understood it. Could it be Sonny's strength, maybe? He wasn't sure. After Michael checked on Maria, who had finally escaped the shock and fallen asleep, Sonny walked with Michael around the colorful hospital gardens for about an hour in quiet companionship. Neither said much, but for some reason, Michael felt comforted by this kind man.

In retrospect, the days following the accident and funeral were hazy. Michael did remember asking the right questions, though. At dusk and in the rain, why didn't the officer have his headlights on? The state law said he should have. Under the stormy conditions, why had his siren and flashing beacon been off? Why hadn't he stopped to investigate the thump he felt, so he could be sure of what he had hit? Not until reaching the empty house and discovering the broken window did the officer return to the scene, where he saw two other police cars and the emergency vehicle. When the investigation was finally complete, Michael had read in the Miami Herald that the Department's Internal Affairs Department could find no evidence to substantiate the officer's negligence under the circumstances.

For three months after the funeral, there was a subtle distance between Maria and Michael. It was as if each was separately cocooned in grief. Michael felt cheated by the loss of his son. There was no justice. The killer of his son went unpunished. Everywhere he turned for help, doors slammed in his face. It was as though a silent law enforcement conspiracy worked against him. His only real comfort came from Sonny. When off duty, Sonny would sometimes stop by, and they would talk for hours. Michael knew he would never forget what Sonny's friendship had meant to him during the darkest period of his life.

One day in a state of depression, Maria said something about not wanting another child. A week later Michael came home and announced that he had undergone a vasectomy. The system would not betray them again. He had made sure of that.

It was five months after Jeffrey's death before Michael and Maria were able to make love again. Maria had cried in Michael's arms far into the night. It was as if the invisible wall between them had finally been removed.

Chapter Two

The forty-foot Hatteras lay quietly in the shallow water off Cat Island in the Bahamas. The Chubby Ann, rising and then falling slowly in the evening swells, waited. The sleek boat, long and graceful, hugged the surface like a giant sea monster. In her silent engine room waited enough power to push her massive hull an easily attainable twenty-seven knots.

The evening sun danced naked on the horizon while painting a spectral panorama on the puffy tropical clouds, its last performance of the day before going to sleep.

Captain Stan Greenlee looked up from his work. To the west, he was awestruck by the beauty of the sunset. Droplets of sweat trickled down his brow, which he frequently flicked away with a forefinger. Turning to the east, he saw thunderheads high in the sky. They were hanging over the tiny mangrove islands that speckle the edge of the Bahamas Bank. The clouds were growing and getting closer. As he knelt on the bow, checking the anchor to see if it was still holding, a cool breeze struck his tanned face announcing the coming storm.

Off the well-appointed, spacious, teak-paneled cabin below, Pete Brownstein was setting the small built-in dining table in the alcove. The lobster he and Stan had speared that afternoon bubbled in salt water on the small stove. White foam circled the boiler as a ghostly shape of steam rose to the ceiling, making the galley unbearably hot. Sitting on the back burner was a small pot of melted butter and garlic. Its aroma reminded Pete of Marcella's Italian Restaurant in North Miami, one of his favorite eating places. Pete tried to seat himself, but he had trouble sticking his long, skinny legs under the small dining table as Stan entered the galley.

"You jerk; can't you wait for me?" chided Stan.

"Hell, I'm starved," Pete retorted. "Diving makes me hungry as hell," he said as he dropped a steamy lobster on his plate before it could burn his long, grimy fingers.

Stan lowered his hefty five-foot-six-inch frame down on the bench at the overcrowded table, while fingering a cold can of Budweiser and enjoying the chill. Dumpy, with a long torso and short, stubby legs, Stan had never been called handsome. His reddish hair was about half gray. The top of his ruddy head was bald, with a thin band of hair around the sides and back that looked like wispy bird feathers.

"It looks like we've got a big one blowing this way," he said as he rolled the cold can across his sweaty forehead. "Damn! This humidity is terrible! How do you stand it down here?"

"Don't you know us skinny guys are always cold?" Pete smirked. Looking at Pete made Stan think of a stork. Over six feet tall, with long, thin arms and legs, he weighed in at about one hundred fifty-five pounds. Pete had light brown hair and sky-blue eyes and would be attractive if he put on about twenty-five pounds and took a shower once in a while. Pete always looked grubby to Stan.

Stan's hazel eyes hardened, piercing into Pete's with contempt. Stan could not remember a time in his life when he had not been overweight. Even as a child, the kids had teased him about it. They had called him tubby. He wished he could be as thin as Pete. He loved to eat, and his love of food since he was young had packed on the pounds. He had good intentions each time he decided to lose weight, but the wonderful aroma and taste of food always made him push his weight loss plan aside. *Oh well,* thought Stan, *Maybe someday.*

Focusing his attention back on Pete's comment, Stan snapped, "Go screw yourself, asshole," as he reached for a lobster.

Stan and Pete ate dinner in silence. They had nothing in common other than the task that lay ahead. This was Stan's last job. He had made enough money in the past couple of years to retire, and since the Feds had begun using the RICO Act to prosecute drug smugglers, he had decided that enough was enough. In the past, you had to get caught with the goods in your hands, but not anymore. Now, with all the new statutes, someone just had to rat you out. That was scary.

Finished, they washed and stowed the dishes, then headed topside.

On deck, Stan heavily climbed the aluminum ladder to the flying bridge. *I've got to lose some weight,* he thought again for the hundredth time. Pete went forward to work the anchor line. On the bridge, Stan propped his bulky body against the captain's chair. As he stretched for the starter buttons, he noticed that the wind had changed from the south and was briskly picking up from the east. Lightning flashed on the horizon, and the cool wind filled with moisture. It was a prelude to the oncoming squall. Suddenly, Stan felt a strange shiver of fear. *What's that about,* he thought? As he pressed the buttons, the twin Caterpillars fired with a thunderous roar.

"Stand by your line!" Stan shouted as the bow turned into the wind.

Minutes passed, and the wind gusted to fifty knots as Pete screamed at the top of his lungs, "The anchor's up!"

The storm arrived in all its fury. The rain beat down on them, stinging like hundreds of needles on their faces. The chilly rain completely engulfed them.

The storm was no surprise to Stan. He knew that in spring and summer, the weather in the Bahamas was at best highly unpredictable. Thunderstorms occur every day, usually in the afternoon or early evening. For boaters, the storms were cause for much concern. It wasn't uncommon for winds to exceed sixty or sixty-five miles an hour. They were usually fast-moving and lasted for only an hour or so, but for inexperienced captains, they were something with which to be reckoned. The danger lay in the speed and intensity with which they arrived, often catching boaters off guard and unprepared.

Blinded by rain, Pete clung to the lifeline to keep from being tossed overboard. The bow of the boat threw him up and then sideways and down again as if he were riding a wild bronco. He grappled his way along, hand over hand, until he finally worked his way back to the stern.

"Take over in the cockpit! I'm coming down!" Stan shouted.

Pete could see Stan's mouth move but could not hear him as the wind screeched around the superstructure. The rain slashed into Stan's eyes and blurred his vision as he almost slid down the ladder. Once on deck, he made his way to the main salon, shivering from the wet and cold.

"Take 090 degrees until I can get a Loran fix," he said to Pete as he shook himself free of the rain, like a wet dog coming out of a pond.

Moments later, Stan appeared with a thick towel and tossed it to Pete. "Here! You look like a drowned rat."

Stan's flabby belly pushed hard against the instrument panel as he reached to switch on the Loran. Then he turned on the CB, tuning it to Channel 26, the designated frequency for the mother ship. "The son of a bitch is gonna be hell to spot in this shit, but with a little luck the weather should clear in an hour or so," he said to no one in particular.

Pete stood in front of the wheel with his long legs spread wide apart. Standing in that position prevented him from having to stay bent over all the time. His back was already hurting from stooping through the doors. "I wish they would make these damn openings with a little more headroom," he grumbled.

A sly, narrow grin crossed Stan's face. *Being short does have its advantages at times,* he thought. He began taking readings from the Loran, correlating them on the chart. Occasionally, a wave broke over the bow, and he had to grab the edge of the chart table to brace his chubby frame. The table creaked under the strain of his weight as if crying for relief. Using a divider and parallel ruler, he worked an intercept course.

"Take 062 degrees. That should put us on target about ten minutes early," he said stepping back, pleased with his computations.

Ten o'clock was the scheduled time for the rendezvous. He looked at his watch. It was 8:55.   Carlos had told him, "Don't discuss the time or location with anyone, not even the crew. You got that?" "Yeah," he remembered saying. He did exactly as Carlos said. He did not want to see Carlos mad. About a year ago, one of the guys who had worked on his boat had disappeared after a heated confrontation with Carlos. Stan had never asked what had happened to him, but he had a fairly good idea. Stan took Carlos at his word. He didn't want to end up being fish food, which is probably what had happened to his crewman.

Stan glanced at the chart and sighed quietly to himself as if speaking might upset his destiny. He had gone to great lengths to avoid drawing suspicion from the Coast Guard.

Stan and Pete had left Miami four days earlier, departing early in the morning and going straight to Bimini. They checked in at Customs upon arriving and applied for a Trans-Aire, which is an authorization from the Bahamian government to cruise the Out Islands for up to thirty days without having to clear Customs at any other port. If checked by the Coast Guard or Bahamian officials, the boat's papers would be in order. The risky parts would be offloading and crossing the Gulf Stream back to the Florida Keys.

After obtaining the Trans-Aire, they bought more fuel at the Bimini Big Game and Fish Club. Finally, they had a hearty lunch at a popular local restaurant, which included fried conch fritters and savory fresh snapper. Just thinking about that meal made Stan's mouth water.

Departing Bimini around one o'clock in the afternoon, Stan and Pete had headed in a northerly direction. When Stan had identified Great Isaac Light, he had changed course to a southeast heading going down the eastern side of the Bahamas. The bright sun was directly overhead, and the clear, turquoise waves were gently breaking on the pure white, and in some areas pink sand beach.

They had cruised around taking their time, trolling for dolphins, changing course often, and hoping they would blend with the local fishermen. The Coast Guard seldom ventured close to the bank where the water was usually too shallow for their deeper draft boats. More than once smugglers had outsmarted the Coast Guard after reaching the bank, and that was what Stan was counting on.

In the master stateroom, Pete straightened his bird-like figure as best he could under the low ceiling and moved ahead, not looking forward to the task at hand. He recognized he was by no means a good sailor, but he liked working on the boat, and Stan was a worthy skipper, even if he was downright rude to Pete at times. The only negative thing about being on the boat was when the weather got rough, he was continuously seasick, sometimes to the point where he could hardly function. Since the arrival of the massive squall, he felt queasy and was sure the next half an hour's work in confined quarters would certainly finish him.

Forward of the master stateroom, half in and half out of the forward storage locker, Pete found three 200-foot rolls of polyurethane plastic and four rolls of duct tape. Backing out of the cramped space, he walked back to the large master stateroom and began unrolling the plastic. Each folded roll measured twelve feet wide by two hundred feet long. The difficult part was unfolding the plastic. Each time he tried to spread the sheet, it kept clinging to the remaining roll due to the inherent static electricity. After several attempts, he took one side and held it up to the overhead and then started taping it to the bulkhead. One side completed, he straightened out the Visqueen and spread it over the bunks and onto the carpeted deck. The idea was to keep the boat clean of marijuana residue. With the vessel unloaded, all they had to do was scoop up the plastic and the boat would be clean.

All at once, Pete's nausea became overpowering. He burst out of the cabin holding his hand over his mouth. His eyes bulged. His only hope was that he could make it to the fantail without vomiting.

Vomiting off the side of the fantail wasn't easy. Pete eventually staggered into the cockpit with the remaining plastic. Bleary-eyed and looking like a dead man, he groaned, "What do you want me to do with the rest of this crap?"

Crap! thought Stan. *I still have to tell him everything.* "Throw it over the side! Just don't get it tangled in the props!" Stan told Pete harshly.

Bristling at the rebuke, Pete nodded and left the cockpit. Out of earshot, he muttered, "Stan can be such a prick sometimes."

Pete's not the only one who's queasy, thought Stan as he squinted into the darkness trying to gauge the height of the enormous waves. It was nearly impossible. He guessed they were about eight to ten feet high. "It'll take some tricky boat handling to keep this baby in one piece while it's next to the mother ship," he mumbled to himself, before quickly stepping out of the bridge to vomit over the side. God, he hated these storms.

"January Delta, January Delta, this is Ditty Box November. Over," said Stan. The only reply on the radio was squelch and static. Stan repeated the call.

"Screw it," he finally said. "They're probably still out of range."

14

As Pete walked back to the bridge, Stan said, "Pete! Take the wheel for a minute." His voice had an edge to it. "I want to take another fix to see how close we are."

Always surprised by Stan's frequent outbursts, Pete hated it when Stan barked at him. *Just because Stan is suffering from anxiety doesn't mean he has to take it out on me,* Pete thought. He understood that as the rendezvous got closer, they would be beyond the point of no return. With the boat loaded, there could be no changing their minds. They would be committed.

As Pete worked the wheel, Stan plotted another fix. The dividers dropped from his hand to the chart, and he looked at Pete. "We're just about in position," he said.

"Want me to cut her back?" Pete asked.

"Yeah, go ahead."

Pete pulled the throttles back to slow. He had to maintain just enough steerage to keep the bow in the waves.

"All we can do now is to wait and keep trying to raise her on the CB," Stan said.

Stan walked like a drunken man, balancing his bulk to counteract the rolling motion of the boat. Still feeling queasy, he slowly walked toward the wheel to stand beside Pete, who also looked a little pale.

The men peered through the cabin windows and gazed into the empty darkness. The only sounds they heard were the high winds whistling through the superstructure, the low rumbling of the engines, the giant waves breaking against the bow of the boat, and the static on the radio. A red glow emanating from the compass light and digital readouts on the Loran and radio tuner cast its dim light throughout the cockpit. It looked like a ghostly spaceship.

As the boat rolled from side to side in the twelve-foot waves, both men fought the spasms of seasickness. Each tried to control the urge to vomit again. Pete's condition was considerably worse than Stan's. Heavy seas were tolerable while underway, but many a seasoned sailor could not take the rolling back-and-forth motion that all ships encounter while drifting in an angry sea. Pete and Stan were no exceptions.

Stan picked up the microphone to transmit, "January Delta, this is Ditty Box November. Do you read me? Over." said Stan again.

Seconds later a clear, foreign voice replied. "Ditty Box November, this is January Delta. I read you. Over."

The two men could hardly believe how clear the heavily accented Spanish voice sounded.

Crap!, they are on top of us, thought Stan. "Roger," he replied. "Turn your running lights on for ten seconds so I can locate you. Over."

"Okay. Over," said the voice.

The two men looked through the windows searching for the lights. Stan stood on the port side, and Pete on the starboard. Twenty seconds later Stan exclaimed. "There she is, just off the port quarter!"

"Son of a bitch!" Pete said excitedly. "We're lucky we didn't run into them. She can't be more than fifty yards."

Stan squinted through the window. Accumulated salt deposits and water droplets were on the glass, making it difficult to determine the direction the freighter was moving.

"January Delta, what's your heading? Over."

"My heading is 050 degrees. Over," said the detached voice on the other end.

Based on his experience, Stan knew that docking two boats next to one another in rough weather could be extremely dangerous and possibly fatal. He pictured how each boat would be rising and falling in the mountainous swells. His vivid imagination could see the larger freighter towering over them, crashing down, tearing, and grinding metal against fiberglass and crushing them into the darkest depths of the Atlantic. He quickly pushed that unimaginable scenario out of his mind.

"January Delta?"

"Yes." said the voice.

"I think we should wait a couple of hours or at least until daylight to make the transfer because of the high seas. Over." said Stan.

There was a long pause, and then the Spanish voice jumped out of the box like a machine gun in rapid fire.

"No! We have other commitments up the coast and a schedule to keep! We cannot wait! Take your merchandise now or forget it."

Damn, thought Stan. *That son of a bitch!* He had to make a fast decision. *What would Carlos do if they came back empty-handed? He would go crazy!* Stan had seen Carlos angry before.

As if it were a computer, Stan's mind raced, trying to sort out the problem and produce a solution. All at once, he knew how simple it would be.

"January Delta, have your line handlers stand by their lines," he told the Spanish voice.

Pete looked at Stan in disbelief.

"Steer three points off the wind and try to maintain about two knots," Stan said. "I'll be the maneuvering vessel. Over."

"Roger," replied the voice.

"Pete, there's some canvas in the engine room. Get it up here right away!" Stan said hurriedly. "We'll have to make a chute."

"You're full of shit!" Pete protested. "It won't work."

"Do as I say, damn it, or I'll have your ass!" Stan commanded.

Pete left the cabin feeling like a scolded dog. After struggling with the heavy canvas, he braced himself on the stern and began cutting the material. He cut a section six feet wide and forty feet long. At each corner, he tied a quarter-inch nylon line twenty feet long.

The Chubby Ann began closing in on the freighter. As they approached it, Stan and Pete could see mass confusion on the rear deck. The crew looked like black ants scurrying around an ant mound. Even with the chaos, a semblance of order appeared. Under the bright cargo lights, twenty-odd Columbians ran about the deck, lifting cargo hatches and moving canvas. All were black, bare-chested men with their pants rolled up to their knees. Some wore sandals, but most were barefoot.

Stacked beside a fifty-five-gallon drum were two crates of live chickens, presumably part of the crew's daily menu. Most Columbian boats had no refrigeration, and the chickens provided the crew with fresh meat and soup. Finally, getting a good look at the huge boat, Stan thought, *My God, how does that thing stay afloat?*

He could not see one speck of paint on the dilapidated boat. The only coat it ever had was probably put on at the time of its commissioning at least thirty years ago. He imagined how she must look on the inside. If outside appearance was a barometer, she defied all principles of flotation.

The Columbian captain was performing a superb job of keeping the enormous ship off the wind. The freighter was riding comfortably at its present heading minimizing her roll.

Stan maneuvered the Chubby Ann within thirty feet of the larger ship. The freighter's main deck was at least twelve feet higher than the Chubby Ann's. As the big ship rolled away from him, her deck would rise at an alarming rate, higher and higher, until the Columbians standing on her deck disappeared. One mistake in Stan's steering would be catastrophic. He had to mentally calculate each wave, judge the roll of the freighter, and anticipate the reactions of the Chubby Ann, all while the two vessels rolled side-by-side in the tumultuous seas. Each wave was different and required Stan's full concentration. All his senses were tuned to his boat. He felt every vibration as the boat crashed into each wave, and he heard the straining of the engines when the propellers dug into the water. His intense concentration made the other events taking place around him essentially non-existent.

Pete stood ready on the stern with a monkey fist in his hand, ready to throw it when the time was right. As the freighter turned in his direction, he drew his arm back and threw the line as hard as he could. Five Columbians, each holding onto the freighter's lifeline, their straining eyes probing the gloomy night, watched as Pete heaved the line. From out of the darkness, the twine-covered weight hit the immense ship's deck with a thud. The Columbians began pulling the canvas chute from the Chubby Ann through the air and across the twenty-foot expanse of water.

In minutes, bales of marijuana were shooting down the slide, one at a time. Eight Columbians held the canvas. They walked together, back, and forth, taking up the slack with each roll of the two ships. The rest of the crew formed a human chain, passing the bales hand over hand from the cargo hole to the edge of the deck. The lead Columbian had one leg wrapped around a lifeline stanchion. When handed a bale, he leaned over the side and dropped the bundle into the chute. Sometimes when he misjudged a roll, the chute, dragging in the middle, would catch a wave, dumping its contents in the ocean.

Each bale weighed between forty-five and sixty pounds. As a bale slid down the chute and gathered momentum, its force was powerful enough to knock the strongest of men to the deck and would certainly cripple Pete if one should hit him.

"Shit!" grunted Pete. He would kick a broken package aside as fast as he could, continually watching for the next projectile.

For over an hour, Pete worked like a madman. Picking up another bale, he began stacking it aside, making room for the next. Sweating and cursing, his mind was oblivious to the time. Exhausted after the last bale had fallen, he cut the chute away and collapsed on the deck.

Stan heard Pete say, "Clear!"

Stan spun the wheel to starboard. Each moment's danger decreased as the two ships separated. When the Chubby Ann reached a safe distance from the freighter, Stan turned the boat into the wind and switched on the automatic pilot. Relieved that the transfer was over, he went aft for a few minutes to rest with Pete.

Exhausted, Pete laid spread eagle on the hard deck. He groaned,

"My fucking back is killing me!"

Spotting the closest live well, Stan lowered his bulk on the cushioned seat and said, "Well, don't get too comfortable. We still have to move all this forward."

"I don't think I could drag my ass that far if I had to," grumbled Pete. Then, as if he suddenly remembered, he sat up with a smile on his face and said, "We're gonna be rich! Rich, man!"

Stan stood and slapped Pete on the back. "Tell you what, fix us some coffee while I work out our return plan, and then I'll help you move this stuff forward. Okay?"

"Forget the coffee. Let's roll a joint."

"You touch that, and I'll throw your ass overboard! That's a promise!" retorted Stan.

"Damn it, Stan! I can't believe it."

"You just make the coffee," Stan ordered. "Until we finish this work, I don't want you screwed up. Understand?"

"Yeah, I understand," Pete mumbled. He turned and went below.

Stan leaned over the chart table and planned the new course. He smelled the wonderful aroma of fresh brewing coffee competing with the stench of pot. His stomach grumbled loudly reminding him how long it had been since he and Pete had eaten those lobsters.

"Hey Pete," Stan yelled, "Bring some of those sweet rolls with you when you come up." *That will hold me until I can eat a proper meal,* he thought.

Stan walked to the pilot wheel, disconnected the automatic pilot, and turned the Chubby Ann to a new course of 225 degrees. As he steadied on the new course, he switched on the autopilot and running lights.

Feeling relieved, he said aloud, "Now I can enjoy my coffee."

The boat rode smoothly in the sea. Once the storm abated, the wind and sea had rapidly calmed. Both men were tired, and their seasickness had finally subsided.

Stan checked his watch. Sunrise would be at 6:40, just under four hours. He had calculated their route to take them in with the local charter boats returning home from a night's fishing.

Pete came back up with coffee and sweet rolls and stood with Stan beside the wheel. "What are we gonna do if we run into the Coast Guard?"

"There's not much that we can do," Stan shrugged. "If they want to come aboard, we're screwed, that's all. Of course, they usually don't mess with you unless they see something suspicious looking."

"What do you mean?" asked Pete with a puzzled look on his face.

"Well, if a boat is overloaded, her water line is low in the water, and they will probably notice it. They'll also notice if the steering is erratic, too. You'd be surprised at how many guys go out and get loaded and come back in so messed up they can't even see straight. That's why I don't allow any smoking on my boat."

"What about us? Do you think we're okay?" Pete said a little uneasily.

Stan sensed Pete's nervousness and said, "I don't think we have anything to worry about as long as nothing mechanical goes wrong. We're not overloaded, and the boat wasn't beat up during the loading. Why?"

"Oh, I don't know. I just keep getting this creepy feeling, that's all. I can't really explain it."

"Well, if it'll ease your mind, the hardest part is over. We cross the Gulf Stream, and then it's smooth sailing the rest of the way."

As Pete leaned against the instrument panel, he heard a rumble that sounded like thunder in the distance. The hum of the twin diesels disguised the direction from which it came.

"What is that?" Pete asked, straightening up and looking a little anxious.

"What?"

"That racket that sounds like an engine backfiring."

"I didn't hear anything," Stan said calmly sipping his coffee. He was unaware of what was about to happen.

Suddenly, Stan looked at Pete as they both heard the sound. Stan's body stiffened, his ears alert as he listened and tried to detect any irregularity in his boat's engines. The next rumble came even closer. Both reached the same conclusion at the same time. The sound they heard was not their engines. It was the engines of another boat.

Stan ran to the port window. Confusion and alarm were in his eyes as he said, "My God, what's happening? Who is that?"

Not more than ten feet off their port quarter, maneuvering to come alongside, was a forty-two-foot Cigarette ocean racer. Directly astern, riding in its wake, Stan saw a thirty-nine-foot Wellcraft speedboat. Three men wearing foul weather suits rode in each boat.

Pete rushed out of the main salon. The magnitude of what was happening escaped him. Unknowingly, he took his last step through the door. As his foot touched the wet deck, his eyes momentarily stared in disbelief as a burst of bullets from an AR-15 entered his head from the front. A microsecond later, his head disintegrated into mush against the bulkhead. His long body tumbled grotesquely onto the transom.

As Pete's lifeless body hit the deck, two menacing Cubans sprang from the deck of the Cigarette racer onto the stern of the Chubby Ann.

In a numbing state of shock, Stan slowly turned from the window to face the intruders as they entered the cabin. *My God, I know him,* thought Stan, looking into one of the men's eyes. The blast of the automatic shotgun was deafening as Stan's legs almost separated from his body. Indeed, it was Stan Greenlee's last trip.

Chapter Three

Crowded with people, the luxurious room's occupants each had a single purpose, and that was to win. Some wore expensive dress attire, but most were dressed in fashionable, casual apparel, the best money could buy. Gucci, Yves St. Laurent, and other well-known designer brands adorned many of the rumored rich and famous privileged, along with sparkling diamonds and gold Presidential Rolex watches. These brand names and expensive trinkets represented status, which may or may not have existed. Even with all the glamour and beautiful people, a pervading tension dominated the gathering. No one knew what the particular outcome would be, but whatever it was, each wanted to look his or her best. It was critical to keep up appearances. About half of the crowd represented the "old money group," some at the tables to increase their wealth, and others hoping to regain it. The rest of the assemblage, secretly hoping to hit the jackpot, put on a show, concealing the fact that they were broke by gambling as though the money they were losing was insignificant. All their hopes and dreams were contingent upon a lucky roll of the dice.

Carlos Martinez sat in the number five blackjack chair. He was no exception. His losses in the forty-five odd minutes he had played were huge, yet insignificant compared to the amounts he pondered in his mind. He did not like crowded places or the high-flying nightlife that Las Vegas offered. He would have preferred being at home in Miami or at his ranch in Costa Rica training his champion cocks, however, his appearance here was necessary and a calculated decision. Sonny Mitchell had suggested they meet here, so he had capitalized on the invitation. Miami could wait. Carlos had big plans for his future, and though boring, this was just one of many steppingstones on the path to attaining his dream. He was going to be rich, and he didn't care what he had to do to achieve it.

A muscular and rather handsome Cuban refugee with a quick smile that hid a Machiavellian personality, Carlos had arrived in Miami in September of 1962, at the youthful age of nineteen. The Cuban missile crisis was at its peak, and the Central Intelligence Agency was desperately seeking bilingual Cuban recruits who were sympathetic to the United States, particularly those who were willing to infiltrate Cuba and help the resistance pass information back to the State Department. The position suited Carlos. Carlos knew that eventually, he would make the right contacts, and ultimately one of those contacts would make him wealthy. He didn't care if it was legal or not.

Upon clearing U.S. Immigration, and after countless FBI debriefings, Carlos had been recruited into the fascinating, if not shadowy world of the CIA. There had been intensive training in the Florida Everglades and the upper and lower Florida Keys. Completing his indoctrination, he made numerous clandestine trips to Cuba, each one top secret. The final and most difficult phase of each operation was getting back into South Florida undetected. Penetrating the Florida coast was his specialty. Public opinion was sensitive to the situation; therefore, the CIA cloaked its activities under the shadow of night.

Michael and Maria Jansen walked through the ornate casino. Its lofty ceilings covered an enormous room, which housed game tables such as poker, blackjack, and roulette. For those who didn't particularly care for card games, there were a variety of slot machines and random number ticket games, such as bingo and keno. Michael felt comfortable in the sophisticated surroundings. They were an extension of his ego. As his beautiful wife walked beside him, the thought flashed through his mind of how hard he had worked, and the risks he had taken to indulge in this luxury. Three years ago, none of this would have been possible, not before meeting Sonny.

Michael Jansen was not a traditionally handsome man. Most people would probably consider him "average or a little above." The gentleness of his dark blue eyes softened his somewhat hard facial tones, which were accentuated by the automatic tensing of the jaw muscles of his oval face. Because of his high cheekbones and tanned body, people sometimes commented that he probably had a little Cherokee in him, but he knew better. His high cheekbones and naturally fair skin had come from his mother, whose ancestors had been Scandinavian. The years in the Florida sun had highlighted his sandy brown hair and turned his oval face bronze. Michael's one hundred sixty-eight pounds perfectly fit his five-foot-ten-inch frame. Lean and sinewy, his broad shoulders were developed from years of scuba diving and water skiing. A kind man by nature, Michael was quiet-spoken, even-tempered, and easy to like, unless he was pushed in a corner.

Sonny Mitchell had once told him, "Damn it, Michael! You're in the wrong business. You're too soft-hearted and lack the backbone for the job." Of course, that had been almost three years ago, and over the years Michael knew he had gotten tougher. He wanted and needed Sonny's respect, but he couldn't completely change his nature. He was aware of his shortcomings and usually gave the other person the benefit of the doubt. He rejected the idea that respect out of fear was the only workable principle in a world where men would take advantage of you, or even sometimes kill you for the slightest reason.

Sonny had said to Michael a couple of years before, "It's only a matter of time before somebody tries to screw you, Michael. Then what are you gonna do?"

On several occasions, Michael had wrestled with those words and his conscience, thinking about just how far he would go to retaliate or protect what was his. Not wanting to face the inevitable, he rationalized his feelings into a false sense of security.

As the young couple slowly walked together, Michael looked down at Maria, and a sudden surge of desire pulsed through his body. His love and admiration for her was unparalleled, far greater than any he had ever experienced with anyone else. Her deep brown, heavily lashed Spanish eyes sparkled, radiating confidence, sincerity, and love. Moist lips framed her perfectly formed white teeth when she smiled. Maria's long, black, shining hair flowed softly over her bare shoulders, accenting flawless, honey-colored skin. Her well-formed perfect breasts, narrow waist, and rounded hips filled the disco dress that had been designed in New York and expertly tailored by her personal seamstress in Miami. Many appreciative stares followed her as they walked through the gaming room. Michael was aware of them, and a brief smile tugged at the corners of his mouth. He knew that what he and Maria shared could never be challenged.

As they approached the blackjack tables, Michael spotted Carlos sitting alone playing against the dealer. Carlos appeared deep in concentration, but Michael sensed his mind was probably somewhere else. Carlos was not Michael's favorite person. There was something about him that made Michael want to keep his distance, but so far, he had not expressed his doubts to Sonny. Michael did not trust Carlos, and he knew that eventually he would show his true colors. For now, though, Michael would just watch and wait.

Brushing away the nagging feeling about Carlos and taking a position next to Maria on Carlos' left, he said, "How are you doing?"

"Not worth a damn," Carlos said with a negligible Cuban accent. "I've been sitting here for over an hour and haven't won more than four hands."

"How much are you down?" Maria asked with a smile, shifting to the stool beside Carlos.

"Oh, maybe eight thousand or so," grumbled Carlos.

Michael seated himself beside Maria. He asked the dealer for a marker for five thousand dollars. The dealer acknowledged the request and gave a silent nod to the pit boss, who immediately appeared with a blank form for him to sign.

Michael usually had a wad of cash when they came to the casino, so Maria asked, "What's a marker?"

Leaning back in his chair, Michael said, "It's a blank check. I got tired of carrying all that cash, so when we registered at the hotel, I deposited some money in the cage over there where all the windows are. Those are the cashiers," he said and pointed beyond the roulette tables. "When you want some chips, the pit boss brings you a voucher to sign against your account. It's strictly for the convenience of the players."

Carlos leaned forward and looked at Michael. "Bullshit! The real reason is that when people sign vouchers, they tend to forget how much money they've pulled from their accounts. It assures the house a bigger take."

Michael did not particularly agree, so he just shrugged and turned to sign the marker as five thousand dollars in chips was counted out to him. The dealer began dealing the cards. As he pulled them from the shoe, Maria conservatively placed a twenty-five-dollar chip on the green velvet table. Michael thought for a moment and then followed Maria's bet with a hundred dollars. Carlos pushed out his usual five hundred in chips. As the cards came around, Maria's totaled fifteen. Michael had fifteen and Carlos had twelve. The dealer showed sixteen, so the three players held their bets. As the final cards were dealt, Maria, in her conservative and decisive manner, held at seventeen. Michael unhesitatingly took a hit and busted with twenty-three. Carlos busted with twenty-two. The dealer, holding at sixteen, drew another card and busted with the ten of spades. Maria and the house were the only winners.

Maria giggled, raised an eyebrow, and with a look of female superiority said, "Well, tough guys, that's why a woman should always manage the money."

"Like hell," protested Michael with a frown. "Are you telling me I don't know play how to blackjack?"

"Of course not, sweetheart," Maria mimicked in a Southern drawl and continued, "It's just that 'us little ole things' have a better sense of the odds, that's all."

Walking up to Carlos, the pit boss said, "Excuse me, Mr. Martinez. There's a phone call for you on the house phone. If you'll follow me, I'll be happy to show you where it's located."

"Thanks," Carlos replied rising from his chair. He handed the pit boss a five-dollar chip.

The man glanced down at the chip.

"Right this way, Sir." The pit boss bowed slightly, thinking to himself what a cheap ass this guy was. *I've watched him lose more than nine thousand dollars in less than half an hour, and he's got the audacity to give me a measly five dollars! Rich people are all alike. I wonder how many people he screwed to get his money,* he thought with loathing.

Like the casino, the lounge was lavishly decorated. Carlos noticed a large-breasted blonde standing behind the bar as the pit boss pointed a stubby finger toward the white, French-style telephone by the cash register.

"Thanks," nodded Carlos to the pit boss.

Disgusted, but not showing it to the casino guest, the pit boss turned and left.

Carlos rested his muscular two hundred pounds on a stool and picked up the receiver. He eyed the blonde while he waited for the operator to answer. The smiling blonde steadily returned his gaze. *Part-time hooker,* he thought.

"Good evening, this is the hotel operator, May I help you?"

"Yes. My name is Carlos Martinez. You have a call for me?"

"Oh, yes, Mr. Martinez. One moment, please."

A familiar voice answered. "Hey," Sonny Mitchell said.

Impatiently, Carlos snapped, "Where the hell are you? I've been waiting for you all day!"

"Well, I guess I got a little sidetracked," Sonny said, laughing.

"Where are you?" Carlos did not attempt to disguise his irritation.

"I'm at the cages here in the hotel. I just got in. Boy, you should see what I brought you! Two of the most beautiful baby dolls you've ever seen," he laughed. "Are Michael and Maria here?"

"Yeah, they're here," Carlos responded with a little less irritation.

"Good. Round them up and meet me in Suite 2135. I'll introduce you to the girls."

Still not pacified, Carlos angrily returned the receiver to its cradle. Dismissing all thoughts of the blonde, he left the bar in search of Michael and Maria. He found them at the blackjack tables gathering their winnings.

"Chubby's here," Carlos said. "He wants us to meet him upstairs."

"I figured that would be him," Michael replied.

"Damn it!" Carlos grumbled. "He's got two broads with him."

"Looks like you're in for a busy night," Maria teased.

Slouched in a comfortable chair, Sonny Mitchell relaxed, sipping his drink, while the girls busied themselves behind the bar pouring champagne from a freshly chilled bottle of Dom Perignon.

The deluxe, oversized Presidential Suite was decorated in ivory and pale blue. On the right side of the entrance was a wet bar containing every brand of liquor imaginable. In the far corner of the room was a beautiful, black Steinway grand piano. Across from the piano sat a large couch covered in ivory velour, with coordinating pillows complementing the numerous chairs in ivory and blue print, strategically placed around the room. Centered in front of the couch was a massive Aubusson rug, in several shades of ivory and blue, with soft pink accents. An elegant crystal chandelier cast soft shadows over the room, blending with indirect light from two French-style lamps, one at each end of the couch, sitting on cherry tables. Contrasting this symmetry, Sonny's scuffed cowboy boots were carelessly thrown aside in the corner.

As the trio entered the room, Sonny looked up and a faint smile flickered across his face. He eased out of the chair and stood in the middle of the room to greet his guests. He cocked his head to one side, and with a boyish grin he watched the reaction of the group. He hoped their first impression of the girls would be positive. Smiling, Sonny stretched out his arms to Maria.

"Hey, Little Bit," he said.

Maria casually walked toward him as she glanced about the suite. She saw the girls standing behind the bar. She went willingly into Sonny's outstretched arms, tiptoed, and kissed him on the cheek.

"Hi, Chubby," Maria said fondly.

Carlos and Michael stood silent and waited to be introduced to Ruth and Margaret.

Ruth was the prettier of the two. She stood about five feet six inches tall, with rosy cheeks, large walnut eyes, and long auburn hair surrounding an astoundingly angelic face.

Margaret, in contrast, was almost six feet tall. Carlos guessed her age to be about thirty. In his opinion, she was on the skinny side. He did not personally find her physically appealing, but she exhibited excellent taste in clothing, which enhanced her slender figure.

Carlos walked over to Ruth. Reaching out, he pulled her to him. He put his arm around her and looked into her dark eyes. "Well, Sonny, where did you find the girls?"

Sonny's face beamed, knowing the confrontation was past. "You guys aren't gonna believe this," he said, seating himself on the nearest bar stool. "I was at the boarding gate in Miami on my way to Los Angeles. Ruth was in line ahead of me getting her seat assignment. I saw her leave the counter and walk over to Margaret."

"Ruth and I still have two days before we have to return to the studio," Margaret said.

Sonny laughed and added that he had looked around the terminal for a second, stuck the money in his pocket, and had gone over to the two girls to explain the change in their seating arrangements. 'It went slick as hell."

"For a minute I thought he was crazy," interjected Ruth.

"He is," Michael smiled.

"So, here we are." Ruth and Margaret were sound engineers at a major recording studio in Los Angeles. Both were thrilled to be away from the demanding artists with whom they had to deal for a few days.

Smiling, Sonny said, "When I reached the counter, I pointed to Ruth and asked the agent where he had seated the girls. He said something about coach, so I told him to put them in first class with me. I paid him the difference in their tickets. Then I slipped him a hundred-dollar bill, and boy, you should have seen his face, Michael," Sonny said laughing. "The guy was squirming all over the place." Ruth failed to catch the joke.

"I didn't know what to think either," Margaret said.

"Anyway," Sonny continued, "by the time we got to Los Angeles, all three of us were shit-faced. We were having such a fun time that I invited them to spend a couple of days. We missed the connecting flight on Hughes Air West, so I chartered a Learjet," explained Sonny. "You know, Michael, as soon as we can get rid of the Queen Air, we ought to look into buying one. Damn, they're nice!"

It was apparent the first-class tickets, Learjet, presidential suite, and champagne were working their magic on Ruth and Margaret, just as Sonny had intended. Each fluttered around the bar taking care of Sonny's every need.

Several minutes of casual conversation ensued. Michael rose from his stool and motioned for Carlos and Sonny to follow. "Hey, guys, I think we need to make a few phone calls, don't you?"

They left Maria and the two girls to themselves and entered the master bedroom. Decorated in dark blue, light blue, and ivory, the room was stunning. Ornate crown molding encircled a ten-foot ceiling. The walls were painted in an incredibly soft light blue. A beautiful, thick, deeply quilted dark blue bedspread covered the plush mattress of an ivory French provincial king-sized bed. Six plush pillows in equal light and dark blue stripes rested against the headboard. Carlos and Michael took seats in matching, striped high-back chairs, next to the sliding glass door framing the balcony. Sonny perched himself on the edge of the bed, and without looking up began reading the direct-dialing instructions printed on the bedside phone.

"How did things go in L.A.?" Carlos asked.

"Good, really good," Sonny answered leafing through his wallet. "I picked up four hundred fifty-five thousand from Dave. That leaves him owing us for about three thousand pounds. His collections have been running a little slow, but he said he'd have the rest of the money by the end of the week. No problem."

Michael crossed his legs. "Why don't we have him deliver the rest of the money in Miami when he comes down in two weeks? I don't see any need to make a special trip out there just to pick up six hundred grand when he'll be in Miami a week later. Shit, Sonny, let him take the transportation risks. Besides, the deal was he'd deliver the money in Miami."

"That's right, Michael, but Dave's one of the best buyers we have, and now he's busier than a cat in heat. Any favors we do for him will help solidify a long-term relationship."

Carlos stood and walked over to look out the sliding glass door.

"Sonny, I promised Mehejas he'd have his money four weeks after the load came in."

Then Carlos turned to look at Sonny. "Five weeks have passed, and now the son of a bitch is screaming for his money. If Dave keeps screwing around with more delays, we're going to have a real problem on our hands."

"Okay," Sonny sighed, leaning back on the bed. "Michael, you fly out next week and pick up the balance. I'll call Dave first thing in the morning and make sure he understands our situation."

"Where's the money you picked up today?" Carlos asked.

"I dropped it off at the cage when I checked in. I ran into Billy in the back office, and he said he'd have it all in hundreds by morning."

"Michael, what's this number?" Sonny asked, pointing to a phone number as he handed Michael a small black book he had taken from his wallet. "I lost my glasses at the airport, and now I can't see a damn thing."

Michael read the number aloud. Sonny dialed the Miami number. While Sonny waited for the phone to be answered, he asked. "Have you guys heard anything yet?"

"Nothing so far," Carlos said, sounding disappointed.

"They should be in by now," Michael said. "The boat was expected just after dark."

Sonny's attention turned to the phone as someone on the line said, "Hello."

"Hey, Asshole!" Sonny laughed into the phone. "How're you doing?"

Carlos and Michael sat back and curiously watched Sonny go into his salesman routine. As usual, he dominated the conversation. Michael pulled a pack of Winston's from his pocket and lit one. As he inhaled deeply, he pondered the silent conflict between Carlos and Sonny. Michael knew Carlos was upset with Sonny. Carlos felt that Sonny did not take the business as seriously as he should have. It seemed that all he wanted to do was party and chase pussy. It burdened the others in the group because they had to take over Sonny's responsibilities. Carlos had too easily forgotten that Sonny had given him his first opportunity to work and had taught Carlos everything he knew about the business. In Michael's mind, Carlos's impatience revealed undercurrents of hidden ambition. Though he never spoke to Sonny about it, Michael intuitively knew that Carlos was cold and greedy.

Michael had recently confided his negative feelings about Carlos to Maria. He respected her judgment of people, and together they had concluded that Carlos' integrity was very questionable. Michael knew he had to watch Carlos closely. He thought about discussing the problem with Sonny, but he dismissed the idea, knowing Sonny would think Michael was jumping to conclusions. Now, Michael wished he had confronted Sonny with his opinion of Carlos. Tonight, there was an unidentifiable, steely look in Carlos' eyes, which troubled Michael. Michael's instincts were never wrong, and he had to find out if Carlos was up to something before, he discussed it with Sonny.

While Sonny spoke on the phone, Carlos and Michael remained silent, each with his own thoughts.

"All right," Sonny was saying, "keep everybody on standby. If you haven't heard anything by morning, have Uncle Bob get Sierra Mike in the air, okay?"

"Yeah, I'll talk with you in the morning," Sonny said, confidently and hung up the phone.

"What's the word?" Michael asked.

"Don't know yet," Sonny said looking puzzled. "Stan hasn't shown up, and John hasn't been able to raise him on the radio." Damn!" exclaimed Michael. "I don't like it."

"Maybe Stan had trouble making contact and is waiting one more night," Carlos said. "He's probably just being cautious."

"No, I doubt that" Sonny sighed. "We'll just have to sit tight and see what happens tomorrow." Sonny had confidence in Stan. He was a good captain, and he wouldn't have taken any unnecessary chances, but Sonny had a strange feeling that whatever had happened had been beyond Stan's control.

"C'mon. There's nothing we can do for now," Sonny said, rising from the bed. "Let's get something to eat."

As the three men walked back into the living room, Maria noticed Michael's worried look. Sensing something was wrong, she snuggled up against him.

"Is everything okay?" she whispered.

"I don't think so," Michael replied quietly. "The Chubby Ann is missing."

Chapter Four

Ten miles due east of Florida Power & Light Company's Turkey Point Nuclear Power Plant, on the south end of Biscayne Bay at Homestead, Florida, two high-speed ocean racers fully loaded with marijuana made their approach into the lower bay. The boats separated and headed toward their respective entrances.

The sleek Cigarette boat entered Caesar's Creek just below Elliott Key. The channel, between forty and seventy feet wide, had shoals on each side and required an experienced captain familiar with the area, particularly at night and at fifty miles an hour.

The second boat, a thirty-nine-foot Wellcraft, entered Angelfish Creek just south of where the Cigarette had entered. A narrow and winding channel about one mile long, Angelfish Creek flowed to the Atlantic through a series of mangroves with numerous tributaries that ran in various directions. As the boat entered the mangroves, its spotlight moved from side to side, allowing the captain to determine the center of the channel. The Wellcraft leaned precariously on her side as she screamed around a sharp bend, spraying water twenty feet in the air. Abruptly, she straightened and prepared for her next maneuver. Any knowledgeable observer would have realized that these maneuvers had been practiced many times.

Erupting from the mangroves, the two boats turned south and headed down the Intracoastal Waterway to the Florida Keys, past Key Largo, and on to Tavernier. The lead boat slowed to a moderate speed and then turned into a privately maintained canal. She finally settled to idle speed, which reduced her exhaust noise. The boats entered a narrow channel about forty feet wide, where there were houses, small docks, and boat ramps on either side. The Cigarette quietly pulled up to a small, reinforced concrete dock. In the dim light, two Cuban men stepped out of the boat and quickly secured her bow and stern lines to the dock.

The Wellcraft continued down the Intracoastal until she reached Islamorada. There she slowed, entering a similar canal.

Chapter Five

After dinner, Sonny and his group were escorted by the maître d' to the Caribbean Room in the Tropicana Hotel. Sonny gave the maître d' a two-hundred-dollar tip to arrange a front-row table for them.

A typical Las Vegas variety extravaganza, the entertainment included long-legged beautiful girls, all topless and each having large, firm breasts, most no doubt the result of modern plastic surgery. The hotel spared no expense for its production. The management wanted the guests to have pleasant memories of their time at the hotel and not leave with antipathy about the place where they may have lost thousands of dollars. If one had to lose, management's goal was to amuse while it was happening, which made good business sense.

When the show was almost over, Carlos excused himself after complaining that his dinner had not agreed with him. Actually, there was nothing wrong with his stomach. He had to make an important call. Reaching his suite, he went directly to the telephone and dialed the number in Miami. His impatience grew as he waited for the phone to be used. After a minute, a male voice responded. "Roberto!" barked Carlos, with his usual short temper.

"Si," replied Roberto in a deep, Spanish voice. Roberto wasn't a man who was easily rattled.

"It's Carlos. Where the hell have you been? " "Hey, brother."

"Don't give me that brother shit. What took you so goddamn long to answer the phone?"

"Hey, relax man. I was on the box with Felipe. The static's so bad I didn't hear the phone."

Carlos regained his composure. "Did it get in?"

"Yeah."

"Okay, I'll see you tomorrow," Carlos replied. "How are our two friends?"

"We took care of them, but do you think that was really necessary?"

"Yes, it was," Carlos snapped. Any problems?"

"No."

"Okay, I'll see you tomorrow," Carlos replied.

He hung up the phone and walked into the bathroom to brush his teeth. As he stared in the mirror, a look of satisfaction came over his face. He prided himself on his rugged good looks, and beneath his clear bronze complexion his ego soared. *Yes, I screwed the Columbians, Michael, and Sonny, and even the Coast Guard. When the Chubby Ann is found, if it ever is, it will probably be written off. I just pulled off the deal of the century, and Sonny and Michael would never know it was me who did it.*

Carlos finished brushing his teeth. He had the urge to celebrate and decided to call Sonny. He felt a perverted pleasure in knowing that Sonny was his victim, and his prey thought he was a friend. He picked up the phone and dialed the Presidential Suite to see if Sonny, Michael, and Maria had gone back to their rooms.

"Yeah," grunted Sonny.

"You guys want some company?"

"I thought you were sick."

"I'm feeling better now." Carlos had almost forgotten the excuse he had made to go call Roberto.

"Oh," Sonny hesitantly replied. "Yeah, come on, but hurry it up!" The line went dead.

Carlos left his room, walked down the hall to the suite, and started to knock when he realized Sonny had left the door ajar.

As Carlos entered the living room and closed the door, he saw that the room was empty. Michael and Maria weren't there. They had probably gone back to their room. Carlos walked behind the bar and started to mix a drink when he heard soft moans coming from the partially open bedroom door. Setting the drink on the bar, he casually walked into the bedroom. Sonny, Ruth, and Margaret were piled together on the king-size bed, completely naked. Sonny was lying on his side. His elbow was extended, and his hand was under his chin watching the two girls. Ruth and Margaret were locked in an embrace, passionately kissing one another on the mouth.

Sonny looked up at Carlos, an amused grin on his face. "Are you going to just stand there gawking, or are you going to get those clothes off? "

Chapter Six

Satisfied that everything was ready, he tried to relax as he leaned against a large coconut palm.

He had reservations about using this particular house, but Carlos had insisted. The house was in a middle-class neighborhood. Orlando Rodriquez stood quietly in the shadows of the moonlit yard watching for the boat. Well-built and average height, Orlando was dark-skinned, with wavy black hair and piercing brown eyes that sometimes looked black. To most, he appeared to fear nothing. He didn't start fights, but he never walked away from one. His relationship with Carlos was the only exception. There was something about Carlos that scared him, and he tried not to get on his bad side.

Not knowing the exact time of the boat's arrival, he and his men waited. His mind went down a mental checklist, trying to remember if he had forgotten some minor but relevant detail located off the main drive, with ample trees and shrubbery around the property providing plenty of privacy. He did not have to worry about the neighbors on either side. They both had gone north for the summer. His men, however, would have to be careful not to be seen by the young couple living across the narrow canal. It was often two o'clock in the morning before they went to bed. He hoped tonight would not be one of those nights. Orlando was cautious because the house was located on a dead-end street. If they drew heat exiting the premises, it would be a problem. To circumvent that possibility, he had stationed one of his men on the bridge pretending to be fishing in the canal. He watched for any unusual traffic or police cars. The sentry had a portable CB. strapped under his shirt, with an earplug in his ear.

Orlando looked to his right and saw the Cigarette slowly moving up the canal. The subtle rumble of its engines was barely audible. Instead of its bow riding high into the air, it plowed headlong, pushing tons of water aside.

Those stupid shits have the damn boat overloaded, thought Orlando as anger welled up inside him. He had given the captain explicit instructions on load distribution and weight. "Now the bastard is plowing up the canal," he mumbled to himself. *St. Simon is probably riding with that shithead,* he thought. The first thing the Coast Guard looks at is a boat's waterline, and by sheer luck or divine intervention, the boat had not been stopped. Orlando stood by the tree as the boat pulled alongside the dock. His eyes scanned the neighborhood watching for any unusual activity.

The captain had trouble maneuvering the boat. Orlando cringed as he threw the engines into reverse and applied the throttles. He tried to back the boat down to keep it from running into the dock. For a moment, Orlando was afraid the roar of the engines would wake up the neighborhood.

The boat finally came to a stop alongside the dock. The crew jumped out and quickly secured the lines. They turned and walked to the house, followed by the captain. Felipe was a short, stocky Cuban, whose face was wrinkled from years in the sun, and who had the disposition of a rattlesnake.

Orlando waited outside a few minutes before entering the house. He wanted to make sure none of the neighbors was curious and that no one had wandered along the bank, unknowingly becoming the victim of his curiosity. *This is the most critical phase of the operation,* he thought. *In many ways, it is the most dangerous, particularly if a raid occurs.* Altogether, in one area were the boat, merchandise, house, vehicles, and most importantly the seven men in the house. If something went wrong now, it would cost them well over a million dollars in equipment and attorney's fees.

Orlando glanced around the room as he closed the door. Fatigue was obvious on the three crewmen's weather-beaten, exhausted-looking faces as they reclined on the couch. They had been without sleep for almost two days.

Mike Mercer and Charley Long sat at a small desk monitoring the recently installed base C.B. radio. Earlier, they had met Orlando at the house to prepare for the arrival of the captain and crew. Now they were waiting for information from Tito Cardenas, the sentry stationed on the bridge. Felipe, the boat captain, leaned over the coffee table. His hands shook from exhaustion and too much cocaine. He groggily prepared a line of toot.

Damn! That crap is going to kill him, thought Orlando. Orlando had a lot of vices, but strangely, he never touched drugs.

The house, built in the 1940s, was a small structure consisting of two tiny bedrooms, one bath, a Florida room, and a combination kitchen-living room. The interior of the house was sparsely furnished, and the beds had been removed to accommodate the volume of marijuana. Bed sheets nailed over the inside bedroom windows provided complete privacy. The kitchen shelves and refrigerator were stocked with enough supplies to last two men for at least a week.

Felipe's attention briefly turned from his cocaine to Orlando, who stood at the end of the coffee table.

"You guys look beat," Orlando said softly in Spanish. Seeing Felipe's condition, he had decided this was not the time, nor the place to start an argument with the captain about overloading the boat. Felipe could be extremely dangerous when he was strung on coke. Orlando made a mental note not to use the man again.

"Yeah, we're tired," grunted Felipe wearily. After almost two days with no sleep, the only thing keeping him upright was the cocaine. He leaned back down over the coffee table.

Orlando crossed the room, stopped at the kitchen sink, and began preparing some espresso. It had been a long two days for him too, and he needed a pick-me-up.

"Mike, has Tito reported in?" Orlando asked.

Mike Mercer stood up, pushed the chair back from the desk, and walked to the kitchen. "Everything's cool. He said some old man on the bridge hooked an eight-foot hammerhead, and there's a small crowd gathered around watching him fight the thing. Other than that, everything's quiet."

"Oh," continued Mike, "Tito wants to know when he's going to get relieved. He needs to take a leak pretty bad."

Orlando thought for a moment as he screwed the lid on the espresso percolator.

"Go ahead and tell him to come on in. We're okay for now. When we get ready to unload, one of you can go back up on the bridge."

Orlando adjusted the flame under the percolator. He crossed the room and pulled a chair in front of Felipe. Felipe was tired and strain showed on his face, but the cocaine had made him more alert.

"How did the trip go, Phil?" Orlando asked cautiously. Now was not the time to have a blow-up with Felipe, not when he was full of cocaine.

Felipe leaned forward, and his eyes narrowed as he looked at Orlando. "Like shit," he said sounding annoyed. "We hit a damn squall last night and almost lost them. If it hadn't been for the cargo lights on the freighter, we probably would have."

"What about Stan and Pete?"

"What the hell do you think?" Felipe growled.

"Okay," Orlando put his hands out in a placating gesture. "Why don't you guys go ahead and get out of here? I'll have your money in a couple of days."

"No longer!" demanded Felipe. He pushed himself up off the couch and signaled Antonio, Pedro, and Juan to follow.

Orlando heard the coffee boiling over on the stove. He jumped out of the chair and ran to the kitchen. "Son of a bitch!" he shouted and grabbed a towel.

As Felipe started through the door, he turned and in a haggard voice said, "Tell Roberto to pull that damn radio out of the boat and throw it away! Damn thing isn't worth a shit! I could barely hear him tonight." Without another word, he disappeared through the door.

Chapter Seven

A luminous green wake veered away from the bow of the eighty-foot Coast Guard cutter Cape Barnes, as her sleek white hull cut through the water at a moderate seventeen knots. Darkness surrounded her, as she cruised in two hundred feet of water along the eastern edge of the Bahamas, on the Atlantic side. Within her hull, eight exhausted crewmen slept. Two other men stood watch on the bridge.

Twenty-six-year-old First-Class Boatswain Mate Herbert Williams had relieved the captain, Chief Boatswain Mate Harry Rogers, for the mid-watch. Williams anxiously waited for his relief, which was due in the next half hour at 0545 hours.

Exhausted, Williams reclined in the captain's chair, his head nodding ever so slightly as he fought the urge to close his eyes and succumb to the sleep he desperately needed. This particular patrol had taxed the crew to their limit. They had been standing watch, six hours on and six hours off, for the past four days. Williams found comfort in knowing that he would be back in Miami that afternoon. He could hardly wait to take his girlfriend Gianna to the new oceanfront restaurant they had talked about last week. It wasn't cheap, but Gianna was worth it. If the evening went as planned, he was going to ask her to marry him. They had been together for almost two years, and he knew she was the only woman for him. She was a real looker, petite and slender with long, black, wavy hair and thick eyelashes that swept across her clear brown eyes. Smart, beautiful, and even-tempered, Gianna loved him despite his many shortcomings, one of which was being gone for days at a time. Yeah, he was a lucky guy.

The bridge was quiet. A humid breeze whipped through the port hatch cooling its inhabitants and the electronic equipment. At night, "lights out" was standard procedure. The single exception was a small compass light that cast an amber halo throughout the structure. The dim green glow of the radarscope and the digital readouts on the electronic equipment were soothing to the bloodshot eyes that were staring out into the darkness, trying to locate any ship that might have escaped their radar.

Seaman Billy Stokes stood poised next to the radar console. As Billy watched the sweep slowly move in a clockwise circle, its dim light emphasized the fatigue on his face. His legs ached from standing for the past five hours, and his eyelids drooped from lack of sleep. Billy shifted his weight from his right foot to his left to relieve the tension.

Lost in thought for a few seconds, Billy always remembered wanting to have a job that was on the water. He loved the water and boats. Being in the Coast Guard was a good match for him. Young and relatively inexperienced, Billy had joined the Coast Guard the year before and still wasn't sure if he had what it took to handle the job. With a small build, carrot-red hair, freckles, and a round, baby face, he always felt like a teenager, who was trying to appease an angry parent, especially when the chief was around. Though he lacked the confidence he needed, he was an outstanding seaman. He worked hard and had slowly begun to gain the respect of the older crewmen, as well as the captain, Chief Rogers.

The mid-watch had been uneventful. Seas were less than three feet, the weather was clear, and the temperature was in the mid-seventies. South Cat Cay showed on the upper right-hand side of the radarscope nineteen miles away.

Stokes sighed. To alleviate his boredom, he took the hundredth range and bearing from South Cat Cay to confirm their course and speed by the navigation chart. As he moved the cursor around, lining it up on the island, Stokes detected a small blip to the left of the land mass. To determine if it was a double-echo or sea return, and to satisfy himself, he watched the sweep go around several more times. A minute later, he was positive it was neither.

"Hey, Boats!" Stokes called, with excitement in his voice. "We've got a contact at 052 degrees at nineteen miles." Williams' eyes popped open as he straightened up in the chair. He stretched his arms and yawned.

"Take a plot and let's see if it's a boat," Williams responded, more alert now.

Stokes nodded. He took another range and bearing on the blip and plotted it on his maneuvering board. A minute later he took another range and bearing, plotted it, and repeated the process again sixty seconds later. After the fourth fix, and using his maneuvering board, Stokes began converting the contact's relative movement into true course and speed.

"Okay," Stokes said, straightening up from the plotting table. "The contact is designated Kilo, bearing 061 degrees and range eighteen miles. The closest point of approach is 5.4 miles at time 0616 off our starboard quarter. I think it's dead in the water. I've got a true speed of 1.5 knots. It looks like it's drifting with the current."

"Very well," replied Williams as he eased out of the chair. Binoculars in hand, he began looking for the contact.

After scanning the horizon for several minutes, he failed to see the object. Williams walked to the radar scope and studied the blip. *Something's not right,* he thought. Judging by the size of the blip, the contact should have been visible. At this range, and with a clear night, he should have been able to see the lights on her superstructure. It made him suspicious that a vessel of that size was not using running lights.

"Stokes, keep an eye on that contact. If there's any change in its course, let me know," Williams instructed. He left the bridge, walked to the starboard catwalk, and resumed his search for the phantom contact.

Diligently searching, Williams stood on the catwalk for fifteen minutes. Every few minutes he called through the hatchway that led to the bridge and asked Stokes for a range and bearing to the contact. Stokes shouted out the information and periodically checked the radar to identify any new ship that might be detected.

A few minutes before the watch reliefs were due, Williams entered the bridge and resumed watching the scope. What he saw bothered him. The contact was at thirteen miles on a bearing of 072 degrees and was still drifting north. As the cutter drew closer, the blip grew larger. At that distance, he still had not made visual contact with the object.

"Goddammit!" Williams said aloud as he took a deep breath. "I knew it, damn it! I knew it! It never fails!"

"What's the matter, Boats?" Stokes asked.

"This shit!" Williams shouted, pointing toward the scope. "We're an hour before changing course for Miami, and now we have this damn thing on the scope. I have to make it back to Miami tonight," he groaned. He could see his perfectly planned evening going up in smoke.

"Ah, don't worry, Boats. We'll make it on time," assured Stokes.

"Damn it," Williams said, sighing in resignation. "The sooner we check out this contact, the sooner we'll get back to Miami. Go on down and wake the chief. Tell him I think he'd better get up here right away."

"Aye, aye," responded Stokes as he hurriedly left the bridge.

The dream was always the same. The little girl appeared on the surface for the third time. Horror filled her eyes as she took in a water-filled breath. Her purple lips formed a silent scream. The only sound from her mouth was the gurgle of salt water from her tiny lungs. Her mother, seven months pregnant, leaned over the lifeline with her arms outstretched, screaming. "God, oh my God, somebody help my baby!" She collapsed on the deck in a state of hysteria. Tears were streaming down her anguished face.

The girl's father frantically fought the tiller as he desperately tried to maneuver the boat closer. The wind was dead ahead, and in his panic, he had put the vessel in irons.

Chief Rogers slowly surfaced back to reality as the urgent knocking on the door awakened him. He shook the nightmare from his brain. The same dream had plagued him for years. Rogers and his wife had been unable to overcome the loss of their four-year-old daughter and had parted ways soon after her death. Taking their son, who was born two months after the tragedy, his wife had moved back to Maine and had eventually remarried. Brushing the past from his mind, he moved his sweat-drenched body to the edge of his bunk and sat up before he answered the knock.

"Enter," he stammered clearing his throat.

Stokes partially opened the door, stuck his head around the frame, and apologized for invading the chief's privacy.

"What is it Stokes?" the chief interrupted more gruffly than he intended.

"Your presence is requested on the bridge, Sir. The boatswain thinks it's important."

Chief Rogers looked quizzically at Stokes. Suddenly wide awake, he said, "Very well, Stokes. I'll be right up."

Minutes later, the chief forced his overweight body up the ladder, carelessly splattering his cup of coffee as he squeezed through the narrow opening to the bridge. He wiped the spilled coffee from his hand onto his khakis and stood motionless for a moment surveying the bridge.

Stokes stood beside the radar unit staring down at the scope. Williams was leaning against the bulkhead on the starboard catwalk. Holding a pair of binoculars to his eyes and panning from side to side, he was searching for something in the gray light of the early dawn.

Stokes saw the chief out of the corner of his eye. Before he could shout, "Captain on the bridge," the chief barked, "Williams, what have you got?" Williams spun around, surprised to see the chief standing there. The Chief waited a moment to collect his thoughts and then entered the bridge.

"Morning Chief."

"Get on with it, man!" Rogers snorted. "You didn't drag me up here to say hello, did you?"

"No Sir, I didn't," replied Williams, recovering from his superior's sarcasm. "There's a contact we've been plotting for the past half hour or so, and I thought you ought to take a look at it."

Williams explained the situation. Chief Rogers remained silent, resting his near-empty coffee cup on the radar console. He watched the blip pulsate with each pass of the sweep.

"All right," the chief sighed. "Stokes, pass the word to the crew to prepare a special boarding party."

Stokes grabbed the microphone, and the ship's public address system blared, breaking the morning silence throughout the ship.

"Now hear this. All hands man the special boarding party. This is not a drill! I repeat, this is not a drill!"

"Mr. Williams, I now have the bridge," commanded the chief.

"Aye, aye Sir," Williams snapped.

Normally, Stokes and Williams would have been relieved by 0600 hours, but due to the special boarding party, a condition similar to general quarters, both their duty stations were now on the bridge. Williams' station was the helm, and Stokes became the starboard lookout. A young seaman apprentice scurried topside to take the port lookout position. Williams released the automatic pilot and resumed their heading of 357 degrees.

"All ahead two-thirds," instructed the chief. "Come to new course 079 degrees. Let me know when you've steadied up."

"Aye, aye Sir," Williams replied.

The chief slid out of his chair, extracted a pair of binoculars from the top drawer of the chart table, and began to search the pre-dawn horizon.

The ship's vibration shook the crew as the cutter's massive engines increased speed to twenty-seven knots. She sliced through the water like a finely honed blade stalking her prey, ready for the kill. The crew had practiced boarding drills hundreds of times, but since this was not a drill, apprehension gripped each man.

Fireman Third Class Johnny Parks appeared on the bridge carrying four webbed belts. Attached to each belt was a Browning 45 caliber automatic pistol, with five clips of ammunition. Parks quickly distributed the belts to every man on the bridge and disappeared as quickly as he had arrived. Johnny Parks was a serious seaman originally from Kings Bay, Georgia. Johnny had done a four-year stint in the Navy, specializing in aviation ordinance. After leaving the Navy, he joined the Coast Guard. He liked his job, but sometimes it was a little boring. Right now, however, it was anything but boring. The air was charged with excitement, and he had to admit a little fear.

Darkness slowly yielded to dawn. Light appearing on the

boundary between the earth and the sky, improved visibility as each minute passed. Chief Rogers scrutinized the deck. Aft of the forecastle, he observed Seaman Avanger manning the fifty-caliber machine gun attached to its deck mount. He turned toward the pump shotguns.

"I've got a visual!" shouted Stokes, excitement in his voice. "It's off the starboard bow at about eight thousand yards."

Rogers hunched forward. He shifted his weight and placed his elbows on the railing, trying to steady his glasses as he scrutinized the area pointed out by Stokes. "There she is," he said as his eyes strained to see.

Squinting, the chief's vision pierced the morning mist. He could barely distinguish the white vessel about four miles away. It appeared dead in the water.

"Steady on new course 079 degrees," Williams announced.

"Very well," acknowledged the chief, without changing his position.

"Come right five degrees," ordered Rogers.

Righting himself, Rogers walked into the bridge and stopped at the radar console. He changed its range to the ten-mile scale, getting a blow-up of the general area and checking the resolution of the contact. The area was clear of other traffic except for the white vessel ahead of them.

"Reduce speed to ahead one-third," commanded the chief.

"All ahead one-third," Williams replied, repeating the order.

Chief Rogers reached over the radarscope, snapped up the inner ship telephone, and dialed the radio room. "Johnson, this is the chief. Get this message off to Miami ASAP. Give them our loran reading and tell them we have visual contact with a suspicious vessel. We are closing to investigate. The ship's readiness is condition two, and we'll keep them advised."

As the morning mist gradually lifted, Chief Rogers could see the boat more clearly. She was rolling ever so gently on the glassy swells as the current pushed her north. *Is she disabled? Maybe drift fishing?* Chief Rogers wondered.

No, he thought if *she is, she would have her lights on.*

Williams interrupted Rogers' speculation. "What do you think, Chief?"

"I'm not sure, Williams, but something's not right."

At one thousand yards, Rogers ordered the cutter's speed to all ahead slow. From this distance, he had a clear view of the vessel. He saw no movement or any sign of activity. Undamaged, her superstructure appeared to be in no danger of sinking.

"Williams, come left to 010 degrees. I want to come abreast of her." .

"Aye, aye, Sir," Williams said, spinning the wheel left.

Leaning over the bridge rail, Rogers shouted to the deck below. "You men stand ready. Avanger, you rest easy on that fifty caliber, you hear? I don't want some son of a bitch accidentally shot!"

Avanger looked up at the chief and nodded his head, acknowledging the warning. Not knowing what lay ahead, he mentally tried to prepare himself.

As the cutter edged to within fifty yards of the vessel, the Chief spoke into his bullhorn,

"Ahoy there, this is the United States Coast Guard Cutter Cape Barnes. Request permission to come aboard."

Seaman Avanger's moist hands gripped the fifty caliber as he stood at ready. Fireman Jaworski and Fireman Third Class Parks stood amidships, each holding his shotgun at waist level, waiting for the chief's next order.

In all his years in the Coast Guard, Rogers had never gotten used to the boarding of another vessel. It was like an invasion of another man's privacy. A man's boat is his home, and from his experiences in the past, other skippers felt the same. He was an intruder, and he resented his task. He was a policeman on the high seas, and like a patrolman approaching a strange vehicle, he had to use caution.

Looking at Williams, the chief said, "Ease up alongside her and mind your helm."

"Yes, Sir," said Williams as he directed his attention to the wheel.

The cutter slowly and quietly approached the other vessel. Parks and Jaworski climbed under the lifeline. Holding to the boat's stanchions, they placed themselves ready for the jump from their deck to the other boat. Not more than five feet away from the other boat, they sprang. Each safely landed in a crouched position.

Williams reversed the cutter's engines for a few seconds, and the Cape Barnes separated from the drifting vessel.

Parks and Jaworski crouched like a S.W.A.T. team going into action. Cautiously, they made their way to the cabin door. Perspiration trickled down Parks' face. His breathing grew rapidly, not knowing what to expect. Jaworski's muscles tightened as he readied himself for the unexpected. They eased their way to opposite sides of the cabin door, placed their backs against the bulkhead, and momentarily squatted down to evaluate their next move.

Bending over slightly, Parks touched his hand to the damp deck and wiped it dry on his pants. Glancing down, his eyes widened in bewilderment. A small whimper came from his throat as he suppressed the urge to cry out. For a moment, he was frozen in shock and fear.

Jaworski heard Parks' strange noise and looked over at him. He stared at his shipmate's bloody hand and knee. Glancing down at the deck, Jaworski saw that Parks was squatting in a pool of coagulated blood. Jaworski reached over, grabbed his friend by the shirt, and shook him. Puzzlement replaced fear as he softly asked, "Where did all this blood come from?" Parks slowly shook his head but didn't speak.

Jaworski rose from his squatting position and stood with his back against the damp bulkhead. He looked over at Parks and jerked his head toward the door. Still shaky, Parks stood. Jaworski motioned for Parks to back him up. He reached for the doorknob and quietly twisted it. After a deep breath, he propelled himself inside the cabin, followed closely by Parks.

After the two men disappeared, Williams eased the cutter to the stern of the drifting vessel. Leaning over the bridge rail, Chief Rogers read her name, which said Chubby Ann.

Chapter Eight

The ringing phone startled him from a comfortable sleep. What an annoying noise, Michael thought as he reached for the phone. The ring quickly silenced as he lifted the receiver. His squinting eyes slowly adjusted to the bedside lamp as he clicked it on.

"Yeah," he mumbled sleepily.

"My ex-wife once told me I was going to get an ulcer from worrying," Sonny said. "Funny thing is the bitch was probably right!"

Michael rose on an elbow and looked at his watch, which showed 4:46 a.m. "Do you know what time it is, Chubby? You didn't call just to tell me that did you?"

"It's quarter to eight in Miami. Get your tail up here right away. We've got problems."

Confused, Michael asked, "What are you talking about?"

"I'll tell you when you get here," Sonny responded as he hung up the phone.

Michael eased the receiver down, wondering what was going on. Maria rolled over to face her husband. Squinting from the light with sleepy eyes, she asked, "Who was that? What's the matter?"

"Don't know," Michael said, reaching for his pants. "Chubby wants me upstairs pronto."

A sense of foreboding enveloped Michael for a moment as he dressed. At this time of the morning, Chubby's call meant something was wrong. Michael brushed it away and looked down at his beautiful wife.

Maria snuggled deeper under the covers. "Don't be long," she said sleepily, "and stay away from those two hair bags."

"Oh, go back to sleep," Michael teased, leaning over to kiss her and resisting the temptation to caress her breast.

Maria rolled over to her left side and pulled the comforter up higher around her neck. Contentment flowed through her as she burrowed her head into her soft pillow.

Settled and cozy, her thoughts drifted to her past, and how she now lived a life of wealth and leisure far different from her roots in Cuba.

Maria was the youngest of thirteen children. Her parents lived in the southwestern part of Cuba called San Juan y Martinez in Pinar Del Rio Province, where the fertile soil and perfect climate made it the tobacco capital of the world.

On a trade route in the 17th Century, a Spanish galleon took two hundred ounces of Cuban tobacco seeds to the shores of the Philippines. Spanish friars decided to cultivate the Cuban seeds in the Cagayan Valley, Isabela, named after Queen Isabela of Spain. This area was a very fertile region north of Manila, where the famous La Flor de La Isabela cigars were first produced.

Maria's father owned twenty-five hundred hectares, or six thousand seventy-five acres of this famous tobacco, plus four thousand nine hundred forty acres of sugar cane. His tobacco farm employed eighteen Filipinos and twenty-one Chinese. All were male and each shared two bunkhouses. One bunkhouse was for the Chinese, and the other was for the Filipinos.

Maria's mother was the head cook for all the workers as well as her own family. Life was hard, but it was good, and food was plentiful. The family lacked nothing important, and their house was always filled with love.

Maria's entrance into the world almost killed her mother. Maria was in a breach position, and the local midwives didn't know what to do. Upset at the sounds of his wife's suffering, Maria's father sent for a doctor in a nearby town.

It took the doctor over five hours to get there, because he was working on another patient who eventually died.

When the doctor finally arrived and examined Maria's mother, he found her extremely weak, and the blood loss had caused her blood pressure to drop critically low. In 1946, a C-Section was unheard of, but the doctor knew he had to do something, or the mother and baby would both be lost. Exhausted and very weak, Maria's mother tearfully told the doctor, "I do not want to lose this baby. Please help me."

Symphysiotomy the doctor thought. "Get everybody out of this room except the midwives!" the doctor barked. "Here, you two," he said pointing to two of the midwives, "hold her arms, and you," the doctor said, pointing to the third midwife, "hold her legs back." Satisfied that he was ready, he reached deep inside his bag and pulled out a metal saw. The use of symphysiotomy was centuries old. This surgical procedure temporarily increased the pelvic diameter by surgically dividing the cartilage of the pelvis. It was both painful and dangerous, but when the baby was in the breach position, and with limited surgical means available, it was performed under local anesthesia.

Unfortunately, the doctor had no anesthetic to give Maria's poor mother. "I am so sorry Senora, but I have no ether. This is a poor country."

The rest of the procedure was a bloody torture for Maria's mother. The doctor reached up inside her and began sawing the fibers of the pubic symphysis. Blood spurted everywhere. Her mother screamed in unbearable pain and passed out. Since that day, Maria's mother had walked with a limp.

At the early age of two, Maria rode her first donkey. It was exhilarating. Her father led her around in circles as she shouted, "Faster, Pappy, faster!" Her father's eyes shone with pride and delight at his beautiful and adventurous little daughter as he pulled the donkey round and round.

On Maria's fifth birthday, her father presented her with a gray pony. She screamed with joy, and with a boost from her father, she leaped upon the pony's bare back and galloped down the dirt road. The swirl of dust left its signature of her freedom to come.

Maria loved to ride her pony early in the morning's brisk air before the temperature rose. The mountains to the north toward Santa Lucia were breathtaking. *That is the most beautiful place on earth,* she thought to herself, *and if there is a God, he lives there.*

All the workers loved to see her coming. She greeted each worker by name as she rode down the different rows of tobacco. During a ride one day, she befriended an old hound dog, who struggled to stay up with Maria and her pony. Every evening, she was faithful in washing her pony and her dog as her father had instructed. Her character was beginning to form, creating the woman she would later become.

By the age of ten, Maria's family had become very prosperous. Her father had a new house built for them. He bought a new, shiny 1956 black Ford pickup and parked it in the front yard. He had several new apartments built for the workers who had families. John Deere tractors replaced the mules in the fields. Electricity had finally been delivered, and the radio became the world's information center. Life was hard, but it was good and bountiful. Maria was an incredibly happy and loved little girl.

The radio mentioned Fidel Castro's name many times, but Maria had no idea what the ramifications of his words would later become.

Maria's mother spent two days preparing the feast for dinner on December 22, 1960. The meal included roasted pork, black beans and rice, croquettes, cold meat rolls, plantains, yucca with garlic sauce and onions, rice pudding, rum cake, and fried sweet dough, among other mouth-watering delights.

Maria's family, along with all the workers and their families, gathered around the many tables in the large main cafeteria to celebrate the Christmas season and enjoy the bountiful meal. With everyone seated, they bowed their heads, thankful for the wonderful spread and the prosperity of the farm, which gave them jobs, steady meals, and nice places to live. Before coming to work for Maria's father, most of the workers and their families had moved from place to place, sleeping in tents and eating whatever they could find. None had enjoyed the opportunities they now had.

As her father asked the blessing, Maria heard a faint, distant sound like the backfire from an old automobile. Not sure what it was, she quietly slipped out of her chair, walked to the eastern side of the building, and gazed out the window. She had never seen an army before, but for some reason, she knew instantly that was the army coming up the road. They were all in uniforms and marching in step, side by side. Each carried a rifle. Though she was young, Maria knew what firearms were and what they could do. Terrified, she turned from the large window of the vast room and in her small, breathless, shaking voice cried, "Pappy! They're coming!" From that distance, few at the tables heard her or even looked up from the blessing. Everyone was hungry, and those who were close enough to hear her thought she was just playing. Instead, they all focused on the savory aromas coming from the abundant food filling each table.

As the blessing ended, all heads rose, and the bowls of delicious fare were quickly passed around to silence the grumbling stomachs. Getting no attention from the crowd, Maria hurriedly ran across the large room to her father and shook his arm.

"They're coming, Pappy, they're coming!" she said. He looked down at her, wrinkling his brow and wondering what in the world Maria was yelling about. At that same instant, the front door exploded, and an ant-like line of militiamen stormed into the huge cafeteria, rifles leveled at everyone around the tables. Confusion and disbelief spread throughout the room. *What the hell is going on?* they wondered. *What are these men doing here with rifles pointed at us?* A moment later, a captain, holding a sheet of paper in his hand, rushed through the line of rifled militiamen.

"Where is Senior Ramos?" he shouted.

Maria's father sat dumbfounded. *What the hell do they want,* he thought? *How dare they intrude on my property and this beautiful Christmas meal!*

In an instant, he jumped up from his chair and turned to face the officer in charge.

"Hijo de puta," he spat at the captain.

A soldier standing behind Senior Ramos raised his rifle, and with the butt of the gun hit Maria's father square in the back of the shoulders. As he hit the floor, Maria screamed and fell beside her father. The captain raised his arm and shouted to no one in particular. "The state has federalized all agriculture, including farms and equipment. The Ramos family has twelve hours to vacate this property. You may take only your clothing and personal effects."

At that very moment, the life Maria had learned to love and cherish had been destroyed, her innocence taken and her trust in humanity gone. Time became an extensive blur. She dimly recalled the flight from Havana to Miami, and she vaguely remembered her family staying with some distant relatives. She also remembered her father saying that when they arrived in Miami, he had only sixty pesos in his pocket.

Maria's mother's priority was putting her children in school. Maria recalled her first day at Norland Elementary in Northwest Miami. She was confused and afraid. The language was foreign, and the food was terrible. Despite everything, she stubbornly refused to cry. For some unknown reason, fate had given her the inner strength to endure that first day.

As time passed, English became Maria's passion. She soon realized that without a command of the English language, she and her family would be destined to poverty. Without fail, every evening when Maria arrived home, she would teach her parents what she had learned that day in school. Life was still hard, but for the Ramos family things had finally begun to look up.

Maria's father eventually got a job at the Doral Country Club working with the ground's maintenance crew. In 1966, he had the opportunity to meet and speak with Lee Trevino. Lee had just won the US Open and was in South Florida practicing for his next tournament. He was so impressed with Maria's father that he offered him a job on the spot as his next caddy.

Maria's mother got a job with a friend who worked evenings cleaning offices. Together, after six months of hard work, they started their own cleaning business. Today, they had over one hundred eighty employees.

Maria graduated from high school with honors. As a Cuban refugee, she qualified for federal assistance from the Department of Education to attend the University of Miami. She studied fashion and graduated with a Bachelor of Arts degree.

She and Michael met while she was styling a photo shoot for Burdines's Department Store in downtown Miami. Michael was a photographer, and his charisma, creativeness, and assertiveness immediately captured her attention. After only a couple of dates, they had a brief, whirlwind affair. Michael immediately proposed, and she immediately accepted. She had known from the first day she met Michael that he was the man with whom she wanted to spend the rest of her life.

As Maria snuggled comfortably in her pillow, she thought, *Yes, life is incredibly good.*

Chapter Nine

As Michael waited for the elevator, he was puzzled over what could be wrong. Sonny hadn't given him a clue. *It could be a thousand things,* he thought. The elevator doors slid open, and he stepped inside. The odor of cheap perfume stung his nostrils as he glanced at the odd couple to the rear of the elevator.

The man was probably in his mid-forties, white, with a paunchy belly and graying hair. The girl, Michael supposed, would not top twenty-five and was strikingly black. She clung to the man's arm as if he might try to get away. *I suppose she has to make a living too,* Michael thought, relieved when the elevator stopped on Sonny's floor. The girl's perfume was overpowering.

Michael walked to the suite. As he reached for the doorknob, a charge of static electricity arced from the tip of his finger to the door.

"Shit!" he shouted, not so much in pain as surprise. Michael did not like surprises. He gently tapped on the door and pushed it open.

The door opened. Sonny stood in the middle of the foyer. He was wearing a pair of men's bikini underwear with the head of an elephant printed on the front. *Who but Sonny would wear elephant bikini underwear?* Michael mused, almost smiling. Sonny's salt and pepper hair looked rumpled as though he constantly had been running his hands through it. Michael guessed he had been without sleep all night.

As he entered the room, Michael saw Carlos reclining on the sofa. *What is going on?* he wondered.

"Where are the girls?" Michael asked quietly.

The elephant's head became an ass as Sonny turned and walked behind the bar. He was barefooted and looked tired. He nodded in the direction of the bedroom.

"In the sack," Sonny said. "You want some coffee?"

"Yeah, that would be good."

Carlos righted himself on the couch and directed his attention to Michael. "We just got a call from the Bear. The Coast Guard found the boat." The Bear was the code name Sonny used for Louis Steinberg, the attorney who handled all the corporate assets. The Chubby Ann was an eight hundred thousand-dollar asset.

"It's all over the news," Sonny said, handing Michael a cup of black coffee. "That's how the Bear found out. The shit has hit the fan!"

Michael looked surprised. "Have arrangements been made to bail out the crew?"

"That's the problem," Sonny said, glancing over at Carlos as their eyes briefly locked.

"What do you mean? What's the problem?" Michael questioned looking puzzled.

Lacking the words, Sonny swallowed and finally said, "There is no crew."

"What the hell are you saying?" Michael asked, his voice rising in confusion and alarm.

Carlos stood, walked to the bar, and poured himself a stiff drink.

"Michael, the Coast Guard found the Chubby Ann completely abandoned," Sonny answered. "The news report was sketchy, but they said bloodstains and marijuana residue were found on the deck. "The cutter Cape Barnes is towing her in."

Michael sat at the bar in silence, mulling over the conversation.

He glanced at Carlos, and then his eyes rested on Sonny.

"What you're saying," he paused, still collecting his thoughts, "is that the Chubby Ann was hijacked, right?"

"That's what it looks like," Sonny replied, knowing that Michael was as upset as he was.

"Damn, I can't believe it," Michael whispered. "I busted my ass on this deal!"

"I know, Michael, I know," Sonny sighed. "There's a leak in our security somewhere, and I damn well mean to find out where."

Carlos leaned across the bar. "Michael, I think you ought to call Lou to see if he can get the boat back."

"No, I don't think so, at least not for now," Michael responded. "When the DEA learns that the boat is registered to a foreign corporation, there's going to be a lot of questions. Let Lou handle it. That's what he gets paid to do."

Michael turned from the bar, walked to the couch, and sat down. "What's our next move?" Michael said as he stared at Sonny.

"Well, the Colombians are going to be pissed, that's for sure," Sonny answered. "I think we ought to get our asses back to Miami and see if we can meet with Mehejas."

Stunned, Michael jumped up from the couch and shouted, "I don't believe a frigging word of what I'm hearing! We've got two crewmen probably dead, maybe murdered, and all you two sons of bitches can talk about is getting the damn boat back and appeasing the frigging Colombians!"

"Listen, Michael!" Sonny snapped. "If I can't control something, I don't worry about it! And the sooner you learn THAT the better off you'll be."

"Yeah, well, tell THAT to your fucking ulcer!" Michael shouted, part from anger and part because he felt helpless.

Chapter Ten

Bernie Colgate slowly read the report marked: SECRET.

Subject: Sonny James Mitchell. Born December 26, 1932, Louisville, Kentucky.

Father: Reverend James P. Mitchell, Pastor, West Louisville Baptist Church.

Mother: Mary Elizabeth Mitchell, formerly Mary Elizabeth Haber.

Sonny James Mitchell is the oldest of three children: Charles Damon Mitchell – Born October 5, 1935, and Bonnie Faye Mitchell – Born November 13, 1937.

The subject graduated from Pinecrest Academy in the top ten percent of his class on June 6, 1950. Voted Mr. Personality in his senior year.

Looking puzzled, Bernie said to no one in particular, "Looks like he comes from a fine family. I wonder what the hell happened." Not expecting an answer, he continued reading.

The subject joined the U.S. Navy on July 15, 1950, Service Number 692-23-46. Completed basic training in San Diego, California.

Attended submarine school in New London, Connecticut.

Subject graduated sub school February 12, 1951.

March 1951, Subject was assigned to the USS Bluefin for duration of four-year enlistment. Service record indicates subject received three disciplinary captain's masts for (a) A.W.O.L; (b) having alcohol aboard ship, and (c) stealing steaks from the captain's galley. Every disciplinary action resulted in a short-term restriction aboard ship.

Subject adapted well and was liked by most of the crew. Subject received an honorable discharge July 14, 1954.

Bernie rose from his chair and walked over to the thick-plated glass window. A yacht caught his attention as he looked out on Key Biscayne. "I'd say this guy's a sociopath if you ask me," Bernie mumbled as he turned, seated himself, and continued reading.

Upon discharge, subject relocated to Miami, Florida to join his parents, who had moved from Louisville during his enlistment in the Navy.

Investigation indicated subject had difficulty finding employment during the first six months following his discharge.

February 12, 1955, subject sat for the City of Miami Police Department's Recruitment Examination Test. On April 1, 1955, subject entered the City of Miami Police Academy and graduated first in the class. Miami Police files suggest, however, that the subject's performance was below average, having the lowest arrest history in the department. On six occasions, subject's performance evaluation was substandard.

On two occasions subject was recommended for termination due to poor evaluations, but in each case, pressure was applied from local Police Benevolent Association and subject was placed on probation status.

Subject is known as being a flirt, and on numerous occasions was reprimanded for having inter-departmental affairs.

Subject married Dorothy Shelby August 2, 1956, and after fathering two children was divorced in 1961. Subject remains single as of this report.

Subject retired from the City of Miami Police Department October 18, 1975.

Intelligence sources report that on September 5, 1975, subject was introduced to Carlos Martinez, a Cuban refugee, and a supposed one-time operative for the CIA. No confirmation of said info as of this date.

On January 3, 1976, subject was arrested with six other co-defendants by West Palm Beach Sheriff's Office for possession of six thousand five hundred pounds of marijuana. After pleading nolo contendere, they were fined three thousand dollars each and placed on probation for one year.

End of Report

"I'm going to get this SOB if it's the last thing I do!" Bernie snapped.

Senior Agent Robert Cunningham of the Drug Enforcement Administration leaned back in his chair. He sat behind a mammoth oak desk on the fourteenth floor of the First Federal Building in downtown Miami.

"What are you thinking?" Cunningham asked Bernie Colgate.

"It'll take a setup with a lot of finesse."

"That's what I thought you'd say." Cunningham smiled. "Tell you what, take a couple of days to think it over and get back to me on Friday with your plan. If I like your idea, the sky's the limit."

Bernie rose. "Okay, by the way," he said heading for the door, turning slightly, "if my plan is approved, I call the shots."

Cunningham looked up from his paperwork. "Let's see the plan first."

Bernie closed the door behind him as he left. *It would be the perfect sting. It has all the necessary ingredients,* Bernie thought. He took the elevator down to the third floor to retrieve his car. He had to figure out a way to infiltrate Sonny Mitchell's organization.

The expense for what he was about to do had not yet been approved, nor had he mentioned it to Cunningham, but if the trip was successful, he'd have no trouble being reimbursed.

The door of the elevator opened, and he stepped out into the indoor parking area. He immediately spotted his sky-blue Mercedes 250 SL. It was early, and the air was still relatively cool in the parking lot. The fresh breeze blowing off Biscayne Bay soothed the city of its incessant humidity. By noon, the temperature would be well over ninety.

I have everything, Bernie thought. *But then again, what do I really have? A confiscated car to drive, and a nice paying job with good benefits, but what's all that?*

He pulled the keys to the plush automobile from his pocket and inserted one in the door. He remembered to duck as he poured his long frame into the roadster. When he had settled in behind the leather-covered wheel, he reached for the ignition and then hesitated. *I miss Marlene and the children,* he thought. His heart ached to be with his wife. He made a mental note to drive up to Fort Lauderdale on Sunday to see them.

Bernie pulled out on Southwest First Street and headed to I-95 North.

After crossing six lanes of traffic at seventy miles an hour, he barely made the exit to the Dolphin Expressway. Finally, he floored the accelerator of the small automobile and sped toward the towering overpass with the Miami River below.

From this vantage point, motorists had an aerial view of downtown Miami. On Bernie's left he saw the Orange Bowl, and he remembered the countless times he and Marlene had watched the Dolphins play. For that very reason, he no longer went there.

To this day, he could not determine what had gone wrong between them. It could have been the long hours or the uncertainty of the future, the not knowing where he might be sent next, or for that matter, if he would return. He knew she hated his lifestyle.

Five minutes later, the sleek automobile pulled into the long-term parking lot at Miami International Airport. He dreaded the next couple of days..

Chapter Eleven

The circular drive of the magnificent hotel was framed by rampant tropical foliage in brilliant colors. As Michael stopped his car under the pinstriped canopy, a valet instantly opened the car door and handed him a ticket. Before Michael could relinquish his seat, the valet quickly moved into the BMW's seat and raced out of sight, leaving Michael standing alone at the base of the steps.

Why Sonny wants to have lunch here, I will never know, thought Michael. *This place is crawling with narcotics officers.*

The Mutiny was one of South Miami's most fashionable hotels. It was the "in" spot where jetsetters and dope smugglers met to rub elbows. It was possible to get a single room for eighty dollars a night or a spacious suite for five hundred dollars. The name alone attracted the rich as well as those who lived on the "edge."

Adjacent to the hotel was the Mutiny Club, an exclusive private dining club. The menu began with escargot, ended with chilled stone crab, and consisted of other delectable dishes in between. If you were feeling down and wanted to lift your spirits, you could order a four-hundred-dollar bottle of Bordeaux.

Michael vaulted up the rustic steps and paused momentarily to survey the surroundings. Directly across from the hotel was an eight-million-dollar spectacle. At least a hundred sailboats waited at anchor in Dinner Key Marina. Because they were so closely situated, if one lost its moorings, countless others would be damaged. *How careless the wealthy,* Michael thought. He made his way around to the side entrance of the club and entered the reception area, where two smiling hosts greeted him. He showed them his membership card and then climbed the staircase to the bar and dining room. At the upper platform, Michael checked his reflection in an antique mirror encased in a Gothic woodcarving. He adjusted his short-sleeved safari jacket and ran his fingers through his sandy hair. Satisfied, he entered the hum of the dining room. The place was always jammed during the lunch hour. Michael made a quick reconnaissance of the room and saw Sonny sitting at the far end of the bar talking to a local disco queen. Michael nudged his way through the crowd toward Sonny. Frustrated people stood three deep at the bar, demanding to be heard over the roar of countless conversations as they tried not to spill their drinks.

Sonny looked up and spotted Michael coming toward him.

"Hey, Mike!" Sonny jokingly bellowed. "Did you bring your wife?"

Michael stopped and nudged himself between Sonny and the girl. He bent forward with a serious frown on his face and looked the girl squarely in her heavily made-up, thick-lashed green eyes.

"Sweetheart, I came over here to warn you about this guy," he said nodding toward Sonny.

"Warn me about what?" the girl asked, looking at Sonny and then back at Michael.

Looking serious, Michael bent down and whispered in her ear, "The minute you turn your back on him he'll screw you, and I won't say where."

The girl's lower jaw dropped, and her face turned crimson. She grabbed her purse and quickly left the bar without a word.

Sonny laughed hysterically, sloshing some of the booze in his glass on the floor. "Why did you say that you asshole?" Michael just grinned.

"What's this shit about my wife?"

"I was only joking," Sonny laughed.

"Well, fuck you and the horse you rode in on," Michael chuckled. The two men left the bar and walked over to a table Sonny had reserved.

After they had seated themselves in the plush leather captains' chairs, Sonny waved to the attractive, young waitress to take their drink order. Sonny chose his usual Dewar's and water. Michael decided on rum and coke.

Michael placed his elbows on the table and leaned forward. "Chubby, why are we having lunch here?" he asked in a hushed tone. "This place is beginning to look like Little Havana," he said as his arms swept the room.

"Oh, come on, Michael, lighten up. Just stop being so damned paranoid. Lou wants to have lunch with us."

"Great, but why here? Shit!"

The waitress brought their drinks, quickly served them, and left.

"I was talking to the Bear this morning," Sonny said. "I've had him check around to see if he can locate our merchandise. Whoever hijacked the Chubby Ann has a boatload of marijuana or knows who has it. Eventually word always gets around."

"Has the Bear come up with anything yet?" Michael questioned.

"Yeah, maybe," Sonny answered without hesitation. "Seems one of his buyers looked at some stuff last night, about three thousand pounds. None of it was in bales, though, just loosely packed in black garbage bags. I figure it's probably ours."

"That makes sense," Michael said, lighting a cigarette. "Whoever ripped us off knew that the Colombians mark each bale with an identifying number that's easily traced. There's no doubt in my mind it's our merchandise. It'll mildew in a couple of days packed like that. Who has the merchandise?" Michael asked.

"Orlando Rodriguez."

"What? Shit, Sonny. That can only mean one thing!" Michael said angrily.

"Yeah, that's what I said, too," Sonny replied, sipping his drink. "Looks like there's a Cuban in the woodpile. I understand from the Bear that Carlos and Orlando used to be running dogs. If that's true, that makes Carlos highly suspect."

"Do you think there's any way we can prove it?"

"The point is," Sonny answered, "what do we do if Carlos did have something to do with the hijacking? Kill him?"

"Sonny," Michael leaned forward and whispered, just loud enough for Sonny to hear, "there's not enough money in this world to make it worth going to jail for murder. I'm not having this conversation with you," Michael said firmly.

"You know I agree with you, Michael, but you and I both know that if a crewman or anybody else wants to rip us off, there's nothing we can do to stop them. That's part of the risk we take in this business."

"So, what are you saying?"

"It's the old adage, 'What goes around comes around. Eventually, Carlos will need a favor, and that's when we stick it to him."

Michael relaxed in his chair. "What about Mehejas? When are we going to tell him?"

"Carlos is meeting with him this afternoon. I don't like the idea of having to depend on Carlos to translate for us. Before we know it, he'll have stolen our connection."

Thinking about what Sonny had just said, Michael glanced over Sonny's shoulder to see Louis Steinberg slowly advancing toward their table. He was adorned in all the accouterments of a winner; Black Florsheim slip-on dress shoes, a gray Pierre Cardin suit, a Gold Rolex watch on his left wrist, and a thick, 18-carat gold bracelet on the right. A two-carat diamond pinky ring completed the projected image.

"Sorry I'm late, fellows," the attorney said, pulling over a chair. "I got stuck in this shit traffic."

Sonny and Michael both rose to greet him.

"Hey Lou," Sonny smiled and reached out to shake his hand.

"You look well," Michael smiled as he offered his hand. Lou chuckled and settled into his chair.

"Needless to say, you fellows have been keeping me busy. I just came from a meeting with our friends in Customs."

"Why is Customs involved?" Sonny asked. "Oh, do you want a drink, Lou?"

"Sure, why not? How about a Stolichnaya?"

"You still drink that Russian shit?" Michael cringed and signaled the waitress as she passed by their table.

Sonny ordered another round for him and Michael and the Stolichnaya for Lou. The waitress quickly took the order and headed to the bar.

"Nobody's claimed the Chubby Ann," Lou continued, "so Customs has confiscated her, pending a declaration of ownership. I can't do anything until you guys tell me how you want to handle it."

"Damn, Lou! I thought you were taking care of all that!" chided Sonny.

Lou's eyebrows rose. "Well, if you remember correctly, the boat is in a Costa Rican corporation. My hands are tied until your attorney in Costa Rica sends me certified copies of the bearer shares, a certified copy of the title, and copies of the leasing agreement. All of that has to be stamped via the Oficina de Registro and the U.S. Consulate. Then I can get somebody up here to represent the corporation."

Puzzled, Michael said, "I thought you were representing the business."

"I am. Indirectly," Lou answered. "I'll ask an attorney friend of mine to be the official representative. This thing has to be handled at arm's length."

"I don't understand," Sonny questioned.

"It's like this," Lou said, trying to explain, so Sonny and Michael could easily understand. "There's already a tie-in between us. If something goes down, I'll be subject to conspiracy charges. Retaining another attorney for the Costa Rican corporation's interest insulates both the Costa Rican corporation's interest and the Costa Rican attorney from us. That way, there's no link between you, me, the Costa Rican company, or the Chubby Ann. Trust me. I know what I'm doing."

"What kind of ticket are we looking at?" Michael asked.

Lou thought for a second. "Oh, for starters I'd say twenty-five thousand."

"Damn, Lou! That's outrageous!" objected Michael.

Lou dropped his head without answering, scowling as if his feelings had been hurt.

"How long will it take?" Sonny asked, interrupting the brief silence.

Lou raised his head to look at Sonny.

"After I get the documents, maybe a couple of weeks, three at the most," Lou said, waiting to see if Sonny was going to object.

"Okay," Sonny said as if to finalize the somewhat heated conversation. "Michael will get the money to you in a couple of days. Right, Michael?"

"Sure," Michael sighed with resignation.

"The Chubby Ann is worth well over eight hundred thousand, Lou. Don't mess this up!" Michael warned.

The waitress stopped at their table. "Would you gentlemen care to order lunch?"

Sonny looked at his companions. Both were quiet in thought.

"Tell you what," Sonny smiled at the pretty waitress and answered, "Give us a few more minutes, would you, sweetheart?"

"Sure, no problem," she said and headed to another table.

Lou relaxed. Now that his fee had been settled, he loosened his tie and motioned for Sonny and Michael to lean forward.

"The main reason I wanted to have lunch with you fellows is because I've got a friend, and I mean a big friend out of Washington that I want to introduce to you. He's with the State Department, and believe me, he has a lot of clout."

"I'm not following you," Sonny said. "What's the deal?"

"To tell you the truth, I don't know. He just asked me to set up a meeting with both of you for this evening, if that's possible."

"What's his name?" Michael asked.

"Manuel Garcia-Lopez," Lou responded.

"Shit, Lou! You know we're trying to stay away from the Cubans."

"I know," interrupted Lou. "This guy's not Cuban. He's half Mexican and half English. His father is from a wealthy family in Mexico City. He married a Vassar girl from Boston. Manuel's been in the political limelight since the middle sixties when I first met him."

"And you have no idea what he wants?" Michael asked.

Lou shook his head. "I do know that you can trust him."

"All right," Sonny said, reaching for the menu. "We'll meet you at my place tonight at eight o'clock."

Chapter Twelve

Tourists driving through Key Largo, Florida, would never have known that only a hundred yards off Highway U.S. 1, on a sandy road hidden by palmetto bushes and scrub oaks, illegal cockfighting was big business.

The arena was round, about twenty feet across, and had a two-foot cement wall encircling the fighting area. For some reason, it was painted red. Sawdust covered the floor. It was hot under the tin-roofed enclosure where one hundred eighty sweaty bodies balanced on makeshift bleachers.

Billy Aiken, an enterprising boat captain and owner of the property stood to the side counting the day's receipts. Ten dollars a head was not bad, plus the profits on all the beer.

And this crowd drank a lot of beer.

Electricity in the Florida Keys is expensive. To eliminate the need for air-conditioning, Billy reached out and flipped a switch on the wall. An electric water pump hummed as the sprinkler system on the roof sprayed the sun-scorched tin ceiling cooling it instantly. A good businessman, Billy was also a good judge of character and much better than Carlos thought. The patrons were all Cuban, except Billy and the Colombian, Mehejas. A short, wiry-built man whose dark eyes mirrored his intelligence, Mehejas was a better judge of the cocks than Carlos, and Carlos was beginning to realize it. Mehejas had already won six thousand dollars. *He is a sharp, cunning bastard,* Carlos decided.

Since Carlos had picked him up after lunch at his hotel, Carlos had not mentioned the loss of the hijacked merchandise. He was unaware that Mehejas already knew about the loss and was waiting for Carlos to broach the subject. Mehejas had as much patience as money, which was saying a lot. Now a forty-four-year-old Colombian from Riohacha, where life expectancy was twenty-six years, he had found out early in life that his patience always paid off.

In the arena, the cock's eye was glazed with fury. The taste of blood had set his adrenalin flowing. His heart raced at 175 beats per minute. He felt no pain in his left eye as it hung by the optic nerve next to his beak. As he whipped his head from side to side, the eye flopped back and forth.

"Dale! Dale duro!" the crowd shouted. "Give him hell!"

Carlos stood silent, watching his rooster fight. Fate was not with his cock today, and Carlos held no hope of winning. A three-thousand-dollar side bet and a fifteen-hundred-dollar rooster both circled round and round in front of Carlos…dying.

"Arriba, arriba!" somebody shouted. "Go for it!"

"Ehijo de Puta!" someone else screamed. "Son of a bitch!" It was difficult to distinguish which was more barbaric, the crowd or the roosters.

Carlos's rooster finally fell to the sawdust and quivered. The opponent pecked at its head until his owner rushed over and picked up the champion. Carlos' rooster was dead. Amid all the mayhem, the losers started paying their bets.

Infuriated at the outcome of the fight, Carlos seated himself beside Mehejas in the front row. Carlos' eyes were red from anger and too many Heinekens. He raised his arms and signaled the old guajiro behind the hurriedly erected bar for another beer. The old man laid his cigar down on a plank and reached into the cooler.

Mehejas watched Carlos through his peripheral vision. *There is something about his eyes,* he thought. *They are almost black and so piercing and angry. He looks as though he is possessed by a demon. Maybe he is,* Mehejas decided.

The crowd settled back in their seats impatiently waiting for the next fight. It was rumored throughout the audience that this was the big fight. Carlos was fighting another of his roosters. Maestro, or teacher as they called the rooster, had the unique ability to jump high into the air, fluttering his wings, and with razor-sharp espuelas, or spurs, and slash his opponent's throat. Maestro usually did this in the first sixty seconds of the fight.

A tall, slender, elderly Cuban called Tico walked into the arena holding his rooster. Carlos' handler, Javier, was overweight and hunched forward. Holding Maestro, he bit into his tobacco as he entered the ring behind Tico.

One spectator whispered to another, "Carlos and Tico have ten thousand riding on this last fight." This information was passed along, whispered with the turning and nodding of heads that looked like dominos following in succession, until everyone in the establishment knew the significance of this fight.

Mehejas bet a thousand dollars on Carlos' rooster out of courtesy. In his mind, cockfighting was okay, but he much preferred watching a good dog fight. Cocks only strutted about, silently flapping their wings and occasionally jumping in the air. As an observer, Mehejas was usually emotionally detached unless he had money riding on the outcome. Dog fighting was a different matter. They were noisier and the fight lasted longer. Watching two good dogs go to it was exciting to Mehejas. Amid growling and biting, everyone could hear bones snap and the howling from pain. *Dog fighting runs closer to a man's soul,* he thought.

Carlos gulped his beer down and ordered another. This was his ninth within the past two hours. His flushed face reflected the alcohol.

Tico cooed to his bird. Javier combed his rooster's feathers with his fingers as if to comfort and reassure the bird. Both men saw the judge nod his head. They walked to the center of the ring and knelt in the sawdust holding the cocks about a foot off the ground. The teasing began.

Grasping the roosters, the men would shove the birds' faces into each other, antagonizing them. The birds would peck at each other in hostility, causing tiny droplets of blood to appear. After a minute or so of this ritual, the men separated with their prized birds and took a position opposite each other alongside the cement wall.

The judge stood ready with his gavel. A moment later the gavel went down with a bang and the cocks were released. Each strutted to the middle of the ring; wings held out from their bodies and feathers ruffled on their backs. A millisecond before meeting head-on, each bird jumped straight up, wings flapping in the air, slashing out with its spurs. Carlos's rooster inflicted a slash on the other bird's chest, knocking it off balance and backward. It seized this opportunity for the kill. Tico's rooster was picking itself up when his adversary landed. As they picked and picked, their spurs became entangled. The judge pounded his gavel.

Carlos disagreed. "Vaya al carajo!" he shouted. "Go to hell!"

Tico and Carlos' trainer were separating the birds.

"No me jodas!" the judge shouted, glaring back at Carlos. "Don't screw with me!"

Carlos rose to his feet. Mehejas grabbed his arm and pulled him back to his seat. "Tranquillo carbon," Mehejas urged. "Quiet, asshole."

Carlos jerked his arm from Mehejas' grasp. "Mierda!" Carlos snarled. "Shit!"

Tico and the trainer were ministering to their birds. Tico examined his bird closely, rubbing its feathers and continuously talking to it as though the cock understood every word he was saying.

Javier stroked his rooster, lifting its wings occasionally to cool it off. He, too, talked softly and continuously to his bird and kept blowing into the cock's face to give him oxygen.

Again, the cocks were ready to fight. The judge stood, gavel in hand, and surveyed the fighters.

Superstition runs a strong current in Cuban culture. Tico was no exception. Before releasing his rooster, he blew his breath into the bird's nostrils. Then he stuck the bird's head in his mouth and held its neck clenched between his teeth. Tico did not know exactly what the gesture was supposed to do, but he had seen it done hundreds of times before, so he did it too.

The gavel sounded and once again the birds were pitted.

"Kill the bastard!" Carlos shouted, rising to his feet. The birds clashed. Pecking and jumping they danced around. As expected, Carlos' rooster jumped high in the air, at least three feet or more.

The crowd roared.

Tico's bird instinctively took the defensive. He raised his head high presenting his opponent a false target.

Fluttering back down, Carlos's bird struck outward with both spurs. Before it could complete the killing arc, Tico's rooster ducked its head and at the same time lowered its body in a graceful bow.

Missing his target and landing off guard, Carlos' cock was unprepared for his challenger.

Filled with excitement and too many beers Carlos shouted, "Dale! Dale! Give it to him!"

As Tico's bird thrust its body upwards, he plunged into his antagonist knocking him into the sawdust. In an instant, the challenger was on top of Carlos' rooster striking a crippling blow to its wing.

Carlos' rooster remained in the sawdust, trembling, with Tico's rooster towering over him. They were shackled together by a deeply embedded spur from Tico's bird.

The trainers ran forward to separate the birds.

The crowd whistled and booed. Carried away with anger, Carlos attempted to hurdle the cement wall to rescue his bird. He tripped in mid-stride, falling on the sawdust, and scraping his arm on the small, rough particles of wood.

The judge saw Carlos leap the wall. To stop him from entering the arena, the judge hammered his gavel.

"Stay out of the ring!" he ordered.

Carlos staggered to his feet, his embarrassment and pain enraging him. "Como mierdo!" he screamed at the judge. "Eat shit!"

The judge was not intimidated by the contrabandista. He rose from behind the temporary desk, which was a card table, and took a defiant stance.

Mehejas remained seated, watching the circus.

Carlos jumped back over the cement wall. He pushed his way through the spectators gathering around the arena, bulldozing his way toward the judge.

The judge made the mistake of thinking that Carlos was a typical Latin, a man of words instead of action. Before the judge realized what was happening, Carlos struck him squarely between the eyes.

The judge shook the fog from his head. Several of his friends wrestled the screaming Carlos to the ground.

Latin blood flowing and outweighing Carlos by forty pounds; the judge threw himself onto the pile. The crowd surged toward the confrontation.

Two shots from Mehejas' nine-millimeter automatic pistol startled and deafened the crowd. The turmoil instantly ceased. Dribbles of water from the roof trickled into the arena.

The human stack of men untangled themselves to see Mehejas standing on the lip of the arena pointing the gun at them. He calmly motioned to Carlos, waving his gun for him to follow.

Carlos picked himself up from the ground. His shirt was torn from the scuffle. Sawdust covered his body, and a slight trickle of blood ran from his nose. "You damn bastards!" he shouted.

On the way out, Mehejas made a decision. He would give Carlos no more merchandise. His business relationship with Carlos was done.

Thirteen

Bernie Colgate parked the Hertz rental car at the bottom of the incline that led to the basement. It was his first visit to the New Orleans Community Correctional Center. He pushed the parking brake with his left foot and reached across the seat for his briefcase.

As he opened the car door, the stench of rotting refuse almost caused him to gag. To his right, a prison trustee was hosing down several greasy garbage cans. The clogged drain made Bernie tiptoe through the milky-looking substance to the loading dock. The six-story jail was no more than five years old but had a dilapidated appearance. To the left of the loading dock was the rear entrance to misery, fear, and occasionally death. Beside the double sliding pneumatic doors, Bernie saw a glass-enclosed cage occupied by an elderly hack wearing a black uniform with dandruff garnishing his shoulders.

Bernie reached for the inside breast pocket of his coat, and through a small square opening in the glass handed the man his identification packet. With unusual effort, the old man fumbled with the wallet revealing a finely engraved gold badge pinned to one side and the I.D. card with Bernie's photograph on the other.

The deputy pressed a button. "Got a gun?" he asked through a speaker.

Bernie nodded and reached for his left armpit, extracted a Colt nine-millimeter automatic pistol, and laid it on the ledge in the opening. He bent over and removed a stainless steel 38 Derringer nestled in an ankle holster on his left leg.

The deputy took the handguns, one at a time, and gave Bernie a metal tag with a number embossed on one side.

"Who do you want to see?"

"Frank Howell," Bernie impatiently responded.

The old man continued at a slow pace as he leafed through some papers and picked up the telephone to call someone. After completing the call, the deputy pressed another button, and the pneumatic doors slid apart.

"Go on in. Somebody will be down in a minute to get you."

Bernie entered the basement receiving area. Stacked against one wall were pallets with brown boxes stamped USDA. in large black letters. *Must be a government subsidy,* he thought.

Soon a tall, middle-aged, heavyset black deputy, who acted as if he would rather be anywhere but there, appeared carrying a large set of keys on an oversized key ring. Bored with his position, he looked forward to retiring and spending time fishing with his son. Wistfully, he thought, *I've just got to hang in there for a few more years.* Finally, giving his full attention to Bernie, he said, "You DEA?"

Bernie nodded, not bothering to hide the fact that he was impatient to speak with Howell.

The deputy turned around and started walking in the direction from which he had come. Bernie followed. After they had rounded the corner, the deputy stopped at one of several elevators. There were no buttons. The man inserted a key from a large ring and twisted it. Moments later, the door opened, and they entered. Deep in thought, they rode to Howell's floor without talking.

Bernie knew that Frank Howell had to be under a lot of pressure. He had been arrested with twenty-six thousand pounds of marijuana aboard a large barge at Houma, Louisiana. After going over

Howell's file, Bernie felt reasonably sure that with the charges against him, he would be a viable candidate for cooperation. Bernie's success or failure depended upon how well he manipulated the interview with Howell.

As the elevator sluggishly moved, and the time for the interview grew nearer, Bernie's anxiety increased. His armpits began to sweat, and bile started to come up in his esophagus. He reached into his coat pocket, retrieved a roll of Rolaids, and popped one in his mouth. *Failure here would cause a tremendous setback to my plan,* he thought grimly. Stiffening his spine, he reminded himself he would not fail.

Bernie detested failure and was determined not to lose. All of his life he had been a winner, and he had no intention of allowing Frank Howell to change his momentum. He would apply as much pressure as necessary to get the job done.

He remembered back when he was a kid playing tennis. The neighborhood kids had reached the point of hating to see him play. He would often have a temper tantrum when he lost. The result would usually end in violence, and some of the kids finally refused to play with him. He had once broken the nose of one boy and given him a black eye because the kid had accused him of cheating. His obsession with winning continued in college. His basketball coach had suspended him for five games for pushing a player into a wall, which resulted in the young man having a broken wrist. Bernie's history of always having to win followed him into his current career.

"Sixth floor is where we keep the federal prisoners," the deputy said.

Bernie managed a slight smile but did not comment.

On the sixth floor, the deputy ushered Bernie into a small reception room. His first impression was "plain." The walls were bare and freshly painted stark white. The combination of floor wax, sweat, and cigarette smoke blended in a strange odor, creating a hostile, detached atmosphere. Bernie noted that every door in the building had a glass, wire mesh-covered window, except the elevator doors.

The deputy motioned Bernie over to a round table with a white Formica top and turned to leave. There were several chairs pushed underneath the table. Bernie laid his briefcase on the table, popped the latches, and seated himself.

In a moment, he heard the door open and looked up from the file he had been reading. Frank Howell stood inside the doorway filling its space and leaving only inches to spare. His denim shirt stopped at his lower forearms. The sleeves were too tight to button. His denim pants legs had the letters "CCC" stenciled in white paint.

Bernie stood. "Mr. Howell?"

Frank Howell's jowls worked like the gills of a fish as he nodded his head. Undecided whether or not he should enter, he hesitated at the door, his eyes darting about the room. Finally stepping inside, he released the door. The "swoosh" broke the silence.

"Come in and have a seat," Bernie said, pushing out a chair with his foot.

The size of the man surprised Bernie. His belly jiggled as he moved across the floor. *He easily weighs three hundred pounds,* Bernie thought, *maybe even more.*

Frank Howell's skin had an unhealthy, scaly, and dry appearance, which was probably caused by the starchy diet he was being fed, and the lack of sun while he had been incarcerated. Bernie would never have guessed that this obese man was a boat captain and a damn good one at that.

Howell sat down. The chair groaned under his weight. "What do you want?" he asked in a baritone voice.

"Mr. Howell, my name is Colgate, Bernie Colgate. I'm with the Justice Department." He watched Howell's reaction. There was none.

"To be blunt and to the point, I need your help." Bernie paused. "I can also help you. That is if you cooperate with me."

Howell moved unceremoniously in his chair, looking questioningly at Bernie. His jaw was set like a moray eel clamped on its prey. Howell's face turned red, and then he heaved himself out of the chair. It slid backward and fell to the floor.

"I'm no snitch!" Howell barked as he turned to leave the room.

"I've got your file," Bernie said loudly, rising to his feet. "You've been in this dump for fourteen weeks now, and where are your friends? Huh? Who's the bigger fool, the guy walking the street or the asshole in prison?"

Frank stopped dead in his tracks.

"You have three counts of conspiracy against you; importing, possessing, and distributing, and each count carries fifteen years. That's forty-five years! Now you tell me, who's the damn asshole?"

In one fluid movement, Howell spun on his heels to face his antagonist. He realized Colgate was telling the truth, no matter how difficult it was to accept. He began to relax and stepped back toward the table.

With confidence, Bernie seated himself again and continued. "Look, there's no reason why you have to spend another night here in jail." His voice softened. "If we can reach an agreement, you can walk out of here right now. It's as simple as that." Assured that he had Howell hooked, Bernie leaned back in his chair, folded his arms, and waited.

Reluctantly, Howell seated himself. Deep in thought, he fitfully moved his huge hands, toying with the ashtray and then popping his knuckles. He was trying to come up with a response.

Taking a deep breath, Howell finally said. "Look, if I talk, I won't last three minutes on the street."

"I don't want you to talk," Bernie said evenly. "I want you to do something for me."

Frank squirmed in his chair. Confused, he looked at Bernie and said, "What do you mean do something? What could I possibly do for you?"

"You'll find out in plenty of time," Bernie answered. "If you're afraid, I can see that you're placed in the Federal Witness Protection Program. That means you'll be relocated to a different state, given a new name, with papers to match and enough money for a fresh start."

"Will you put that in writing?"

"Yes, if we come to an agreement now."

Howell sighed. "Okay," he paused and then continued, "get me the hell out of here." Not sure he had made the right decision; he looked into Bernie's cold, dead eyes. They frightened him, and chills rolled up his spine.

With the conversation almost over, Bernie's voice took on a knife's edge. "Let's get one thing straight, you fat prick. If you try to run or try to screw me, you'll never live to see the inside of a jail again."

Fourteen

Sonny called it "The Little House." Built in the late forties, it had sold for seventy-five hundred dollars. It looked just like the other two hundred fifty matchbox houses built in the same reasonably priced neighborhood.

With time, however, most families outgrew the tiny two bedrooms. By the mid-1960s, the area had taken on a different appearance. An epidemic of bedroom additions, carports, and Florida rooms spread like a contagious disease.

Today, thanks to inflation, "The Little House" was worth over two hundred thousand dollars.

When Sonny bought the house in 1977, he had given an interior decorator carte blanche. In a matter of months, an additional one hundred fifty thousand dollars had been hammered, pasted, glued, hung, rearranged, torn out, and painted throughout the structure. This made it one of the most attractive, yet unobtrusive, homes in Miami's Southwest Section. Still, it was small. "Cozy," Sonny said.

Michael and Sonny sat at the teak bar. The wood that Sonny had shipped in from Costa Rica was like much of the other woodwork within the house. Sonny sipped a scotch and soda. Michael nursed a vodka on the rocks. They waited for Lou Steinberg and Manuel Lopez.

"I just had the place swept," Sonny mused. "I'll bet I've spent twenty grand. Hell, maybe more, and I've yet to find one of those little boogers."

Michael went to the icemaker to get more ice . "Be glad you

haven't," he smiled. "You find one and it's the old I gotcha bullshit!" He twisted the top off of a new bottle of Smirnoff.

"Chubby, have you ever thought about what you'd do if we got caught?"

"Hell yes! Costa Rica is where it's happening. As soon as I become a pensionado, those bastards won't ever be able to touch me. You should start making plans for yourself, my man. This isn't going to last forever, you know. That's why I've been so reluctant to get you too heavily involved, being married and all. I'd hate to see anything happen to you and Maria."

Michael was touched by what Sonny had said. It was not often that Chubby showed his inner feelings. "Ah, stop worrying. Another year and we'll both retire."

"I'm not worrying, but I do want you to look into buying more land in San Jose next time we fly down there, you hear?"

Michael and Maria had been to Costa Rica many times. Sonny's ex-wife had introduced them to that wonderful country several years ago. They fell in love with the people, the climate, and especially the democratic government that stabilized the country. Michael and Sonny had partnered in a joint venture and had built a beautiful home there. Maria loved the place.

"Yes, Dad," Michael joked. Momentarily, his forehead wrinkled. "I've been trying to figure out what's going on with this guy Lopez we're supposed to be meeting. What's he got on his mind?"

The sound of an automobile parking in the driveway caught their attention.

"You'll find out in a few minutes," Sonny said, sliding from his stool.

Lou Steinberg was wearing the same clothes he had worn at lunch. He entered the house first, followed by a middle-aged aristocratic-looking man wearing a pleasant smile.

Michael and Sonny remained standing at the bar as the two men entered. Lou bent down and set his briefcase beside a chair. He and

Lopez seemed relaxed, enjoying the casualness of old friends.

"Fellows, I'd like you to meet an old chum of mine. Manuel, meet Sonny Mitchell and Michael Jansen."

Manuel Lopez had an infectious smile. His upper lip sported a well-trimmed mustache, slightly graying and matching his razor-cut hair. Deep brown eyes reflected confidence. He was wearing black patent leather shoes, grey slacks, and a freshly pressed white linen Vera Cruz shirt.

"Good evening," he said, bowing slightly and extending his hand. "I've been looking forward to meeting you gentlemen. I'm sure you are curious as to the purpose of my visit."

"As a matter of fact, yes," Sonny replied, motioning to them to have a seat. "May I offer you a drink?"

"Yes, please," Manuel answered. "A little sherry, if you don't mind."

"And you, Lou?" Michael asked.

"Oh, Tanqueray and tonic will be fine. You're starting to give me a complex about my Stoli."

"Michael, would you do the honors?" Sonny waved his hand toward the refrigerator.

"Certainly," Michael said as he reached for two glasses.

"Lou tells me you work for the State Department," Sonny said, looking at Manuel.

"Yes, I do. Unofficially, that is. You see, I'm an attorney by profession. Due to my family ties in Mexico, I occasionally serve in an unofficial government capacity."

Michael placed the drinks on the table and then lifted his glass. "Salud, here's to Mexico," he said.

"Thank you for your hospitality," Manuel smiled and returned the gesture.

"Tell me," Sonny said, attempting to steer the conversation. "What brings you to Miami?"

"I'm glad you asked," Manuel replied, shifting his weight on the stool. He pulled a Meerschaum pipe from his pocket. "May I?" "Of course," Sonny nodded. He was familiar with Meerschaum pipes because his father had owned one. It had been given as a gift to him by a member of his church congregation when his father had admired it. Meerschaum came from tiny shells of fossilized sea creatures that fell to the floor of the ocean, and over millions of years were covered with many layers of silt. As the crust of the earth rose to sea level, it was eventually mined. The white stone was then beautifully carved into the incomparable Meerschaum pipes.

Lighting his pipe, Manuel Lopez continued. "Mr. Mitchell, we have a mutual friend whose name I am not at liberty to disclose. He suggested I talk with you. I made some inquiries here and there, and I concluded that you and your organization are indeed the right people to approach with this proposal."

Sonny and Michael unconsciously straightened on their stools, listening intently.

"You and your group," Manuel continued, "are not the typical run-of-the-mill dope smugglers. By this, I mean that you are non-violent and honest in your dealings. Fair might be a better word. What I propose is of a magnitude inconceivable to most men in your profession or anyone else for that matter."

"Excuse me, Mr. Lopez," Sonny interrupted. "Are you going to explain your reasons all night, or are you going to tell us your proposition? Please come to the point."

Manuel's face reddened slightly. "Forgive me. I tend to ramble at times, but it is the most delicate subject." He cleared his throat with a sip of sherry.

"As you know," Manuel said, "the Coast Guard is making it difficult for anyone to get through the Yucatan Channel and the Windward Passage. That leaves the Mona Pass or some other pass hundreds of miles to the east of Puerto Rico. This makes for a much longer cruise and innumerable delays. What would you say if I can guarantee safe passage, plus storage of your merchandise on the island of Cuba, all sanctioned by Fidel Castro?"

The men were immobilized by Lopez's words. Michael and Sonny looked at each other for a moment and then turned their gaze toward Lou. The implications of Lopez's plan were mind-boggling.

"Son of a bitch," Sonny murmured, dragging out his words. The potential of Lopez's suggestion held them in awe.

Manuel remained silent, waiting for his words to reap their full harvest.

Sonny was the first to recuperate from the astonishment and magnitude of the proposal. "That's an interesting statement, Mr. Lopez. That is if you can do what you say. You do know it's borderline treason, don't you?"

"That is true, Mr. Mitchell," Manuel smiled. "However, we are also speaking about the potential of making millions of dollars in a very short time."

"How many people know about this?" Sonny asked steadily.

"Just the four of us and a few of my friends at the Cuban Embassy in Mexico City," Lopez said with a smile. "That is all."

"Assuming we agree," Sonny said, "what's the deal?"

"It's simple. The percentages I quote are based on net profits."

"Which are?" Sonny pressed. "The Cuban government wants fifty percent, and I want five, plus a minimal finder's fee for my friend Lou here." Manuel looked at Lou and winked.

"How far up the Cuban totem pole does this thing go? Politically, I mean?" Michael asked.

Manuel re-lit his pipe, taking his time before answering.

"I have personally discussed the proposal with Mr. Castro and have his approval. It was originally his idea."

Again, the men fell silent.

Lou broke the spell. "I need another drink."

"Help yourself," Sonny replied thoughtfully.

"I'll give the son of a bitch credit for one thing," Michael said, meaning Fidel Castro. "He's smart. The Mariel boatlift was a con job, but this…Man, he's pushing it!"

"If the newspapers are correct," interjected Lou, "Castro is hurting for cash. A marijuana pipeline would funnel millions of dollars into Cuba, offsetting its balance of payments deficit. More than likely, he thinks that by flooding the United States with drugs, the country will go down the toilet and at the same time boost his economy."

"Hell!" Sonny snorted. "Marijuana's not the problem with this country. It's the politicians! Booze is the number one problem with teenagers today. When was the last time you read in the paper that some liquor store clerk was arrested for selling booze to a minor? There's no profit in it for the politicians! Hell no! They get the graft, kickbacks, and all the bureaucratic positions in the Justice Department, all for waging war with the excuse that 'it's all society's problem. Crime is big business for these damn crooks in Washington!"

Manuel laughed. "You sound hostile."

"Damn right I'm hostile," Sonny frowned. "The fundamental role of government is to protect the citizens from each other. It's not supposed to take away my freedom of choice or protect me from myself. Shit! If I want to smoke pot, damn it, or even eat cow shit, that ought to be my decision, not some overweight, jerked off, pimpled-faced bunch of bureaucratic sons of bitches in Washington dictating morality to me."

"I tend to agree with you, Mr. Mitchell," Manuel said. "That is why my conscience is clear about the marijuana dilemma."

"Why don't we do this?" Manuel continued. "I'm going to be in town for two more days. Why don't we get back with Lou in a day or so, and by that time you will have reached your decision."

"That'll be fine," Sonny answered.

Lou and Manuel Lopez rose to leave.

Sonny and Michael sat in silence after the meeting had broken up. They each pondered the importance of their discussion with

Manuel Lopez. Occasionally, one would ask the other a question and then sink back into silence.

"You know, Chubby, this is a kid glove situation, but I like it. Damn, I like it!"

"There's a hell of a lot to consider, Michael." Sonny reached for a bottle of Old Par. "I mean, logistically. Think about it. There's the problem of security. This is not a regular pissant smuggling operation that every asshole and his brother is trying to pull. Shit! The feds will go crazy if they get wind of this. They'll act like we betrayed Old Glory. If we do this, things will sure as hell be different."

"Huh," Michael grunted, lighting a cigarette. "I remember how gung-ho I used to be. Just point me in the right direction and boy, I was ready to go."

"That's the problem today," Sonny mumbled, pouring another drink. "People think if you can drive a boat or fly an airplane you can be a smuggler. That used to be true, but it sure as shit isn't anymore. Hell, I wish that were all there was to it! Sure, some guys luck out, but most of them end up getting busted.

"Sonny was slurring his words. He propped his elbow on the bar and rested his head tiredly in his hand. "I remember when only a handful of people were in the business. It was sort of like a private club. You didn't have to worry about getting screwed. Now, half the country is involved in one way or another. That's why this thing's got to be airtight."

Michael stubbed his cigarette out. He had a foul taste in his mouth. "Okay, Chubby."

"Okay, what?" Sonny blinked.

Surprising even himself, Michael said, "You handle the security, stash houses, boats, and personnel. I'll take care of the other end."

"How do you expect to do that? You don't even speak Spanish."

"That's the point, Sonny, neither do you. We need someone who can handle the Cubans and the Colombians, someone who's trustworthy and can't be motivated by money. We need Maria!"

"What!" Sonny yelled, his face beet red. " You gotta be out of your mind, Michael!"

"Think about it for a minute, Chubby," Michael persisted. "Who else do you know that speaks Spanish fluently and won't screw us? Carlos?"

"Shit!" Sonny grimaced. "I'm waiting for my 'come around' on that one. Let's do it!"

Fifteen

Maria Jansen walked slowly through Burdines in the Dadeland Shopping Mall. Her arms ached from carrying the bulky packages she had hastily bought. Three pairs of pantyhose, several lightweight blouses, two pairs of slacks, and two boxes of shoes made up her load. Maria's favorite pastime had always been shopping. It was the only conflict she and Michael ever had. Michael was happy never to set foot in a store, but Maria could and did easily get lost for hours upon hours, completely absorbed in new shopping experiences.

Her last stop was the men's section to pick out some new cologne for Michael. Tired of his Aramis, she sought something different, maybe something French or English. Whatever she chose would have to be selected quickly. Otherwise, she and Michael would miss Pan Am flight 803 to Panama scheduled to depart at 2:35 that afternoon. *I've got to hurry,* she thought.

"Yes, may I help you?" the effeminate, well-dressed, blonde man said from behind the counter. Maria shuffled her bags and sat them on the counter. Her arms thanked her. Though she could shop all day, her arms were tired from the full shopping bag she was carrying.

"Do you have anything from France?" Maria smiled politely at the tall, handsome man. She wondered why gay men got along so well with women when they preferred their own sex.

"Oh, yes, we just got this in from Paris yesterday," he said, smiling with bright white teeth, much too perfect to be his natural teeth. "Yves Saint Laurent is just wonderful! Here, try this." His eyes twinkled in delight as he gave Maria the bottle.

Maria sprayed a tiny bit on her left wrist, and with the other rubbed it together to diffuse and dry the sample. Sniffing lightly, she checked its aroma.

"You're right," she smiled. "It's nice. I'll take it."

"Cash or charge?"

"Cash, please."

"Let's see now," he said, running his hand down a tax guide. "That'll be $37.95 with tax."

Maria handed him a hundred-dollar bill.

As the clerk rang up the purchase, Maria thought of the other errands she had to take care of before going home. Glancing at her watch, she said aloud, "Oh, the cleaners, I can't forget the cleaners." The clerk looked at her and smiled as she rattled off the errands she still had to do before going home.

It was not unlike Michael to abruptly phone or come home and say, "Pack me a bag," or "We're catching a plane in two hours." Only God and Michael knew where they were going. Maria was used to the sometimes-hectic lifestyle she and Michael lived. She enjoyed traveling with Michael to new places, and of course, shopping while Michael was working. She only objected when he left her at home alone. Often though, he would call her after being away for only several days and say, "Sweetheart, I miss you. Grab the next flight out," and she would hurry to the airport. Her life was always in a constant state of flux, but she loved Michael with all her being and would follow him anywhere.

"Here you are," the clerk said, handing her the purchase.

"Thank you." Maria nestled the cologne in an already overstuffed shopping bag. She gathered up her packages and threaded her way through the grand department store, looking left and right at the creative displays as she carried her cumbersome load. A moment later, a stunning pair of shoes caught her eye. She tilted her head around a package and twisted her wrist to check and see if there was enough time to try on the gorgeous shoes that beckoned her. *No,* she sighed, disappointed that there wasn't time. *Another day, another wonderful shopping day,* she thought wistfully.

As Maria stepped on the down escalator, she didn't notice the human shadow that had been with her for the past hour.

When Maria reached the front door of the department store, she stopped, turned, and started to back out of the entrance to protect her packages. She saw a man a few paces away moving in her direction. After hesitating a moment, she allowed the Cuban gentleman to assist her through the portal.

"Gracias," she said, grateful for the assistance.

As the door closed behind them, Maria turned to walk toward her car and felt resistance on her arm. She glanced over her packages to see what was going on.

The Cuban had taken her arm in his hand and was guiding her by the elbow in a different direction. Maria instinctively resisted, not knowing what was happening. It was too late.

"Mrs. Jansen, no harm will come to you if you remain quiet and come with us," the man said forcefully under his breath. Shocked, Marie said, "What do you mean? Who are you?"

Two other men joined the Cuban, one on each side of Maria. The three men steered her to the street.

"Kidnapped" shot through Maria's mind. A silent scream formed on her lips. *Does this have something to do with Michael? What do they think Michael has done to deserve such retaliation? Maybe it's for ransom. How does this man know my name?* As her mind raced, her knees buckled slightly, and her captors supported her weight.

The Cuban conducted a soundless symphony. At the wave of his arm, a light brown Buick stopped at the curb, and Maria was hustled inside.

Sixteen

Bernie Colgate sat in a white wicker back chair. It had a chrome frame and wooden arms; a replica of the type found in many doctors' offices. He figured Cunningham replaced the overstuffed chair with this new one because it was uncomfortable, making it less likely that its occupant would want to prolong his visit. Bernie rotated onto his left hip as he listened to Cunningham speak. *Why can't the man get on with it?* Bernie was ready to get started on his plan, and Cunningham kept going on and on about it. *Doesn't Cunningham realize that I know what I'm doing?*

"So, you think your plan will work?" Cunningham said again from across his desk.

"Of course, it'll work," Bernie said, smugly. It flashed through Bernie's mind for the second time that Cunningham was an idiot for doubting him.

"Well, it had better! The prosecutor in New Orleans has an airtight case against your snitch, and after dropping charges and giving him immunity, if this one falls through, he'll want your head."

Bernie nodded, impatient to leave. "You'll see my expense receipts in the back of Howell's folder. I'll also need some front money. Two thousand for starters should work."

"All right," Cunningham sighed. "What else?"

"For now, that's all." Bernie knew his plan would work. His plans always worked. If Bernie had any shortcomings, confidence certainly wasn't one of them.

Cunningham began writing a voucher for the money.

"I've got Hans Ferguson available to work with you on this one." He ripped the voucher from its pad. "He's one of the best federal prosecutors in Dade County. Stay connected with him daily, you hear? I don't want any slipups." He hoped Bernie knew what he was doing.

Seventeen

Michael finished counting out ten thousand dollars in cash for the trip to Panama. He separated it into ten stacks, a hundred per pile, and returned the surplus to his safe. It was a Mosler; thirty-two inches high by twenty inches wide. It was bolted to the concrete foundation of the house to discourage thieves. The salesman had told him that it could withstand a temperature of up to two thousand degrees Fahrenheit for three hours. To further reassure Michael, he had also told him that a Mosler bank vault had withstood the atomic bomb in Hiroshima. The primary purpose of the safe was to protect its contents from fire, and this safe would certainly do that. If thieves entered the house while he or Maria was there, they could have the money. Under any other conditions, thieves would have one hell of a time getting the money out of the house.

Michael knelt on the plush, beige carpet in his studio. Before replacing the bundle held in his hand, he leaned down and began counting the other stacks. Each time he removed money from the safe, he always took a quick inventory. To his knowledge, although Maria knew the combination, she had never opened the safe.

Today's count was about four hundred twenty thousand dollars. The safe was not the only place where he had stashed his cash. If he and Maria were ever robbed, the thieves would only get what was in the safe. Michael had an additional five hundred thousand dollars in two separate places out in the backyard. He will never forget the day he buried the money.

He smiled to himself, remembering. His second deal had just

come in; Maria was out shopping, and Sonny had stopped by with the money. He had brought along a six-foot length of six-inch PVC pipe, four caps, and liquid adhesive.

"Didn't know you were a plumber," Michael joked, wondering why Sonny had brought the plumbing supplies.

"I'm gonna show you a trick of the trade, wiseass!" Sonny laughed. "Just follow me."

Michael walked with Sonny through the house to the garage. Sonny grabbed a hacksaw, quickly cut the pipe in half, and glued a cap on one end of each piece. Picking up the other two caps, the glue, and the pipe, Sonny motioned to Michael to follow him.

Puzzled, Michael just stared at Sonny, not moving, wondering what Sonny was up to.

With an elusive smile on his face, Sonny said, "Come on, let's go."

What the hell? Michael thought as he followed Sonny down the hall to the bathroom, where Sonny directed him to have a seat on the closed toilet lid.

"I love you," Sonny said, looking at Michael.

Shocked, Michael said, "What the hell do you mean by that?" *What the hell is going on?* he thought. *Is this a joke or has Sonny lost his mind?* Michael didn't know what to think.

Sonny couldn't control his laughter. "My ex-wife," he laughed, above the noise of the running water, "says that if you can say I love you to somebody sitting on the toilet, you must really love him. I just wanted to prove the bitch wrong!"

Michael burst out laughing at how ridiculous he must look sitting there on the john with his pants up.

Sonny began filling the tub with hot water. When the tub was half full, Sonny shut the water off.

"How much do you want to stack?"

"Stack? Shit, I don't know. I just want to see what the hell you're up to."

Sonny lowered the capped ends of the pipes into the water. "Let's wait a few minutes until they get hot. Meantime, get me the money you want to hide."

Still not completely understanding what Sonny was doing, Michael went to get the money. Sonny was testing the temperature of the PVC when Michael returned.

"They're ready," Sonny said, removing the pipes from the water and drying them with a towel. "The idea is to cap the money inside the pipe while the tube is still hot. Then, as it cools, a vacuum is created. It's like a can of vacuum-packed coffee. No moisture can enter to damage the money. And too, since the PVC is non-ferrous, a metal detector can't pick it up."

"Very clever," Michael said, appreciating the new trick Sonny had taught him.

That evening, after the burial of the two canisters, each holding two hundred fifty thousand dollars, Michael and Maria celebrated with several tall glasses of champagne and an hour of passionate, yet tender lovemaking. Just remembering caused an ache in Michael's groins.

Slowly, as his mind returned to the present, Michael eased the bundle of cash he held in his hand into the safe, closed the door, and spun the combination mechanism to ensure it was locked.

Moving back behind the oversized oak desk, he looked at his watch and wondered what was keeping Maria. *Leave it to a woman,* he thought. As he began to gather up the money they needed for the trip, a slight uneasiness about Maria's delay caused him to shiver.

Shaking off the feeling, he reached out and raked up the money for the trip, stacked it into a neat pile, and set it next to his and Maria's passports.

He leaned back and looked around the studio. It was his special place, set aside from all the rest of the twelve-room house. Mementos of his past stared back at him, framed commendations from Vietnam, a blowgun from the Amazon basin, and Indian pottery from the Dominican Republic. All these things only scratched the surface of this man's quiet personality.

In Michael's early twenties, he had been a professional photographer and many of the most favored moments he had captured lined the walls. There was an 8x10 black and white of Michael standing beside a Piper Cherokee Warrior. He was holding a ripped shirttail commemorating his first solo flight. Another photo showed him standing on the stern of a boat holding an eighty-five-pound grouper he had speared off the Dry Tortugas in the Gulf of Mexico.

As his eyes wandered about the room, they stopped at a picture that touched the depths of his soul. It was a photo of Maria and their five-year-old son Jeffrey. Michael had taken it the day before Jeffrey's death as he danced about the room, celebrating another chess win over his buddy, Dennis. Part of Michael had died that day. He still couldn't believe his son was gone. Jeffrey's death had created an emptiness that could never be filled. If only it hadn't been raining that night; if only Jeffrey had been at home instead of across the street; if only....

The telephone rang, jarring Michael back to the present.

"Hello," he said absentmindedly, glancing at his watch. It was 12:33. *Where is Maria?* Michael wondered. Worry began to fill his thoughts.

"We've got your wife," a husky Latin voice said.

"Who is this?" Michael shouted into the phone, not fully realizing the impact of what had been said.

"We've got your wife," the man said again. "She will not be harmed if you do exactly as I say. You will never see her again if you don't do exactly as I say."

"Who the hell is this?" Michael shouted into the phone, rising to his feet. His breathing quickened as anger and fear welled up inside him; anger at the bastards who had kidnapped Maria and fear that he might lose her.

"Shut up!" the man commanded. "Do not be a fool, Mr. Jansen," he said more casually. "Listen very carefully to me."

"What do you want?" Michael said, his heart beating wildly.

"Do not call the police. It would not be in your best interest, contrabandista!"

Michael stood paralyzed, listening to the man speak.

"I will call you back with instructions."

"Where is…" Michael had not finished when he heard the steady hum on the line.

His mind reeled as he stared at Maria's picture on his desk. *This couldn't possibly be about Maria,* he thought. *No,* he decided. *It has to be about me. Who would want to hurt me? Contrabandista? They know what I do,* he thought. *That has to be it.*

"You son of a bitch! I'll kill you if you hurt Maria!" he shouted to the walls.

He started pacing about the studio, trying to decide what course of action he needed to take. Walking behind the desk, he snatched up the phone and rapidly dialed the familiar number. The line clicked at the other end.

"Yeah?"

"Chubby, I just got a call. Somebody's got Maria."

"Where are you?"

"I'm at home, damn it! Hurry!"

Why in the hell would somebody kidnap Maria? Sonny thought. "I'm already out the door," he said.

The phone clicked as Sonny raced around the room gathering up what he knew he and Michael would need.

Eighteen

Roberto Ruiz hung up the phone. Tilting his cap forward, he shaded his eyes from the glare of the sun reflected off the aluminum siding of a refrigerated truck parked next to the gas pumps. The sun's rays magnified tenfold. As Roberto passed through the invisible beams of sunlight, he was forced to squint until he was clear of the vehicle.

Parked by the phone booth, Carlos sat in a metallic gray 250 SL Mercedes. The air conditioner hummed as he waited for Roberto to return. The on-and-off cycle of the A/C irritated him.

Carlos' thoughts drifted to how smoothly the kidnapping had gone. From a safe distance, Carlos had watched Philippi, Juan, and Antonio grab Maria from the Burdines' parking lot as the driver, Charlie, waited in the car. As they pulled out of the parking area, he and Roberto had moved in behind them, serving as backup. Carlos had no intention of letting Maria see him. Once this scam was over, it would be business as usual for Sonny and Michael.

The two cars had headed for the Keys where Philippi had a rundown safe house on Little Torch Key. Reaching Marathon, Carlos peeled out of the traffic and turned into a 7-Eleven parking lot so that Roberto could call Michael again.

A knocking on the window interrupted his thoughts as Roberto motioned to him to unlock the door.

Nineteen

Sonny whipped the four-wheel drive Blazer into Michael's driveway, skidding to a halt. Before the truck stopped, Sonny swung the door open and jumped out of the vehicle as if some unseen force had thrown him out. His feet hit the pavement three feet from the Blazer as it kicked backward several inches. Sonny hurried up the walkway.

This house is too large for Michael and Maria. There has to be a ghost connected to it, perhaps the spirit of their young son. Sonny thought back to the day that he had been called to the scene of the horrible accident and had later met Michael for the first time at the hospital. Neither Michael nor Maria ever mentioned their son, but Sonny knew they were still grieving for him.

He had often seen Michael and Maria tending the lawn and flowers, and on one occasion even painting the Spanish-style structure. He remembered asking Michael why he hadn't had a contractor do it. Michael brushed the question aside saying, "I can do it *better*. Besides, I've got the time now."

Sonny jumped the two steps to the porch as Michael opened the front door. Michael wore a worried look on his face. Even the suntan over his fair face couldn't hide the flush on his cheeks caused by his anxiety. "You okay?" Sonny asked, closing the door behind them.

"Just a bit shaken up. Want some coffee? I've got a fresh pot on."

"Sure, why not," Sonny answered, following Michael through the tastefully decorated living room.

Sonny smelled jasmine drifting in from the backyard through the open sliding glass doors leading out to the pool and patio area. *The breeze makes it cool and comfortable in here,* he thought as he wondered about Maria. *Why the hell had someone kidnapped her? Was she okay? She damn well better be,* he thought, *or I'll kill the bastards!*

In the kitchen, Michael poured coffee, then reached inside the commercial-size refrigerator and removed a small pitcher of cream. The room resembled a photograph in Architecture Today; everything was neatly in its place, almost unlived in.

Sonny stood by the sink, watching Michael's movements.

Deliberate, he thought. *He's trying not to lose it.*

"Don't clam up on me, Michael. Tell me exactly what happened," he said quietly.

Michael looked at Sonny for a moment and then picked up the cups and moved them to a small dinette in the corner.

"There's not much to tell yet, Chubby."

"All right," Sonny sighed, "try to start at the beginning."

Michael seated himself and sipped his coffee. Sonny, lingering, stood with his back to the sink, arms stretched back and gripping the edge of the counter.

"Well, Maria went shopping at Burdines this morning to pick up some last-minute items, the same as she always does. I was sitting here waiting for her when the phone rang, and some son of a bitch says, "We've got Maria.""

"Tell me about the man's voice," Sonny urged, sitting down beside Michael.

"It was Latin, probably Cuban. He said nothing would happen to Maria if I did as I was told."

"What did he tell you to do?"

"He said he'd call back later with instructions. Then he told me not to call the police, and that it wouldn't be in my best interest."

"The son of a bitch is right about that!" Sonny smiled, trying to change the tempo of the conversation.

"He called me a contrabandista," Michael said, looking at Sonny. "They know what I do. It means smuggler in Spanish."

"Hah! Now we're getting somewhere. That narrows it down a lot. Any ideas?"

"None," Michael responded.

A thousand thoughts were going through Sonny's mind as he leaned back in his chair.

Finally, he spoke. "Do you have a tape recorder?"

"Of course, I've … Oh, I see what you mean. Tape the call, right?"

"You got it. I doubt if it will do much good, but whoever it is just might slip up." Sonny stirred the coffee, took a sip, and frowned.

"Damn! This coffee tastes like shit, Michael."

Michael managed a smile. "Sorry, Chubby, I guess I made it a little strong."

"Hell, I guess you did!"

Sonny rose to his feet, reached into his pants, and pulled a coin purse from his pocket. It was leather, dyed black, with "Concorde" embossed in gold on each side.

"Got any extra quarters? I'm running low."

Michael sighed, wondering why Chubby was worrying about quarters at a time like this. He lifted himself from his chair.

"Yeah, I've got some back in the studio. How much do you need?"

"Enough to top off this pouch. I gotta make a couple of calls."

Michael finished rigging up the tape recorder to the phone and checked it several times, making sure it worked properly by calling the local time number. Satisfied, he sat behind his desk trying to think of what he could do next. *Nothing,* he supposed; *nothing but wait.* He could not keep himself from fidgeting about the room. One moment he would be thumbing through some current photographs, the next he would be staring around the room, almost in a daze. Finally, he got up and paced the floor. He stayed busy doing nothing.

He was just trying to avoid going crazy over the situation with Maria. It would kill him if anything ever happened to her. He didn't want to think about how empty his life would be if she were gone. Losing Jeffrey, their young son, had been devastating. He had been the nucleus of their life together. Michael couldn't go through another loss. He couldn't lose Maria too. Whatever it took, he had to make sure she was safe.

As he walked around the room, his eyes suddenly rested on his gun rack. The cold, stainless steel Colt .357 Trooper held his attention.

Now is the time of reckoning, Michael thought. He never thought he would have to kill again. He had thought that was all behind him. His stomach became queasy as the past volcanically erupted in front of him. His mind spun, and he lost his balance. Half falling, he sat down on the carpet and lowered his head between his knees. When Michael closed his eyes, he saw the eyes of the old Vietnamese man staring back at him. That was a memory that had haunted him for years. On May 8, 1965, fifty kilometers outside of Lo Ann, South Vietnam, Michael had looked into the eyes of that old man. It was a day he longed to forget but knew he never would.

———————

Students and young people throughout America were displaying their innocence and horror against the immorality of their government's participation in Vietnam. During that time, Michael was crawling on his belly through mud and underbrush; picking off leeches and ticks in what he thought was an effort to bring peace and freedom to the people of South Vietnam. This ideology was short-lived. After several months of watching his friends and classmates maimed and slaughtered fighting a political and unwinnable guerilla war, Michael realized that his government's propaganda had been false. With restrictions on the bombing of certain key targets and strongholds in North Vietnam and Cambodia, any hope of victory had been lost. His general conviction and that of his platoon was to lay back and try to live through the shit for another ten days, and then rotation.

That day in May, a young Captain from San Diego had brought orders to search and destroy a small village along the Dingle River fifteen kilometers from their bivouac. In this war, the term meant to destroy and then search. Intelligence reports indicated that the village was being used at night as a staging area for "Charlie."

His men were reluctant to go. Only two days before, Michael and his platoon had searched the village. They had found only one old man and some women.

Michael had finally told his men to get their gear and move out. He didn't want to go either, but orders were orders, and they had to obey them.

Grumbling to themselves, they walked single file out of the bivouac. To instill the confidence necessary for the mission, Michael had no choice but to take the point, which was the most dangerous position. Though none of them wanted to go, the men in his platoon respected his leadership and slowly moved at a distance behind him.

Dusk was premature under the dense foliage. Decaying leaves and undergrowth were spongy beneath his feet. The rank odor of mildew and rot filled his nostrils. Gnats, flies, and mosquitoes swarmed around his face, thriving on his sweat and blood.

Each step he took was calculated to produce the least possible noise. Eyes constantly in motion, never resting on any particular object, and scanning the brush for the slightest movement, he advanced. The snap of a twig sounded like a shot. Blood pounded in his ears, amplified a thousand-fold. His head was dizzy with adrenalin. He was stimulated in part by fear of dying and in part by the unknown that lay ahead. The next step could be the end of his life, either by a booby trap or Charlie.

After three hours of grueling torture, Michael eased out of the jungle onto the bank of the Tingli. The full moon cast its muddy reflection across the fifty-foot-wide river. In reality, it was no more than a creek. The surface was still, stinking of death, bloated cattle, and human feces.

Michael heard a rustle behind him. He wheeled, ready to fire. It was Walker, the radio operator.

"Quite!" Michael whispered.

Walker crawled alongside him. A tall, gangly twenty-two-year-old from Fort Worth, Texas, Billy Walker, and his father had worked together on their horse ranch before he had been drafted and sent to this hot, humid place full of Vietcong, who wanted to kill him. He didn't want to be in Vietnam. He wanted to be back in Texas with his parents and Nicole, his young wife, who had been his high school sweetheart. He was ready to get the hell out of this mosquito-infested jungle.

"Where the hell are we?" Walker hissed.

"About a mile downriver from the LZ."

The rest of the platoon moved in along the river, taking up positions at various intervals and then resting. Fear permeated the group as each took his turn in the front at a distance behind Michael and Walker.

Twenty minutes later, followed by Walker and the rest of the platoon, Michael made his way along the riverbed. Crouching low, he frequently stepped in the water and waded around bushes and limbs extending out above the river.

The bugs were ferocious. He stopped for a moment to swat at them. Their stinging and biting were almost unbearable. He removed an olive-green bandana from his field jacket and wrapped the material around his face to keep the mosquitoes out of his mouth. The swarming insects relentlessly sang a high-pitched buzz, drowning out all other river noises.

Slowly, Michael moved forward, and Walker took Michael's position. The men to the rear repeated this process. Gradually, the human chain snaked its way onward. Michael smelled smoke drifting down the river. Moments later, they rounded a bend, and the village came into view.

Slowly moving forward, bending low, and eventually coming to rest atop a small hill overlooking the village, Michael gazed down at the huts. There were several smoldering fires, but for some reason, the village looked deserted. Walker crawled up beside him.

Michael dropped his head down out of view. Whispering, Michael said, "Take five men and skirt the right side. I'll put two men here and take three with me to the left. When you get behind that big hut," he rose slightly and pointed, "wait 'til I make my move."

Walker swallowed in fear and nodded in assent.

Michael raised a hand revealing five fingers and motioned them towards Walker. Five almost invisible men moved up alongside them and then vanished with the radio operator.

Two more fingers went up. Moments later Bradley and Fanello squatted beside him.

"You two guys stay put," he whispered.

They quickly took a position on each side of the knoll.

Michael motioned the other three men forward. They moved under the cover of the bank until reaching the far side of the village. Finally, there, they took a moment to catch their wind. Michael could tell by their breathing that they were scared. Hell, he was scared too, but he couldn't let his men see the fear in his eyes. He flipped the selector on his M-16 to semi-automatic and crawled up over the embankment.

He had moved no more than forty meters in from the river past the first hut when he was startled. His backup started screaming. His shrieking broke the silence. Michael spun and dropped to a knee, ready to fire. He cast a glance around the village, saw no movement, and then made his way back fifteen feet to his companion.

Standing silently, the soldier was immobile, shaking and staring down at his foot. Michael winced at what he saw. He stooped down and began to free the foot. The man had stepped on a punji stick trap. Narrow slivers of needle-sharp bamboo had entered the sole of his boot and extended six inches out of the top. A booby trap had been placed in a ten-inch hole and then covered with sticks and leaves. This soldier was lucky. Most of the time, the bamboo was covered with feces.

Michael grabbed the boot and intended to free the man. From the bamboo, all hell broke loose. Automatic rifle fire from a nearby hut sprayed the undergrowth where he was kneeling. He jerked the man's foot from the trap. The soldier cried out from the pain and collapsed on top of Michael. The soldier's outcry brought fire from the other huts.

Hugging the ground, Michael closed his eyes and buried his face in the rotten muck. Bullets sprayed all around him. He kept thinking that the next round was his. How many more bullets could miss him before he took one? *Shit, what a mess!* he thought. Suddenly the village was aglow in white light, brighter than day. A starburst flare began drifting lazily down, streaming a silver trail. Walker's men opened fire into the huts. Michael's group recovered their wits and quickly began firing at random. Several VCs ran from a hut, which had caught fire from tracer bullets. A long burst of fire from an M-16 across the way brought them down.

"Corpsman!" Michael shouted above the noise of the rifle fire. "God dammit, I need a corpsman now!"

A corpsman came running. Michael pointed to the soldier lying beside him.

"Shit!" the Corpsman groaned as he looked at the soldier's injured foot.

Michael grabbed up his M-16 and started fishtailing across the ground toward the rear of the closest hut. He heard someone screaming from the direction of the knoll. It sounded like Fanello, but he wasn't sure. The shrill sound of incoming mortar drew his attention. He had barely hit the ground when it exploded dead center in the village. He couldn't tell if it was theirs or the VC's. Dirt and debris showered him. Michael heard another one of his men cry out, probably hit by fragments of the mortar.

A heavy barrage of fire was coming from a makeshift shed at the end of the compound. Michael stepped out with his M-16 fully automatic and opened fire. He emptied the clip and then stepped back to protection.

Walker was shouting orders to the men as they rushed the weathered building. There was heavy gunfire and then silence.

Another starburst exploded, drenching the village in bright light. Michael turned and stepped to the opposite end of the hut. When he reached the corner, he froze. A long shadow fell beyond the corner of the hut. The figure was standing at the side of the hut holding a rifle. It moved toward him. *This is a kill-or-be-killed situation,* Michael thought, and knew what he had to do. He dove forward, hit the ground, and fired as he rolled to one side. The blast hit the man across his mid-section, toppling him to the ground. The flare faded about a hundred feet above the ground.

Michael crawled over to look at the enemy. In the dim moonlight, shame and regret overwhelmed him. He stared down into the eyes of a small, old man. It was the same old man he had seen two days ago. Now he lay before Michael dying, with a crooked cane clutched in his hand. Michael reached down, not knowing what to do. He lifted the limp figure by the shoulders and pulled him up onto his lap. The old man blinked up at Michael and in a hoarse voice said in Vietnamese, "I had no place to hide." A tear glistened on his cheek, his eyes closed, and he died in Michael's arms.

That night, at the moment of the old man's death, something happened to Michael, something that would impact him for the rest of his life.

Twenty

A room key was tossed on the table, followed by the brushing sound of a chair being pulled across the nylon against his armrest. Still, he continued to gaze out through the large, tinted plate glass window as he watched a twenty-six-foot runabout making its way into the man-made basin at Plantation Yacht Harbor.

"Why are you shaking your head?" Roberto asked, taking a seat.

"I'm waiting for this guy," Carlos smiled, nodding toward the boat, "to crack up on the dock. It's amazing how insurance companies ever make any money."

"You're in Room 231," Roberto said, glancing around the restaurant for a waitress. He returned his attention to the boat.

A fat man with a deep suntan, wearing a T-shirt and Bermuda shorts, walked past them on the dock next to the plate glass windows. He stopped at the gas pump, where he was probably waiting for the runabout. *Harbor Master,* Carlos thought. *He's probably just another working slob making a hundred fifty bucks a week.* Carlos turned toward Roberto.

"Go down to the house. Call Jansen when you get there and let him talk to the girl. Give him the instructions as planned and keep me posted."

Roberto shifted to the edge of his chair and hesitated before he spoke. "Think he'll go to the police?"

"Nah, I don't think he'll risk it. He's no fool. There'd be too many things to explain. He'll pay. I know he will."

Roberto rose to leave.

"Oh," Carlos hesitated, eyeing Roberto, "make sure Philippi keeps his hands off that girl. If he doesn't, he's a dead man." The look in Carlos' eyes told Roberto that he meant it.

"I'll call you," Roberto responded as he turned and walked out of the restaurant.

Twenty-One

Still sitting on the floor, Michael was hugging himself, trying to ease the pain. Swaying back and forth. In his mind, he was still cradling the old Vietnamese man in his arms.

He had no idea how long he had been sitting there when he heard the sound of the Blazer in the drive. *I can't let Sonny see me this way,* he thought and wiped a single tear from his cheek. Hearing the front door close, he shoved himself up off the floor and headed for the bathroom.

When Michael came out of the bathroom Sonny was sitting in a chair. A large black suitcase lay on Michael's desk. *What the hell is in that suitcase?* he thought Just looking at it gave Michael a sense of foreboding.

Sonny looked up at Michael for a moment and said, matter-of-factly, "You look like shit! What happened?"

"Nothing, I'll be all right. What's in the case?"

"Just some goodies," Sonny said vaguely. "Any calls?"

Michael shook his head.

Sonny flipped the latches and raised the lip of the case.

Michael was drawn to the suitcase, unresisting. As he glanced inside, a wave of nausea passed over him, but he checked it.

"Where in the hell did you get these?" A glitter in his eye replaced the wave of nausea.

"From a friend," Sonny answered, standing by the case.

"Holy shit!" Michael mumbled, reaching out to touch the glistening metal. It was cold to his touch. *Cold, quiet death,* he thought.

Sonny reached into the suitcase and extracted the gun that Michael had considered. Sonny held an AK 47 Russian Kalashnikov machine gun in his right hand. With his left, he picked up a clip and jammed it into the bottom of the gun. It seated with a solid, metallic "thump." He soundlessly screwed on the fourteen-inch silencer.

"Six hundred rounds per minute," Sonny said, almost in a whisper as though he were in awe of the weapon. He placed it on the desk.

The next item Sonny removed was a Remington eighteen-inch, twelve-gauge riot shotgun. He held it admiringly.

"This is the real jewel," he said quietly, reaching into the suitcase once again. "Three-inch magnum, number two buckshot in a banana clip for close-up work. The only problem is if you fire it inside a room, your ears will ring for a damn week." He gave the gun to Michael.

"This is more my style," Michael finally grinned.

He brought it to his hip, checking the balance.

"This baby here is mine," Sonny said, showing Michael a nine-millimeter Mauser.

Michael put the shotgun on the desk.

"Czechoslovakian," Sonny continued, handing the pistol to Michael. "Seven-inch barrel, semi-automatic, eighteen rounds per clip. Here's the silencer," Sonny said as he held it up for Michael to see.

Michael fumbled with the clip, which was just forward of the trigger.

Finally realizing the amount of firepower in front of him, Michael said, "Damn, Sonny! I don't want to start a war. All I want is to pay the bastards what they want and get Maria back!"

Sonny gave Michael a stern look, thinking how naïve he was.

"I've got more experience in these situations. Trust me, I know what I'm doing!"

Michael sighed and shrugged his shoulders as if conceding.

"Yeah, I guess you're right, Sonny. I was just trying to avoid this sort of thing."

Sonny went back to the suitcase and pulled out the last of the weapons.

"Colt .380 semi-automatic with nine rounds per clip," Sonny said, admiring the gun. "You'll use this one." Sonny handed Michael the pistol and the shotgun.

Sonny picked up the Kalashnikov, broke it down expertly, and was replacing it in the suitcase when the telephone rang. Michael was moving toward the phone to answer it when Sonny threw his hand in front of the instrument to stop Michael from picking it up. Sonny raised his eyebrows as he looked at Michael.

"Try to keep him on the line as long as possible," he whispered, and then moved away, so Michael could answer.

Michael looked quizzically at Sonny as his two fingers pressed the buttons of the tape recorder.

"I have a surprise for you," the Hispanic voice said.

Michael could hear a rustle from the other mouthpiece as if a hand had carelessly brushed across it. Michael's heart leaped at the next sound.

"Michael, are you there?"

"Yes, sweetheart, I'm here," Michael answered, his heart pounding.

"Michael, I'm so scared."

He could sense that Maria was about to cry. There was a rustling sound and then no sound at all. Michael knew someone's hand was clamped tightly over the mouthpiece. Moments passed until he could no longer stand the silence.

"Hello? Hello!" He shouted into the phone.

"There is no need to shout, Mr. Jansen. Maria is all right and will stay that way as long as you follow my instructions. Do you understand?"

"Yes," Michael exhaled.

"Tomorrow morning at eight o'clock you are to deliver five hundred thousand dollars. Now listen very closely. There is a wayside park on U.S. 1, just before you pass Indian Key Channel. Do you know where it is?"

"Yes."

"Good. Heading south, you are to put the money in the third trash can on the right-hand side. Be sure the money is in a large brown grocery bag. After putting the money in the can, turn around and go back up the road to Papa Joe's Restaurant. There you will receive a call telling you where you can pick up your wife."

"Oh, Mr. Jansen, one more thing…"

"Yes," Michael replied, looking at Sonny.

"It would be a pity if you disappointed us."

The line went silent.

Michael sagged against the desk as he dropped the receiver in its cradle. Sonny reached over and flipped the recorder off.

"I'll kill that son of a bitch if I get my hands on him," Michael said with steel in his voice.

Sonny was intent on rewinding the recorder. Michael began pacing around the studio, his mind already replaying the conversation, thinking of what he should do next.

Sonny pushed the "play" button. He heard the Hispanic accent for the first time. The ringing of the telephone drowned out Maria's voice. Sonny punched the "stop" button and simultaneously reached for the phone.

"Yeah?"

Sonny listened for a moment, a small smile on his face. It froze there as he reached for a pad and began jotting something down.

"Thanks, Henry, I owe you one." He hung up the phone.

"Who was that?"

Tearing the paper off the pad and handing it to Michael, Sonny said, "That's where they're holding Maria."

Twenty-Two

Maria had given up trying to watch television. She could not concentrate. Anyway, the reception was so poor she could hardly make out the picture. Her mind kept wandering back to her predicament. *Is Michael in danger?* She knew he must be frantic with worry about her. She also knew Michael would move heaven and earth to get to her, but she was afraid for him. *What do these people want?*

Her captors had reluctantly allowed her to go to the bathroom. Leaning over the filthy basin washing her face, she shifted her weight from one foot to the other and felt the rotten floor give way slightly to her insignificant load. Maria looked down as she shifted her weight on the ball of each foot and watched the torn linoleum sag from the pressure of her toes. She automatically held to the edge of the basin, hoping she wouldn't fall through the spongy floor. Images of unimaginable creatures living under the house pulling at her legs and feet flashed through her mind. Unconsciously, she spread her feet apart and continued to wash herself.

The bathroom contained a tiny, grimy shower that looked as if it had never been cleaned, a washbasin, and a toilet that had a ring of rust in the bowl, all compressed into the closet-sized room. Above the toilet, there was a small window covered by a dirty curtain, no more than the size of a porthole. Maria took the chance that the commode would hold her weight and stepped up on the lid. The floor squeaked its thanks. She moved the musty-smelling curtain aside to look out, but to her disappointment years of accumulated dust and dirt blocked her view.

Maria quietly eased back down, supposing that if worse came to worse she might try to climb out the window, although she had no idea what lay beneath it. She had concluded from previous sounds that the house was built partially over water. Earlier she had heard a motorboat pass and felt the house sway a tiny bit from the boat's wake.

Maria knew she was in the Keys, but where she had no idea. The older Cuban had forced her to wear a pair of reflector-type sunglasses; the kind motorcycle policemen sometimes wear. The ones given to her had black paint sprayed on the inside, and only through her peripheral vision had she managed to generalize where she was taken.

The man who had made the phone call to Michael tapped on the door. "Hurry up, lady, we ain't got all night."

"I'm coming," Maria answered, straightening her clothing. She rubbed her wrists which were sore from the handcuffs, took a deep breath for composure, and opened the door.

The medium-built man whom Maria presumed to be in his early thirties, "the caller," as she had named him, pointed to a little bed, the one from which she had been released. It had a cast-iron frame, with a heavy length of chain attached that led up to the mattress. As Maria sat on the edge of the bed, the caller withdrew the handcuffs from his pocket. He locked one side to Maria's left wrist, then fed the other cuff through a link of chain and fastened it to Maria's other hand. She winced with pain as he tightened the cuffs to her wrists. Finished, he stepped back to appraise his handiwork.

"Please, can't you loosen them just a little?" Maria asked, looking down and then back at the caller. "They're too tight," she pleaded in Spanish, with a look of discomfort on her face.

"Sorry lady," he said in English. "That's the way they have to stay."

Maria had named the older man Gordo, meaning "fatty" in

Spanish. She had heard Gordo call him Philippi. Short, sweaty, and obese with greasy hair, he sat on an old, torn, black car seat being used as a couch. He was reading a paperback novel with a picture of two men on horses on the front cover. The other two men, at whom Maria had not gotten a good look, had left shortly after her arrival.

She settled on the bed but kept moving about trying to find a comfortable position. The weight of the chain was a continuous source of irritation to her wrists. *Somehow, I've got to get out of here,* she thought, scanning the room. It was not much larger than the bathroom. *Rat trap* flashed through her mind. Next to her bed was a narrow, single cot. Gordo had taken possession of it. He sat there, thumbing through a Hustler magazine.

To the left, and in another room, was a small kitchen. It had a range, refrigerator, and table that would accommodate four people. A wooden plank was nailed across a wall for additional storage space. In the far corner, was an outdated kitchen sink and tile counter, with an assortment of plates and glasses, surprisingly neatly stacked to one side.

Philippi sighed, heaved himself up from the makeshift couch, and looked at Gordo.

"Want some espresso?"

"Yeah," he replied, without looking up.

Philippi turned and walked into the kitchen. The house shook on its pilings as he moved about. Maria was surprised the floor did not give way under the heavy man's weight. She listened intently to his banging around, the opening and closing of the refrigerator, and finally to the sound of a chair being dragged out from the table; and then there was silence.

He must be sitting down, she thought, glancing up at the ceiling, which was no more than five feet above her. Watermarks had left dark brown stains that looked like a road map running from wall to wall, indicating the roof was in severe need of repair.

Maria froze as she heard a car pull to a stop outside the house.

She heard the slam of one car door and then another. *The other two must be back,* she thought and rolled her face ostrich-like into the pillow. She closed her eyes and continued her prayer to the Virgin Mary, a prayer that had rarely ceased since late that morning.

Twenty-Three

While Sonny drove, Michael sat quietly listening to the hypnotic hum of the deep lug tires on the four-by-four vehicle as they gripped the pavement, moving them closer to their destination. Key Largo was in the rear-view mirror, and Plantation Key was ahead. The tires sang a shrieking song as the Blazer crossed another bridge grating at seventy miles an hour. The farther south they went, the more frequent the song.

Michael looked over his shoulder to the back seat, reminding himself that the suitcase Sonny had brought with him was still sitting on the slowly darkening left side of the back seat. It made him think of a coffin, ready to be opened. He glanced over at Sonny, who was concentrating on his driving. Then he brought his attention back to the road. Coral Shores High School zipped past Sonny's window.

Michael thought about the subtle change that had taken place in Sonny within the past eight hours. He was perplexed at how fast Sonny had acquired the weapons in the suitcase. Surely, at some point in the past, Sonny would have mentioned them to him. Sonny liked to brag about things like that. Then, there was the phone call.

What possible source did Sonny have to access an address from the phone call made to Michael by the kidnapper? The telephone system in the Keys is at best antiquated. It would take more than just a friend to trace a call like that. It puzzled him.

Michael's mind snapped back to reality as Sonny began slowing the Blazer. Islamorada came into view. Michael noticed that The Tiki Bar parking lot was full. Continuing on the bridge, Sonny drove past the Chesapeake Seafood House and headed toward Long Key. Thinking of Maria, Michael ached inside, imagining what might lie ahead.

Sonny increased his speed. Papa Joe's loomed up ahead, and they quickly sped past. Michael counted the three trashcans on the right, and then they suddenly disappeared.

Sonny finally broke the silence.

"You know we gotta kill 'em, don't you?"

The statement stunned Michael. "Just like that, huh?" he stared at Sonny.

"Just like that," Sonny responded and looked straight ahead as if he might change his mind if Michael gave him the slightest option. But, like Sonny, Michael knew there were no other options.

"Suppose we get them? Then what are we gonna do? Hand them over to the police? You know as well as I do, that's out. Turn them loose? Shit! They'd be gunning for us on the next street corner. Remember, Michael, he said forcefully, "Maria can identify them."

Michael continued to stare at Sonny. What he said made sense. Michael turned his gaze back to the road.

Sonny stomped the high beams and then the dim again.

"Shit!" he mumbled as a semi-truck heading north passed them, its turbulence rocking the Blazer.

Michael was quiet for a while.

"Thanks for everything, Chubby," he said finally. He was almost apologetic.

At 9:03 p.m. Sonny turned the truck off U.S. 1 onto Pelican Drive. He slowed the Blazer to fifteen miles an hour and flashed on his high beams. There were no streetlights along the drive, and only an occasional shack or mobile home emitted light. The pavement ended, but the road continued, carpeted by needles from the thick, Australian pines that lined and hung over both sides of the road. Both men were unfamiliar with the area but had studied a map and knew the drive circled to the end of a small peninsula.

"You check the right, I'll take the left," Sonny said, straining his eyes at the mailboxes.

"There it is," Michael said, just above a whisper.

Sonny maintained his speed as they passed the ramshackle house over the water. Neither man got a close look at the house.

They drove on around the peninsula for about a quarter of a mile, when Sonny spotted and turned into a deserted boat ramp, braking to a stop.

Michael already had the map spread out when Sonny switched on the dome light. They both leaned to the side to avoid casting shadows onto the paper.

"This is where we are," Sonny said, pointing his finger to a spot on the map. "That's the house there," he said, running a finger along the edge.

"Look, there is a canal running right by the house," interjected Michael, "out to the Intracoastal."

"Yeah, that's right," Sonny mumbled, looking down at his watch. He straightened up in his seat, thought for a moment, and made a decision.

"Give me a fifteen-minute head start and then pick me up where the pavement begins."

Sonny reached around the bucket seat for the suitcase.

"What if somebody drives down the road?" Michael questioned. "If we screw up now…"

Sonny cut him short. "There are plenty of scrubs to hide in if that happens," he said, pulling the Mauser from the case.

Climbing out of the Blazer, Sonny eased the door closed and disappeared into the night.

Michael slid over in the driver's seat and looked at his watch which showed 9:26 p.m. He propped his elbow on the doorframe, rested his head against his knuckles, and began listening to the night sounds. A mosquito buzzed threateningly nearby. His mind was jumbled with a collage of thoughts as he recapped the past nine hours. *Amazing,* he thought, *how fucked up one's life could become in such a short time.* He fought to keep his emotions under control. *You've got to stay focused,* he told himself. He and Sonny would get Maria away from those bastards no matter what it took.

The acid in his arm suddenly began to burn. Before the mosquito could withdraw its proboscis, and as if the little bug were the cause of all his pain, Michael smashed it into oblivion.

He sat with his eyes closed. Anxiety and anticipation gripped him. *Right now,* he thought, *Maria's life is like a coin tossed into the air, reaching its apex and flipping end over end, with a fifty-fifty chance of landing on the correct side.* It was as if all his willpower and energies were being directed toward that coin. Even then there was no guaranteed outcome.

Michael could no longer sit still. Following Sonny's previous movements, he reached behind the seat and pulled the suitcase up between the bucket seats. He withdrew the Colt .380 and found comfort in its touch. He nestled it gently under his shirt. He fastened the lid and turned to replace the suitcase to its corner on the rear seat.

It's time to go, he thought as he looked at his watch. *Three minutes.* He started the Blazer and retraced the route that he and Sonny had previously taken, being careful to drive slowly, remembering the landmarks leading back to the right house. *It's the next one,* he thought.

As it came into view, Michael estimated that the house sat back off the road about fifty yards. A yellow bug light hanging under a neglected porch had been turned on. The light outlined the silhouette of a late-model automobile. His adrenalin rushed at the thought of Maria only being a few yards from him. Questions flared within his consciousness. *Is she hurt? Is she still alive? Is she tied up?* Quickly, the house was out of view.

Several minutes later Michael stopped the Blazer where the pavement began. He left the motor idling, and his hand slipped down to the Colt. A moment later, he saw Sonny rise from behind a palmetto bush next to the road and head toward the truck.

"Let's go," Sonny whispered, climbing into the vehicle. "Damn mosquitoes are eating my ass up." He swatted at the back of his neck and then scratched his forehead.

Michael put the Blazer in gear and continued around the drive.

"What did you see?"

"Not much. I didn't want to take a chance by getting too close." Sonny looked at his watch.

"I think we ought to go up the road and figure out what we're gonna do."

Michael bounced the Blazer onto U.S. 1 and headed north. Sonny remained in silent thought as he scratched his mosquito bites. Michael glanced at the fuel gauge and pulled into the gas pumps at a 7-Eleven.

"Filler up. I'm going to get some insect repellent," he said, slamming the door behind him.

Michael grabbed a bottle of mosquito repellant, paid the attendant, and returned to the Blazer. He handed the bottle to Sonny, who immediately began to apply a liberal dose of mosquito repellent to his face and hands. Michael climbed in beside him.

"Here, put some of this on," Sonny said, tossing the half-empty bottle to Michael.

He turned on the engine, pulled over to the side of the parking lot by a phone booth, and turned to face Michael.

"I didn't see a guard, but that doesn't mean they don't have one. If I were doing what those bastards are doing, I'd damn sure have one somewhere with a CB. If we go walking up to the house and they've got a sentry, any alarm might make it too late to get Maria out."

Michael nodded in agreement.

"That's why I think we ought to approach the house from the water. It's probably their most vulnerable point."

"Where are we going to get a boat?" Michael questioned.

"There's a skiff we can use about three houses up from the shack."

"You really think that's the best way?"

Sonny's eyes looked into Michael's. "Yes, I do."

"Then, let's do it," Michael nodded in agreement.

Sonny didn't want to kill the dog, but the son of a bitch left him no choice. Michael sat down in the front of the boat. Sonny was about to push off when the little bastard came from out of nowhere and grabbed him by the ankle. Sonny almost shouted, not so much from the pain as from surprise. Fortunately, the dog's grip was more on the hem of Sonny's pants than on his ankle, but Sonny knew the skin had torn.

In the dark, he had been unable to make out exactly what kind of dog it was. He couldn't tell if it was a puppy or a miniature. It didn't matter. Sonny just wanted to get the thing off of him as quickly as possible. He withdrew the Mauser and hoped that he wouldn't shoot himself in the foot. He fired point-blank at the dog. The Mauser, with its silencer, made less noise than the dog's grunting and growling. Sonny scooped the dog up and held it under the water until it stopped squirming. The entire incident took less than forty-five seconds.

Hearing a noise, Michael spun in his seat to find out what was causing the ruckus. Sonny put his bad leg on the transom of the bone-fishing skiff and pushed off with his right foot. By the time Sonny pushed the boat off, Michael had removed the pole used for working the flats and began to push the skiff along the bank.

By moonlight, Sonny checked his wound. The skin was broken in a couple of places. *Not bad,* he decided. There was barely a trickle of blood. Rabies crossed his mind. *No time to think about that shit now,* he thought.

The skiff seemed to maneuver best when poled from the bow. Michael sat on the bow, poling smoothly and with care as Sonny crouched low in the stern resting the Kalashnikov across his knees.

In the darkness, Michael could vaguely see Sonny pointing to the right. He changed the course of the skiff in the direction Sonny was pointing. Michael heard the sounds of brush scraping against the stern and saw Sonny standing up to push the boat away. *Too much noise,* Michael winced.

The stern moved farther out into the water. Both men could see the yellow porch light reflecting off the water on the other side of the canal. The closer they came, the brighter the light.

As they approached the end of the dock, they saw the back of the house extending over the water. Michael nosed the boat in closer to the overhanging bushes. His poling had all but ceased as they inched their way to the dock. Sonny reached out and grabbed a piling. Michael eased the bow over, grabbed another piling, and quietly dropped the pole into the boat.

The house and dock overhung the water by about ten feet. Since it was low tide with a margin of three to four feet clearance under the dock, Sonny thought it was an ideal place to hide the boat. Laying the Kalashnikov on his seat, he motioned to Michael for help.

After some difficult maneuverings, they got the boat safely underneath the dock and tied it to the pilings. The side porch light shone down through the cracks of the dock, which created striped reflections on the water. Sonny twisted around on his seat and lifted his legs into the water. He grimaced. His wound stung from the cold saltwater. Holding his breath, he lowered himself into the water and felt for the bottom. Three feet down, his feet touched the soggy mush. His weight caused him to bog down in the muck just above his ankles.

Michael slid into the water close to the side entrance. He did not seem to be having as much trouble as Sonny. He picked up the shotgun, and standing in a stooped position waded to the narrow end of the dock. He waited for Sonny to catch up.

In this situation, Sonny's height was not to his advantage. Carrying his rifle in a fording position, he duck-walked past the boat.

Michael heard a deep thump, and looking back over his shoulder he saw Sonny grimace and rub his forehead. About two inches above his head was a large re-enforcement beam, which Sonny must have hit. Moments later, Sonny waded up beside him, took Michael's hand, and placed it on his brow. There was a goose egg-sized knot at Sonny's hairline.

Sonny released Michael's hand and pointed up. Reaching up and grabbing a plank, Sonny began raising himself, but he froze at the squeaking of a screen door opening. He jerked his hand back. Whoever it was eased the door closed.

They heard the dull drumming footsteps as someone walked on the dock. The footsteps stopped, and then there was the hiss of a cigarette butt in the water. The footsteps drew closer.

Sonny took a deep breath to steady his respiration. He double-checked the silencer on the Kalashnikov. Michael silently moved several steps to the side to avoid being bunched up.

Both men cautiously drew back a bit farther under the dock as the footsteps grew louder. A shadow fell over them as a man stopped at the edge of the dock. There was a pause, the zip of a zipper, and a stream of urine gushed out into the water making circles and figure eights.

Michael thought the man would piss forever. The stream started slowing down, hitting the planks of the dock, making a hollow noise, and then dribbling down on his head. He closed his eyes, not daring to move. Gritting his teeth and resisting the urge to fire, he held his breath as the man continued urinating. Finally, the dribble ended with two spurts and a flick.

The man coughed, bringing mucus up from his lungs, then spat the phlegm into the water. Pausing a moment more, he turned and slowly began walking back toward the house.

Michael could stand his repulsion no longer. He silently dropped his face into the water and gently washed his eyes and mouth.

Sonny stepped out from under the dock, eased up, and saw the man's back silhouetted in the light. *A perfect shot,* he thought, bringing the Kalashnikov to his shoulder. The next few moments were mechanically spontaneous. He held his breath, aligned the sights on the highest dark spot, and pulled the trigger.

The man's head violently snapped forward. From its center, dark liquid quickly sprayed out in all directions. Sonny knew it was not sweat. Then the man's head exploded like a dropped watermelon. A short stub remained where his head had been. Nothing more. He momentarily froze, suspended in the air, and then sank to the dock like a crumpled blanket.

Sonny heaved himself up on the dock and squatted at the edge as Michael followed. Both waited to see if the sound had roused anyone from inside the house. He put his hand out and motioned to Michael to stay put. He quietly walked on the balls of his feet across the planks to where the body lay. Michael held the shotgun level at the screen door, covering Sonny.

Sonny laid his rifle down, picked up the man's feet, and began dragging him toward a large marine storage box at the edge of the dock.

Michael moved under the porch as Sonny reached the box. He kept a safe distance between them in case they drew fire from inside the house.

Sonny dropped the man's legs and lifted the lid of the box back in one fluid movement. Reaching down and struggling with the dead weight, he lifted the legs and pulled the body closer to the box. He draped the back of the man's knees over into the box and began stuffing him inside. Moments later, he lowered the lid and went back to retrieve his rifle from the sticky goop.

Sonny was wiping his rifle stock clean when Michael joined him by the frame of the screen door. They waited a minute to collect their composure and to evaluate their situation. There was a low hum from the window air conditioner coming from the other side of the shack. Any noise Sonny had made must have been muffled by the air conditioner. Whoever was inside would be expecting the corpse to return, so their entrance would not be unexpected. They had the element of surprise.

Michael's heart pounded in his ears. He looked at Sonny and nodded his head. Sonny took the shotgun from Michael and handed him the Kalashnikov. He leaned the shotgun against the wall and removed his Mauser from his belt. Now they both had guns with silencers. Sonny nodded to Michael.

The screen door creaked open. Sonny stepped in front of the wooden door, twisted its knob, and walked inside. Michael followed closely.

The kitchen was empty. Michael closed the door behind them as the corpse would have done.

From the size of the tiny, dilapidated house, Sonny concluded there was only one other room. He held up three fingers and rhythmically counted them down. When there were no more fingers, he and Michael walked through the threshold into the other room. What happened next happened in milliseconds.

Philippi was snoring lightly on the cot facing the wall. Charlie Long sat next to him reading the paper. Maria lay on the bed. She was semi-conscious and huddled to one side.

Antonio reclined on the car seat, his legs hanging over the armrest.

Charlie looked up in disbelief. Before he could rise, Sonny pulled the trigger on the Mauser. Its decompressing gases sealed Charlie's fate. Half his face spattered against the wall leaving red mush dripping down to the floor. The impact flung his body against Philippi, which abruptly awakened him. "What the …" Philippi was dead before uttering the third word. The bullet hit him high in his left rib cage, exploding his heart.

Maria stirred.

Antonio jumped from the car seat seeking cover behind the bed. Michael fired the Kalashnikov. Several bullets hit Antonio, slamming him between the bed and the wall. Blood splattered on Maria's dress.

Michael and Sonny spun around, ready to fire again, if necessary. Michael saw Maria's mouth open as she pointed at the bathroom. Michael dropped to a knee and fired. He held the trigger depressed, spraying the paper-thin wall. Wood and plaster exploded. The door fell from its hinges onto the floor, and then there was complete silence.

Roberto Ruiz lay grotesquely on the bathroom floor; his head wedged between the wall and the toilet. He never finished what he had started. His pants were still around his ankles.

Sonny looked around at the shambles. Maria was standing on the bed with her hands covering her mouth. Vomit was running down her breasts and onto her stomach. Unable to speak, she held out her cuffed hands and nodded slightly toward Philippi. Sonny walked over to the body and fumbled for the keys.

Still on his knees, Michael rose, staring into the bathroom. Sonny unlocked the cuffs.

"Let's go!" he commanded, grabbing Maria by the arm and pulling her off the bed. He turned Michael around and shoved Maria to him.

"Take her to the car!"

As Michael half carried Maria into the kitchen to the back door,

Sonny pulled a handkerchief from his pocket, lifted the receiver, and placed a call.

Twenty-Four

Sonny sat at the patio table staring out at the pool. He was suffering from a severe hangover caused by the stress of the previous night. His body felt weak and burnt out from too much adrenalin.

Michael walked out of the house, bare-chested and barefoot, in white tennis shorts, carrying a wooden tray of coffee and cream. He set the tray on the table.

"How's Maria?" Sonny asked, making a casual effort to assist Michael with a chair.

"She's still shaken up a bit and thanking God to be alive. She keeps begging me to quit."

"What did you tell her?"

"Nothing, what could I say? Shit! She's right!"

Sonny said nothing as he poured the coffee, but his mind began racing at the thought of Michael leaving just when they were getting ready to get the Cuban deal started.

"Cream?"

Michael nodded his head. "Yeah, a little." He slumped back in his chair.

"I'm sending Maria over to her mother's for a few days. It'll be good for her."

"That's a good idea. I've got a feeling we didn't get all of them. I'm thinking maybe we missed the leader. I don't think any of those bastards have the brains to orchestrate a kidnapping." Sonny hadn't told Michael that he had recognized Philippi.

Alarm crossed Michael's face. "What do you mean?" Michael said.

"Just think about it for a minute, Michael. If you were kidnapping someone, would you have been there?" Sonny answered his question. "Hell no! You'd have somebody else doing the dirty work, just like any other deal. Nah, I figure the leader was probably hanging around somewhere close by, probably at a motel or something."

Michael gulped down his coffee. Feeling a rush of fear, he rose from his chair. "I'd better go check on Maria," he said.

Sonny took his arm, pulling him back down.

"Michael, I need your help, especially now," he said. "We're right in the middle of this Cuban thing. Help me get it going, and then you can bail out if you still want to."

Michael stared intensely at Sonny. He knew he owed him for Maria's life. His face softened.

"I'll talk to Maria."

Twenty-Five

When Sonny arrived home that afternoon, he headed straight to the answering machine. It showed that fifteen calls had been automatically answered. Grabbing a pen and pressing the rewind button, he seated himself on the edge of the bed, ready to take notes. The first two calls had been from girlfriends; one was from his mother, and another was from Lou. The remainder of the tape was blank. *Odd,* he thought. *Eleven calls and nobody wanted to leave a message.* The telephone rang, interrupting his thoughts.

"Yeah?"

"Chubby?"

"Yeah, who's this?"

"It's Frank Howell. Remember me?"

"Frank Howell? Sonny said, wrinkling his forehead and trying to remember. "Frank Howell? Oh, now I remember. The 'Bonnie Lee,' right?"

"Yeah, that's right."

"Where have you been hiding?" Sonny laughed. "I haven't seen you in a couple of years."

"Oh, just doing a little work here and there. Listen, Chubby, I need to see you. Any possibility you can meet me tonight?"

Sonny thought for a moment. "I'll be at the Alley around nine. You can meet me there."

"Okay. See you tonight."

The line went silent. *What does he want?* Sonny asked himself.

Twenty-Six

Frank Howell met Sonny, Michael, and Maria at the Alley, located in an industrial area in Coral Gables, just behind the Coral Gables Lincoln and Mercury dealership. The restaurant was a nondescript building, which matched most of the other rundown paint shops, mechanic garages, tire stores, and other assorted small businesses that usually made up an industrial park. The exception with the Alley was that, after dark, the building took on an entirely different atmosphere. Clear Christmas bulbs lined Banyan trees, shrubs, walkways, and even the building itself. Their lights cast a soothing, soft ambiance throughout the vicinity. If you landed there at night in a helicopter, you'd never know you had landed in a dilapidated industrial park.

Howell pulled his car up to the main entrance to the restaurant and parked. Before he could remove his heavy bulk from the Lincoln, a young parking valet was holding the door open for him.

With a slight grunt, Howell extricated himself from the automobile. The valet handed him a ticket as Howell moved around the car.

Pulling the two heavy oak doors open to facilitate his size, Howell stepped inside and heard a quiet swoosh as the two massive doors closed behind him. He stood there for a moment waiting for his eyes to adjust to the dim light. Soft disco music played throughout the restaurant.

Moments later, he took several steps into the restaurant. To his left, he saw a large horseshoe bar. Two bartenders were serving customers sitting in plush high-back chairs lined around the bar. All were dressed to a tee. No expense had been spared on the posh decorations. Indirect lighting pervaded the room. He looked around in the dim light and finally spotted Sonny and his entourage sitting around a circular table. Behind them was a large sliding glass door, which overlooked a small garden planted with exotic plants strategically placed to create a false image of the restaurant's surroundings.

Howell maneuvered his large bulk around the tables and finally arrived at Sonny's table. He noticed a telephone sitting in the center of the table. Surprised, everyone looked up at the massive figure standing before them.

It took Sonny a moment to realize it was Frank Howell. Two years had made a drastic difference in Frank's appearance. *About a hundred fifty pounds or more*, thought Sonny.

"Hey, Frank," Sonny said, standing to shake his hand.

"Hey Chubby," Howell responded. "It's been a long time."

Sonny looked around the table and introduced Maria, who nodded and remained seated.

"Pull up a chair," Sonny offered. "This place has the best prime rib in South Florida."

Howell reached for the back of the captain's chair and pulled it out.

Maria stood up. "If you gentlemen will excuse me, I'm going to powder my nose." She quickly turned and walked away from the table.

Howell held to the arms of his chair as he eased himself into the plush seat. "I can't stay very long Chubby."

"So," Sonny paused, "what can I do for you, Frank?"

Howell waited a moment before answering. He was trying to remember exactly what he and Colgate had rehearsed.

"A couple of years ago I decided to get out of the business. I haven't worked since then. Now my ex-wife is trying to take me to the cleaners to the tune of a quarter million dollars. Of course, I can't afford that, so I thought of you. If I could make a couple of trips, then I'd be in the black."

Michael had been leaning back in his chair listening to what Howell was saying. "So, what have you been doing with yourself for the past two years?" he asked.

Howell looked over at Michael suspiciously. "Well, I have a little place down in Belize. I opened a small restaurant and have just been lying low. I understand the IRS wants to talk to me."

Michael smiled. "Yeah, I guess eventually all of us are going to have the same problem."

Sonny leaned over in his chair. "Maybe I can help you out, Frank. We've got some big things going down very soon. And I do mean big things. I'll call you in a couple of days."

Maria was restless. She had waited in the powder room long enough. *Hopefully, they'll be done with whatever they were going to discuss.*

When Maria reached the table, Frank Howell was already gone.

Twenty-Seven

Bernie Colgate stepped into a phone booth outside the El Globo Supermarket on Southwest 19th Avenue and 6th Street. The El Globo was in the heart of Miami's Little Havana district, the vast, expanding community where thousands of Cuban refugees had settled to escape the communist dictatorship of the Castro regime. To most of the immigrants, Miami, Florida's Little Havana was a dream come true.

After dropping a dime in the coin slot, he pushed the folding door completely open, allowing the rank fumes of old urine and wine to escape from the confined quarters. Shouldering the receiver to his ear, he dialed the number.

"Good morning, U.S. Attorney's Office," answered an indifferent female voice.

"I'd like to speak to Hans Ferguson. This is Bernie Colgate calling."

"He's on another line. Would you like to hold?"

"Yes, I..." Bernie was too late. The woman on the other end had immediately placed him on hold. Music had already begun playing. on the line. The smooth melody was no consolation for enduring the urine odor of the phone booth.

While Bernie waited for Ferguson to come on the line, he watched with fascination as laborers milled about in front of the Cuban-style sidewalk café. Some were smoking long, black, Havana cigars, which were made locally, while others smoked domestic cigarettes. They all shared a common passion for drinking strong

Espresso served in tiny plastic cups. Most of them had paunches capping their belts in the proclamation of America's prosperity.

"Good morning, Mr. Colgate," Hans Ferguson said.

"I've got to make this quick! The damn stench in this phone booth is killing me," Bernie grumbled. "My man Howell had a meeting with Sonny Mitchell last night at the Alley."

Ferguson interrupted him. "Did you get a tape of the meeting?"

"No. I didn't bother with a wire because I knew there would be too much background noise. There is always in a place like that. I'll see what I can do next time."

"How long do you think it will take to gain Mitchell's confidence?"

"Probably won't be long. Howell has made a couple of offshore trips for Mitchell in the past, so I'd say sooner than we expect. Also, something big, I'm not sure exactly what, but something big is about to go down."

"Any guesses?"

"Nope, but Howell said that Mitchell seems confident as hell."

"Anything else?" Ferguson's questions were brief.

"Nothing, but I'm anxious to get started." Bernie sensed Ferguson's impatience.

"I'll see what Customs and Immigration can come up with," Ferguson volunteered. "Maybe if I can get Judge Carr off her ass by this afternoon, we'll have a go-ahead for a phone tap," Bernie said, anxious to get the operation going. He didn't want any delays to hold him up. He had to get Mitchell.

Ferguson paused for a moment. "Oh, and Colgate, I don't want any grounds for entrapment, understand?"

"Yes! I understand," Bernie said a little too sharply. It pissed him off for Ferguson to question him. Hell, he knew more than Ferguson. Why didn't Ferguson just let him handle things his way? *I know what I'm doing,* Bernie thought with confidence. He couldn't wait to see the look on Ferguson's face when he caught Sonny Mitchell red-handed!

"And another thing, Colgate, you're supposed to check in with me daily, damn it!"

"Yeah, sure thing," Bernie replied with a hint of sarcasm and quickly hung up. "I'll show that bastard how a real op is run," mumbled Bernie to himself.

Since childhood, Bernie had always had an inflated opinion of himself. He always had to be right, and he always had to win.

Twenty-Eight

An announcement came over the intercom. "Ladies and Gentlemen, at this time we are beginning our descent into Barranquilla. Please return to your seats and observe the 'No Smoking' sign. Thank you." The announcement was repeated in Spanish.

Michael shifted in his seat. Emerging from sleep, he unfolded his arms, unconsciously tightened his seat belt, and re-adjusted his pillow. *It is cold,* he thought, shivering a little as tiny goose pimples stood the hairs on his arms at attention. He straightened his cramped legs under the seat in front of him, stretching out the stiffness from the fifty-minute flight from Panama. *Ah, that feels good,* he said to himself, relaxing his muscles. Rearranging himself in his seat, he leaned over and looked out the window at the Caribbean below. A line of barren terrain was broken just forward of the wing, contrasting with a wide band of muddy sediment washing out into the ocean from the many streams and tributaries from within the interior.

The Aerocondor 707 began a slow descent to the south. The left wing lifted, and the horizon quickly vanished. Michael's attention was drawn to the tiny ice crystals that formed between the two pieces of safety glass. They reminded him of snowflakes as sunlight refracted through them causing microscopic colors to flare outward like precious stones. *There is beauty in nature's simple things,* he thought.

Michael's inner ears started to compress as the airplane began its descent. The familiar noise of the compartment turned into a deep hum, becoming indistinguishable as the pressure increased. He clasped his nose with his finger and thumb in an attempt to equalize the pressure. It did not work. He turned his head toward the window so the stewardess couldn't see the exaggerated faces he was making. He moved his jaw from side to side, opening his mouth excessively wide and yawning. He heard and felt a crackling sound while holding his mouth stretched open, and then he heard a sound like air escaping from inside a balloon.

Relief came. The normal sounds from the compartment returned.

He gazed out of the window as the pilot leveled the wings. A toy-like freighter just below the wing tip, spearheading a lazy wake, made its way toward Santa Marta.

Michael's mind wandered, jumping randomly from the events of the past four days to the present and then on to possibilities in the future. His mind seemed as though it was free floating in his head, working like a 35mm projector flashing a still image on his skull, and a moment later another replaced it.

As always, Maria was on his mind. *She's strong,* he thought. *She rebounded quickly from the "incident," as they called it. At least, she appeared to rebound after the kidnapping. Sometimes Maria kept things inside.* On that horrible, rainy night, when their son Jeffrey had been killed by the police car, she had insulated herself in a cocoon of grief, and he had been unable to reach her for months.

Following the "incident," Michael spent two days by her side, constantly talking with her and giving her love and reassurance. He had done his best to help her accept the events of the kidnapping and put them in the proper perspective.

Finally, when they discussed the possibility of his delaying his retirement with Sonny, she had understood. Although she was afraid, Maria had agreed that Michael should continue helping Sonny. Sonny had been a very good friend to both of them; however, as soon as the Cuban deal was set up, she told Michael that she wanted him to get out. He had agreed with her. Their life together was more perfect than he could ever have imagined, and he didn't want anything to happen to either of them. In the business with Sonny, in which he was currently involved, danger lurked around every corner. Michael had been uneasy about the shootings when he and Sonny had rescued Maria. He had watched the papers for the past four days. There had been no mention of the bodies at the little shack. He couldn't figure out why. He did not think of what had happened as murder. He was more inclined to think of it as extermination. He believed his actions were morally justified. Because of his actions, society was better served without such scum. On the other hand, the possibility of being charged with murder was still very disturbing.

Looking out of the window of the plane as it was preparing to land, Michael saw the city of Barranquilla draped across the barren, rolling hills. *Colombia's largest seaport,* he thought. The inequality of poverty depressed him. *Barranquilla is a city of a million and a half people, and ninety-nine percent of them are illiterate,* Michael thought, recalling his previous experiences. *It's a place where the average laborer only earns a dollar a day. A policeman considers himself lucky to be making forty dollars a month. Corruption is the acceptable main staple of the police and the army because there is no other way to supplement their income. The concept of a middle class is virtually non-existent. Either one is wealthy, or one is poor. In this seaport city, the wealthy virtually control everything.*

Michael cringed at the thought of taking a gypsy taxi to the hotel. Thinking back, he remembered when he took his last trip on the thoroughfare into Barranquilla. He recalled the old school buses painted in colors of the rainbow, with peasants packed like cordwood, leaning precariously and favoring the weaker side. He had the impression that if one of the buses happened to hit a bump, it would immediately topple on its side. Clouds of dust and black exhaust followed the caravans as they moved with tortoise-like slowness. The road had recently been flattened and widened. Dusty swirls of sand and dirt swept the road, with the concrete pavement occasionally showing through it.

Barranquilla's main road was a no man's land of dilapidated cars of the 50's and 60's. Carts were being pulled by donkeys and buses, and he. trucks were steered at random, anywhere a path of least resistance presented itself. Honking and dodging, the taxi had darted in and out of the traffic at breakneck speed. As the taxi had drawn closer to the city, the thoroughfare had narrowed into two lanes. The traffic had become increasingly heavy, slowing their progress. The impatient driver had used his horn more frequently as his driving had become more aggressive.

The flat, scrubby terrain had yielded to the slums. Shacks of mud and cardboard had lined the view. There had been little black children playing in the red clay yards. The smell of poverty had been overwhelming. Michael had caught himself holding his hand over his nose and mouth. He was hoping the stench of open sewers and diesel exhaust would go away, or that the traffic would speed up. He longed for anything that would be a relief.

Michael remembered taking a shower for over an hour after he had finally reached the Hotel El Prado. He had scrubbed his body clean, but the smells in his nostrils still lingered. Michael had sighed, dreading what lay ahead.

Snapping out of the unpleasant memories of his first trip, Michael felt the airplane making another banking turn, lining up for its final approach. He guessed that the altitude was no more than four hundred feet as he saw the outer marker rush by under the wing. He heard the whir of flaps being fully extended. A moment later, he felt the plane bump twice before setting down on the hot runway.

Michael drifted back in thought. He vaguely heard the

stewardess's voice over the roar of the thrust reversers. "Kindly refrain from…." The stewardess's voice droned on.

Michael had not needed the 'heat' of coming to Colombia to negotiate a deal, but in this case, it was necessary. At first, Mehejas was adamant about Michael not coming, but through Maria's efforts over the telephone with him, she had been able to change Mehejas' mind.

Michael thought there was a slight possibility that Mehejas might want to take his life in retribution for the lost cargo. He had considered it carefully and finally concluded that it was not likely. If Mehejas wanted him dead, a thousand dollars and a round-trip plane ticket from Barranquilla to Miami, paid to the right person, could quickly and easily get it done.

Michael watched the isolated terminal as the plane drew closer. The passengers, against the urging of the stewardess, began gathering their belongings and moving about the cabin while the plane was still taxiing. Some began forming a single line in the forward compartment, all waiting to escape the confines and closeness. Michael remained seated. He had no intention of continuing to contemplate his upcoming meeting with Mehejas.

Eventually, after everyone had disembarked, Michael stood to leave. He stepped out of the Boeing 707 onto an aluminum platform, only to be met by a slap in the face from a dry, hot wind blowing off the tarmac. Shouldering his carry-on bag, he carefully began to make his way down the shaky, aluminum ramp to the hot pavement. *Careful,* he thought. He remembered how his grandmother had accidentally fallen while making a similar transition, breaking her hip. She had ultimately died, not from a fracture, but an embolism caused by complications from the fall. The world was happening as his heartbeat quickened.

A Columbian Army colonel dressed in American fatigues looked directly into Michael's eyes.

"Señor Jansen?"

"Yes," Michael answered. *What in the hell is going on?* Puzzled and a little uneasy, he stood his ground until the colonel spoke.

"Allow me," the colonel said, pointing to the rear of the vehicle.

The driver sitting beside the colonel jumped from the seat to meet Michael at the rear of the vehicle. He took Michael's bag and handed it to a companion sitting in the back seat.

Michael climbed in the back and looked at the colonel. He was still wondering why a Columbian Army colonel had picked him up, but he kept silent. The vehicle lurched forward and headed toward the terminal. Trying not to be obvious, Michael studied the colonel and occasionally looked to the side watching the two soldiers through his peripheral vision. Nothing more was said until the jeep braked to a halt adjacent to an open-air baggage pick-up.

"Señor Jansen," the colonel said, facing Michael, "please give your passport to my sergeant. He will have it stamped for you."

Breathing a shallow sigh of relief, Michael leaned forward and unquestioningly removed his passport from his pocket and gave it to the soldier.

"Forgive me," the colonel smiled. "My name is Colonel Gomez. Señor Mehejas has asked me to escort you to your hotel. I do hope that will be satisfactory for you."

"Yes, of course," Michael sighed with relief. *So that's what this is all about,* he thought. *Nothing like having the heavy brass meet me. I wonder who else Mehejas has on the pad.*

Michael guessed the colonel was probably in his late forties. Except for his accent, he could have passed as a graduate of West Point. The colonel sat erectly in his seat as he eyed the tourists collecting their luggage. Michael intuitively knew his family was politically connected.

A soldier in army greens, with an AR-15 slung over his shoulder, walked with the sergeant among the tourists. They slowly worked their way toward the jeep. The soldier in green wore a white armband just below his left shoulder. "Policia de Tourista," it read.

He continued around the jeep with the sergeant to stand by the colonel. He saluted the colonel and then gave him Michael's passport. They spoke in Spanish for a moment. The soldier saluted again and stepped back from the vehicle. Colonel Gomez pocketed Michael's passport.

Michael grabbed the back of the colonel's seat to keep from being thrown from the vehicle as the driver accelerated the jeep in a sharp turn.

Twenty-Nine

Michael awoke to a knocking on the door. His eyes fluttered for a moment, slowly becoming accustomed to the early morning light. He looked up at the high ceiling and remembered he was in the El Prado Hotel. He felt comfortable and relaxed, and his consciousness wanted to return to the total peace from which it had just emerged. He closed his eyes, and the knocking resumed.

Inhaling deeply, Michael sat up on the edge of the bed. "Just a minute," he groaned as he cleared his throat. Not wanting to open his eyes, he drunkenly staggered in bare feet to the door. The lock resisted his attempts to open the door. Cursing under his breath, he finally got the door open. Mehejas stood in the middle of the hall, a henchman on either side of him. Suddenly Michael became fully awake. He had not expected Mehejas so early. He stared at the men for a moment. Mehejas 'smile broke the tension.

Relaxing, Michael smiled, extending his hand.
Taking a step forward, Mehejas accepted Michael's hand. He said nothing, so Michael stepped aside, allowing the group to enter the room. Mehejas walked past him. The other two men, whom Michael presumed to be bodyguards, looked to each end of the hall, and then entered. Michael realized that no matter what happened, he was in Mehejas' backyard.

The three men walked to the middle of the room and then turned to face Michael as he closed the door behind them.

Michael pointed to the sofa and chair, seating himself on the bed. Mehejas took the chair, and the other two men sat on the sofa.

"Well," Michael said, looking at Mehejas, "can I offer you something to drink?"

"Yes, please," Mehejas answered. He said something in Spanish to the man nearest Michael. The man got up, walked to the phone, and placed a call. The other Columbian sitting on the couch was the next to speak.

"My name is Peter," he said in perfect English. "Mehejas has asked me to interpret whenever it is necessary." He pointed to the Columbian with the bulldog face that was making the call. "That's Lucas. He's calling room service for drinks. Is Scotch all right?" he asked as he leaned back on the sofa.

"That'll be fine." *Nothing like a shot of Scotch first thing in the morning,* Michael thought.

Peter seemed congenial enough. His wiry physique reminded Michael of his brother Gary, but that was where the similarity stopped. Peter's natural blonde, shoulder-length hair was combed back, framing his oval, rather boyish face. Michael supposed that one of his parents must be of Scandinavian or German descent.

Peter said something to Lucas, interrupting his conversation on the phone.

Michael sat on the bed, remaining quiet and watching his guests curiously until the drinks had been ordered.

Lucas hung up the phone and walked back toward the sofa.

"Lucas, do you speak English?" Michael asked.

Lucas shook his head no as he seated himself beside Peter.

Mehejas crossed his legs, looked at Peter, and spoke again in Spanish. Peter listened intently, waiting for Mehejas to finish.

"Mehejas wants to know if you intend to pay for the lost shipment."

Michael looked from Peter to Mehejas, "Ask him how he expects us to pay for something we never received?"

"Mehejas' position is that he sent the merchandise in good faith, and he believes you should at least pay his cost for the product."

160

"I understand that, but Mehejas has to also understand that our risk and losses are just as great as his, if not more. We lost a boat and two crewmen, plus the expense of setting up the operation." Michael did not tell him they would probably get the Chubby Ann back. He wanted to maintain a firm bargaining position.

Peter, turning to Mehejas, translated what Michael had said. They spoke back and forth for a moment. Lucas remained silent.

Peter looked at Michael. "He says that his cost is about one hundred eighty thousand dollars. Will you split the difference?"

"Of course," Michael answered, "if he'll split the difference in our costs."

Peter said, "Si," to Mehejas. Mehejas' expression softened. Then he asked another question.

Peter explained the question to Michael, "He wants to know what your costs were."

Michael looked Mehejas straight in the eyes as he replied. "Around three hundred thousand."

Peter paused for a moment. Mehejas already understood Michael's answer. He bolted upright in his chair, knowing he had been trapped. He looked at Michael with contempt.

"We can no longer do business," he said, rising to his feet. Lucas was up with the speed of a cat beside Mehejas.

Michael put both palms out to stop Mehejas.

"Tell Señor Mehejas I did not come here to argue like children. Tell him I have a proposal for which only a fool would not listen!"

Peter spoke rapidly in Spanish. Mehejas hesitated for a moment, letting Peter's words sink in.

"You are either a fool or a very brave man," Peter cautioned. "No one talks to Mehejas that way."

Michael's eyes had not wavered from Mehejas. Mehejas glared back for a moment, and then he seemed to relax as he lowered himself back into his chair.

"I am not a fool," Mehejas finally said, just above a whisper.

Lucas finally relaxed and also sat back down.

There was a knock on the door. Michael slowly let out a sigh of relief, and his blood pressure fell at least thirty points. Lucas stood again when Michael eased off the bed and headed for the door.

Drinks had arrived. As Michael opened the door, a dark-complexioned Columbian man wearing an orange kitchen jacket squeezed a pushcart past him and brought it to a stop in the center of the room. The cart held several bottles of Old Par Scotch Whiskey, a bucket of ice, glasses, and napkins. As the waiter removed a large half-moon plastic cover, an assortment of fresh, colorful tropical fruits, including papaya, melons, and plums were revealed.

Michael signed the check, circled a dollar tip at the bottom, and handed it to the waiter on his way out.

Michael assumed the role of bartender. He attempted to hide his unsteadiness by holding a glass flat on the cart with one hand and pouring the whiskey with the other. He kept the mouth of the bottle against the rim of the glass to stop his hand from shaking. He had regained most of his composure by the time he had served his guests.

While Michael had been busy mixing drinks, Mehejas and his companions had been devouring the beautiful assortment of fruits. There was not much left by the time Michael had finished mixing his drink. *It didn't matter that I wasn't particularly hungry; it was just the idea,* he thought to himself. The interruption seemed to have eased the tension somewhat. All three men appeared less tense. Michael pushed the cart over by the drapes and seated himself on the bed in the same place as before. In a moment, after completing his discussion with Mehejas, Peter turned and addressed Michael.

"Señor Mehejas will hear your proposal."

Michael took a sip of his drink. He slowly began telling Peter a step-by-step sequence of the events leading up to this meeting. He would stop after a few sentences, giving Peter time to explain to Mehejas. When Peter looked back at Michael, Michael would continue.

When Michael began to speak of Cuba, he sensed from Mehejas' subtle reaction that the meeting had developed a different attitude. The hostilities of the three men vanished. Mehejas was, after all, no fool. Michael completed his offer.

Mehejas entered into a heated debate with Peter, gesturing with his hands.

Watching them, Michael eased off the edge of the bed and began preparing another round of drinks.

"He wants to know how many pounds you want in the first load," Peter questioned Michael.

"I'd like to make a trial run with about twenty thousand pounds. Then, if there are no problems with the Cubans, we should maintain a stockpile on the island of at least two hundred thousand pounds. For planning purposes, tell Mehejas I think he should get commitments of at least one million pounds from his growers on this new crop. Also, let him know that he is to supply the transportation to Cuba. Tell him we'll get back with him on what the port of entry will be, with more specific dates and all the other information that he will need to safely enter Cuban waters."

Mehejas listened intently, interrupting Peter occasionally to clarify something Michael had said.

Then, deep in thought, Mehejas fell silent for a moment before coming to a decision. He finally gave Peter his response to translate.

"He says you have a deal on two conditions. One, the price is eighty dollars a pound. Two, he wants one million dollars in cash up front."

"What!" Michael shouted, rising from the bed. "Where the hell are we going to get a million dollars in cash?"

"Señor Mehejas insists. Otherwise, there will be no deal."

Michael knew that what Mehejas was asking was reasonable, considering the past blown deal. He had his commitments to the growers and the necessary expenses for the freighter, and so forth.

The problem as he saw it was that Sonny was adamant about not giving out front money. They had been burned in the past. Anyway, where were they going to come up with that kind of money? Certainly not from his nest egg!

"All right," Michael responded, "but first I'll have to talk with Sonny. If he agrees, it's a deal."

Understanding what Michael had said, Mehejas offered a small smile.

Thirty

Michael looked at his watch. It was 12:32 a.m. He listened to the antiquated clicking as the International Operator placed his call. At a little past six the previous evening, he had put in a call to Sonny in Miami, and now the operator was finally connecting the call. *No wonder this country is so archaic,* he thought. Throughout Michael's travels, he had concluded an indisputable theory; transportation and communication were the vital elements necessary for the economic growth of any nation. In parts of the world where these elements were missing, violence and poverty were dominant. He rose to a sitting position on the edge of the bed and reached for a cigarette.

At the same time, Sonny was wondering what was going on with Michael and Mehejas. Michael was a good negotiator, and Sonny trusted him implicitly. The phone rang.

"Yeah," Sonny answered.

"It's your long-lost friend. Remember me?"

"Hey guy, how's the vacation?"

"Not too bad. How's Maria?"

"She's fine. I called her this afternoon. She's waiting for you to get your ass back."

"What's going on?" Sonny questioned.

"I spoke with our client. Everything is a go except for one small item."

"What's that?"

"He wants a letter of credit for one million dollars." He knew Sonny would know what he meant.

"Shit, Michael, did he agree to all the terms of the contract? "Yes, even to the million bushels of coffee."

"How soon does he need the letter of credit?"

"He didn't specify. I would imagine within the next several days."

Wrinkling his forehead in thought, Sonny was silent.

"Are you still there?" Michael asked after a moment had passed.

"Yeah, I was just thinking about how to handle it, that's all. Where does he want it?"

"Well, if we can do it, send it to the Banco de Bogotá, the same way we've always done it."

"All right," Sonny sighed. "Tell him he'll have it in a day or so."

"Are you sure?" Michael hesitated, wondering how Chubby would come up with the money.

"Yeah, go ahead and tell him."

"Okay, do me a favor and connect me with Maria."

Sonny put Michael on hold.

Michael had a mental picture of Sonny dialing Maria's mother's number through Southern Bell's electronic switching system. He heard Maria's sleepy voice.

"Baby, is that you?"

"Hi, sweetheart," Michael said, forcing himself to sound as cheerful as he could. How's my baby doing?"

"When are you coming home?"

"I'm not sure, love, probably in a couple of days. I have to go to the Peninsula tomorrow."

"Please hurry home, okay? I love you, Michael."

"I will sweetheart, just as soon as I finish everything here. I love you too."

"Don't worry about anything here," Sonny said on the three-party lines. "If Maria needs anything, all she has to do is pick up the phone."

Michael replaced the receiver, lit another cigarette, and lay back on the bed. He was fully awake now as the events of the day and the phone call occupied his mind. He thought about the merry-go-round that his passport had taken. *Why had the Colonel kept it? Why had Mehejas given Michael's passport back after their meeting?* Mehejas knew Michael was helpless without it. He surmised it had been Mehejas' way of playing a cat-and-mouse game, and, of course, Michael was the mouse.

He stubbed his cigarette out and killed the bedside lamp. *I need to get some rest,* he thought. *Tomorrow is going to be one hell of a long day.*

Thirty-One

Michael stepped out of the Bronco in Riohacha, La Guajira, located on the Northeastern Peninsular of Columbia, South America. Wiping a salty drop of sweat from his eye, he squinted up at the barn-like warehouse in which the marijuana was stored. His back ached from ten hours of cramped driving, and his face felt grimy. His mouth had a sticky, chalky taste from drinking Guaro, a low alcoholic liquor distilled from sugar cane and sometimes referred to as "soft vodka." The Guaro bottle had been passed around continuously during the long and hectic trip, and everyone had imbibed liberally. *What a ride,* he thought, sighing in relief as he wiped his face on his shirttail. He drew a deep breath of the dusty air and silently thanked God that the long journey had ended. He was also thankful that he had survived the blasting noise of an eight-track tape playing Vallenatos. The Columbian folk music had begun that morning at seven o'clock when they left Michael's hotel. Glancing at his watch, Michael noted it was now five in the evening. He had thought the flute and accordion would drive him crazy.

Five heavily armed Colombians had accompanied Peter, his interpreter. They had fetched Michael from the hotel in Barranquilla with instructions from Mehejas to take him to Riohacha. They were to inspect the first shipment there. Apparently, Mehejas wanted no arguments over the quality of the merchandise once the shipment arrived in the States. It was good thinking on Mehejas' part, Michael decided, to take such special precautions. He knew of instances where bloodshed had occurred over misunderstandings of quality and price. He was somewhat relieved that Mehejas wanted to do business in such a clear-cut manner.

A Toyota Jeep braked to a skidding halt behind the Bronco. A massive dust cloud trailing the vehicle overtook them. It added another layer of grime to Michael's damp clothing and face.

Two men leaped from the vehicle with guns drawn. Peter stepped forward, speaking rapidly in Spanish. There was an intense argument. Michael nervously leaned against the dusty Bronco and waited for the two men to decide what to do. He thought for a moment that there would be a shootout.

Michael looked around feeling helpless. He was in a foreign city, a foreign country, and unable to speak the language, which amplified his distress. It was impossible to determine who his enemy was. Without realizing it, he had placed his life in Peter's hands. He didn't like that one bit. An involuntary shiver passed through his body as he watched the exchange between the three men.

Riohacha was like a 70's Twilight Zone. It reminded Michael of the old West where law and order were seen as a way of life. If one hadn't learned it by the age of twelve, the consequences could be dire. This was a place where twentieth-century man had returned to the 1800s, except Chevy Blazers and Ford Broncos had replaced horses. Rumors said that the guajeos begged the Gringo boat captains and pilots for guns and ammunition. Upon delivery, they would kill the Gringos to avoid paying for their high-priced weapons. One thing was certain. Riohacha was a town empty of old men.

Eventually and without incident, the driver of the Toyota jeep broke away from the group and began leading the way to a huge tin-covered door. It was closed and locked with a large, rusty chain and padlock. He unlocked the padlock and walked the door open.

Still a little uneasy, Michael followed Peter into the warehouse. The pungent odor of burlap bags, stacked to the height and length of a semi-trailer, betrayed their contents. The group's attention shifted to Michael.

"May I open a couple of bales?" Michael asked, touching one of the hard-pressed packages.

Peter spoke in Spanish, motioning toward the bale on which Michael had his hand. The chauffeur of the Bronco took out a penknife and began cutting the burlap cover. Michael moved closer to inspect the contents.

What he saw confirmed what he had suspected. The marijuana had been prematurely cut. Ripping further into the package, he discovered layered levels of leaves and stems, indicating the marijuana had been packed too tightly. There were few buds, the color was bad, and heat damage from internal combustion was evident. His assessment of the merchandise was at best low-grade commercial. Further inspection of other bales revealed the same low-grade product.

Michael looked at Peter indifferently.

"I don't know," he said, shaking his head in a manner suggestive of refusal. "By the time this hits the streets, it will be full of mildew. How much do you have?"

Peter turned to the Toyota driver. The man shrugged his shoulders and answered. Peter translated and said, "About twenty-five thousand kilos."

Thoughtfully, Michael looked at him and finally spoke. "Tell Mehejas we'll take it at fifty dollars a pound."

Peter nodded, turned, and walked out of the building. Michael followed close behind. When they reached the Bronco, the driver of the Toyota caught up with them. He appeared agitated. He spoke rapidly and with authority, occasionally throwing his arms in the air as if he were trying to convince Peter of something.

They argued for five minutes or more. Finally, Peter turned to Michael. "My friend, it appears we are in for a slight delay," he said reluctantly. "Chemas here," pointing toward the driver, "has a DC-7 coming in tomorrow. He needs a translator. Since it is Mehejas' load, I have no choice but to go." He smiled at Michael. "You are welcome to come along for the show."

Michael sank back against the Bronco, thinking about a cold shower when another thought popped into his mind. *This is better for me,* he thought. *The DC-7 can take this shit, and I won't have to deal with it.*

Looking at Peter, Michael said, "Sure, why not? I've got nothing else to do." *Damn,* he thought, *I need a bath.*

———————

Later, Michael finally got his bath, although it wasn't quite what he had expected. His "bath" had been in a narrow creek snaking its way about a mile to the ocean. He sat in six inches of cool water, watching the hot, golden sun drop below the sparse scrubby trees. A young, straight-haired Indian boy scooped up water in an old lard can and poured it over Michael's head. He was grinning and laughing, all the while looking at the much lighter-complexioned man. Though fair, Michael was well-tanned, but the Columbians were much darker. In retrospect, Michael had thoroughly enjoyed himself. He wished he were back there now because he was already hot and dusty again.

Last night was spent in Riohacha. Chemas gratuitously provided lodging at his home for Peter and Michael. Michael had no idea where the others had gone. The small house was comfortable and surprisingly clean.

Michael later learned that Chemas's status was that of a "mayor," and he was considered a confidante to Mehejas. Chemas's authority

171

in the surrounding area was almost god-like. Nothing was done without his explicit permission. At some point during the rowdy evening of eating and drinking, Chemas had displayed his battle scars from the past twenty-two years, which had been his entire life. Peter said jokingly that Chemas had four more years to live. The average lifespan in Riohacha was short, and frequently it ended violently.

Chemas was driving. Peter sat in the front passenger seat, and Michael was wedged in the back. Two Columbians sat to his left and one to his right. Another guard was scrunched up in the luggage department wrestling an ice chest filled with Heineken's. The dirt road was worse than a washboard. To avoid being thrown against the roof of the vehicle, Michael buckled his seat belt as tightly as he could. He held one hand against the roof of the Bronco, pushing hard against it to counteract each bounce. Each time a vehicle hit a bump, the guard and ice chest would leave the luggage floor, momentarily suspended in midair. They both would crash down amid grunts of pain and the swooshing of the water melting the ice. The rollercoaster ride had reached the point of being ridiculous. *All this chaos is a symphony in the third degree,* Michael thought.

Salt flats loomed ahead. The processing plant was silhouetted on the horizon, and the calm ocean was on the left. As the terrain leveled out at the salt flats, the Bronco reached eighty miles per hour. Michael cringed at the thought of Chemas losing control and crashing into a pit. The scene resembled a giant waffle extending forty miles. Each pit was about the size of a football field surrounded by a six-foot embankment. It was crowned with a dirt road, barely wide enough to allow one vehicle to move over. Salt-water canals wove throughout the maze. Each pit had a metal gate, which could be opened or closed. After the saltwater evaporated, the Indians would rake up the salt and then re-flood the pit. This process was timeless and endless. The roads, or levies, resembled a maze capable of trapping a driver without a guide. It would take an inexperienced person several days to find his way out.

Chemas drove in a northeasterly direction keeping close to the ocean. They passed sporadic clusters of Indians dressed in brightly colored clothing, who were raking up salt from the infrequently dry pits. Michael wondered where they got their fresh water in such a godforsaken, dry environment.

Eventually, they passed the salt pits. Rocky hills replaced the flats as the Bronco twisted its way over the harsh tundra. Thorn trees and cacti were impenetrable in many places. Goat trails led off in every direction. Frequently, the roads became indistinguishable from the trails. The elevation rose slowly to two hundred feet above the ocean.

Suddenly the Bronco broke out of the scrub onto a mud-colored plateau. Michael took in the vista. The area had been cleared over a mile. He realized they had arrived on a clandestine runway, which had been bulldozed out of this abandoned wilderness. The ground, packed hard as concrete, was perfect for a heavy airplane.

Seven men piled out of the truck. Grunting and sighing with relief, they began stretching their legs and urinating. Michael thought it was almost ridiculously funny that he walked to the back of the truck to relieve himself, while the other men peed where they stood. Oddly enough, he found Peter standing at the back with him. Little explosions of dust rose from the impact of the warm yellow streams.

"How long is the runway?" Michael asked, zipping up his fly.

"Six thousand feet," Peter answered, shaking himself.

Michael joined the others at the front of the vehicle. They had broken out the beer. For some reason Michael did not understand, this occasion had turned into a festive affair.

Chemas spoke to one of the guards. The man broke away from the group and walked to the rear of the truck. Moments later he returned, proudly carrying an M-16 rifle and a Heineken. He handed Michael the beer, then passed the rifle around for inspection. It went from hand to hand. Occasionally, a man would point it at some make-believe target, probably wondering when he would have to use it.

Suddenly, Michael heard the high-pitched whine of a vehicle. Looking up, he saw a jeep dart out from the bush onto the runway about three hundred yards away. A cloud of dust pursued the jeep and its six occupants. Michael knew they were soldiers and instinctively stepped back behind the Bronco for protection.

The Colombians froze. Chemas lowered the barrel of the M-16 to the ground, taking a passive stance. When the jeep was within fifty yards of the group, Michael was relieved to see Colonel Gomez sitting in the front passenger seat. A smile flicked across Gomez's face when he recognized Michael. The vehicle slid to a dusty halt next to Chemas. The dust cloud over Michael temporarily blocked his vision.

Momentarily blinded by the dust, Michael slowly walked toward the jeep.

"Mr. Jansen," the colonel smiled and extended a hand. "It is so good to see you again."

"Hello, Colonel," Michael replied, shaking the man's hand.

The four soldiers climbed haphazardly out of the jeep, accidentally banging their vintage M-1 carbines against the side of the vehicle. The men set an example of supposedly well-trained fighting men. Their enthusiasm reflected the forty dollars a month salary each received.

Chemas walked around the jeep to speak with the colonel. Michael eased over to stand beside Peter next to the Bronco.

"What time will the plane be here?" Gomez asked Chemas.

Peter pitched his empty Heineken bottle into the bushes. "Maybe in another half hour."

Chemas responded. "Want a beer?"

"Can't stand the shit," the colonel said with a slight smile.

Michael turned to the sounds of several trucks grinding through the bush. He could only see a dust cloud and thick, black exhaust smoke rising above the scrub. Two Mack flatbed trucks, loaded with cargo and covered with tarpaulins, lumbered out on the runway. The smoking exhaust began making its way toward the men. About thirty Indians, who resembled baby spiders clinging to their mother, held fast to the tarp straps.

Thirty-Two

Michael lay on his side, propped up on his elbow under the eaves of a truck. He was hiding from the oppressive afternoon sun. It was too hot to talk. Peter, Chemas, and the colonel lay alongside him. The soldiers sought refuge from the sun under the other truck, while the Indians squatted around what little shade they could find under the thorny bushes growing from the dry, dusty terrain. This was just another example of Columbia's class system.

Peter removed a green box from the Bronco and set it up next to the rear tires. A portable VHF radio, compatible with those found in private and commercial aircraft, was set to 122.6 MHZ. Squelch occasionally leaked from the speaker as they waited for the DC-7. The radio was the aircraft's only link to the ground. With numerous clandestine runways in the area, the pilot would be blind without a radio on the ground. The navigator would use his radio direction finder to locate the proper runway.

Michael's eyes rested on the sway-backed fuel truck parked at the edge of the bush. It was a step up from the fifty-five-gallon drums that had formerly been used in the past. He looked at his watch, wondering where the plane was. It was two hours overdue, and in another half hour, the sun would be setting over Santa Marta. If the airplane arrived after dark, it would be too late. It would be thirsty for fuel and looking for a place to land. In the absence of runway lights, the big bird would be destined for burial at sea.

"Big Red, Big Red. This is Big Blue. Over."

Peter reached for the microphone. The colonel and his men began stirring, sitting up, and listening to the unfamiliar language.

"This is Big Red," Peter said. "Go ahead."

"Roger, Big Red," said a confident Texas drawl. "We're about ten miles out. We should be with you in about four or five minutes. Over."

"All right," Peter replied.

Colonel Gomez crawled out from under the truck, barking orders in Spanish to his men. Hot and sweaty, they dragged themselves from the shelter, stretching and yawning from their afternoon siesta. Reluctantly, they began scattering along the runway.

Michael heard the low rumble of the airplane. He looked toward the ocean and saw it in the distance, just above the water. It gained altitude as it approached the plateau. Thirty seconds later it tracked to the left of the runway several hundred feet above the scrub. Trucks, men, and the ground shook as the huge plane passed.

"Big Blue, we have you in sight," Peter said. "Make a right-hand turn and come in the direction from which you came. We'll have a jeep on the runway for your reference. Over."

The pilot effortlessly swung the four-engine monster to the right as if it were a single-engine Piper Cub.

"No problem," said the Texas drawl. "We got y'all in sight. We'll be with you in a minute."

The plane dropped behind a rise, then reappeared about a quarter of a mile from the strip. The Indians, out of hiding, watched the silver aircraft make its landing.

With the landing gear down and the flaps fully extended, the huge plane lumbered for its final approach. It slipped sideways over the trees as the engines were cut. It gently glided to the ground trailing an incredible cloud of dust.

The airplane looks abnormally large, Michael thought. *More than likely, it's the largest thing within miles,* he reasoned. Although he had nothing to do with this operation and was only along as an observer, his adrenaline was pumping. There was an overwhelming excitement, which he could not explain. Perhaps it was standing here completely detached, watching the hopes and dreams of others held together by an invisible trail leading to this clandestine runway in this primitive wilderness. The thought crossed his mind of how many other airplanes had landed here and how many more were yet to come. *This runway,* he thought, *is a symbol of the free enterprise system at its best.* It was indicative of the risks small groups of freethinkers were willing to take; a professional gambler placing a final stake on the last card. These were men fighting against the system. They were willing to forfeit their lives if they lost, which many, thus far, had done.

The DC-7 taxied to the end of the strip and stopped. It sat there for a moment, seemingly out of place, deciding where to go. The engines roared, and it moved around to face back in the direction from which it had come. Slowly, the airplane bumped its way along the rough surface toward them, eventually coming to a stop parallel to the fuel truck.

One by one, the four huge radial Wright R-3350 Duplex Cyclone engines, each boosting one thousand horsepower, were shut down. As the last propeller came to a stop, Peter and Chemas, followed by Michael, walked toward the cargo hatch aft of the starboard wing. It swung open to reveal a tall, slim man who looked to be in his late thirties, smiling with a sense of relief.

Two other crewmen joined him. In the waning light, Michael saw the apprehension fading from their faces. The shortest of the three nudged past the first man and dropped the seven feet to the ground.

Straightening up, he offered his hand to Peter.

"Howdy," he said. His smile revealed even white teeth. "My

name's Fisher." Wearing a short buzz cut, Tom Fisher was a thirty-nine-year-old retired military pilot who had fallen on tough times due to a costly divorce. The owner of the airplane, a wealthy businessman from Dallas, and a friend of Fisher's, had given him a way out. The substantial proposal to fly to Columbia had cinched the deal for Fisher.

The other two men jumped down, and Captain Fisher was introduced to the group. The co-pilot turned out to be the tall, slender man named Billy. The third man, the flight engineer, was named John. He seemed to be the most nervous of the three.

To ease their anxiety, Michael asked, "How was the flight? Can I offer you a beer?"

"I sure could use one," Billy said.

Captain Fisher looked at him with a brief moment of displeasure, and then he sighed.

"Hell, why not?" he said. "We're gonna be here all night anyway." They followed Michael to the truck.

Chemas shouted a command, and a flurry of activity began. One of the Mack trucks fired to life and began backing its way toward the cargo door. Colonel Gomez pulled the jeep up at an angle to the plane, shining the headlights on the loading area. Several Indians started a fire upwind on the edge of the scrub.

"How much weight do you have?" Fisher asked Peter.

"About forty thousand pounds."

"ABOUT forty thousand pounds? Shit! I have to know exactly," snapped Fisher.

Muttering under his breath, Fisher turned and walked to the truck parked next to the cargo door. When he reached the truck, he climbed up on the tailgate, balanced his beer, and disappeared into the fuselage of the plane to supervise the cargo loading.

A cool breeze began blowing off the Caribbean forcing the few remaining idle hands to surround the fire seeking warmth. Peter walked over to the fire carrying several blankets that he spread on the ground. He motioned for his guests to be seated. Billy and John joined Michael on the pallet. It was going to be a long night.

Michael sat listening to the night sounds and watching the hypnotic rhythm of the fire. Occasionally, he would see a soldier with a carbine slung over his shoulder moving about at the foot of the shadows cast by the flames. His stomach growled, reminding him that his last meal had been the hastily eaten breakfast early that morning. He looked over to see John and Billy fast asleep, exhausted from the ten-hour flight. He wondered what motivation had been used to compel them to be here.

An Indian broke the barrier of darkness carrying an armload of sticks and dropping them on the fire. Sparks and cinders were caught up in the cooling, stiff breeze sailing them into oblivion. The Indian disappeared as quickly as the sparks had vanished. As insignificant as they may have seemed, the randomness of these events sent cold shivers racing through Michael. *Cause and effect,* he thought, realizing how elusive his life really was.

The Mack truck came to life again and slowly moved away from the plane. Michael saw Captain Fisher standing in the beam of the jeep's headlights. He was leaning against the hatchway fighting fatigue. Michael figured it would be another hour and a half before the pilot could get some needed sleep. *The captain is a prudent man,* Michael thought. *If the bales are improperly loaded, the aircraft's center of gravity will be out of balance, almost assuring a fatal takeoff. This is not child's play, nor a task for the inexperienced. Lives are at stake,* Michael thought as he watched the activity around him.

A second truck replaced the first and the loading continued.

Michael sleepily roused in the early dawn to the shaking of his foot.

Peter squatted beside him.

"Hey, it is time to get up," he said, handing Michael a rusty can filled with something that smelled like coffee. Michael shivered from the cold breeze still moving in off the ocean. He fingered the hot container, crabbing his way closer to the fire, hoping that its heat would quickly dry his dew-covered clothing. Michael glanced over at the flight crew as they groggily began uncurling from fetal positions, grunting, groaning, and assessing the new perspectives of the plateau. Michael looked around in the fading gray light.

All the Indians had vanished. A lone soldier sat sound asleep under a wing, carbine across his lap.

"Good morning," Michael said to no one in particular.

"This ground's as hard as a gourd's ass," Fisher grumbled, moving next to the fire.

"Y'all got any more coffee?"

Peter tossed his remaining coffee out and replenished the can. He handed it to Fisher, who took a swig.

"Shit!" He spat and passed it on to Billy.

"Where did the colonel go?" Michael asked, looking at Peter.

"There is a hut about a mile from here. He and Chemas always spend the night there when we are working. Do not worry, they will be here shortly."

Wide awake, Captain Fisher looked at his watch and said, "We gotta get movin' y'all, if we're gonna make that dry lakebed by dark."

He rose and stretched, soon followed by the rest of the crew. Together, they walked toward the aircraft to begin their pre-flight checklist. The captain slowly walked around the plane, checking for any damage that might have occurred during the night's loading. He didn't trust the drivers of the trucks. *Some idiot could have backed into a wing, or who knows what else?* He found nothing out of place and no apparent damage.

A rickety ladder had been placed at the cargo door during the night. After his exterior inspection, Captain Fisher ascended the ladder. His personality took on an air of professionalism as he strapped himself in the left-hand seat.

"Let's see if we can get this son of a bitch off the ground," he sighed.

Billy squeezed into the seat to the right of the Captain.

John took the flight engineer's seat in the center cockpit, just aft of the pilot and co-pilot. He pushed a release lever and spun the chair forward to face the instrument panels lined with numerous switches and gauges. The nerve center of the aircraft lay dormant in front of him. It occurred to John that within a matter of a few feet, he had stepped through an invisible chasm, from the primitive into the space age.

Fisher reached over and put the emergency hydraulic selector in 'Brake and Systems Only.'

"Emergency hydraulic switch on," he said, looking at Billy.

Fisher leaned back, turning his head toward the flight engineer.

"John, let's skip the E.H.S. Since we're making a cold start from the batteries only, conservation of power is critical."

"All right," John said and pressed the switch back to the off position.

The captain spread a chart over the center console.

"Billy, I think we ought to…," and the captain began going over their return route.

John left the cockpit with a fuel stick in hand to start his pre-flight check. He opened the port escape hatch and stepped out onto the wing. The over-the-wing inspection went routinely. The port fuel tanks had been topped off at two thousand gallons with fuel caps securely replaced. The oil stick showed engines number one and two at their proper levels.

He retraced his steps on the wing and entered the fuselage. The same procedure was repeated on the starboard wing.

On his way back to the cargo hatch, he stopped to inspect the marijuana. He checked the cargo nets to make sure the tie-down straps were secure.

Michael watched him climb down the rickety ladder. Walking forward, John stopped under a wing, and using the fuel stick he began pushing on a C-4 strainer located under the wing. Gasoline poured down through the stick onto the ground. After a moment, he knelt to the ground and inspected the discharge. Satisfied, he moved to the next strainer and repeated the process until all five strainers on that wing had been checked.

Reaching the wheel well, he pulled a flashlight from his back pocket and examined the dark depths of the hole. Next, he worked his way down the hydraulic lines to the brake drums, making sure there were no leaks. The tires were in good condition. *Hell,* he thought. *What difference does it make whether or not the tires are okay? If something is wrong with them, what do we do, call Firestone for a service call? I don't think so,* he chuckled to himself.

His inspection route took him to the nose gear, back to the starboard wheel well, out under the other wing, and then back under the fuselage. He checked the hydraulic compartment door and all the luggage compartments, making sure no stowaways were on board, or no other contraband or explosives had been secretly stashed. The tail section looked clean. Content that the airplane was airworthy, he climbed back aboard and pushed the ladder out and away from the plane. It landed with a thud in a swirling cloud of dust. He closed and locked the cargo door.

"How does she look?" Fisher asked as John strapped himself in.

"All is a go," he answered.

"All right, let's get this bitch in the air," Fisher smiled.

"Stand by to count props."

"Roger," Billy responded, looking out to the number three engine.

"Give me eight blades," Fisher ordered.

John held the number three starter switch. The propeller began to move slowly, and then faster. Oil had settled in each cylinder and exploded out of the exhaust manifold in thick blue smoke, startling the men on the ground. The propeller spun faster as its full ignition shook the large aircraft.

"Oil pressure's rising," John said above the roar and vibration. "Generator's online."

"All right," the captain replied. He was also watching the instruments.

As the manifold pressure increased, the engine began to run smoothly, and the vibration all but ceased.

"Start number four," the captain instructed. The procedure was repeated. Engines number two and one followed.

Completing the Before-Taxi checklist, Captain Fisher looked around the cockpit and then at his crew. Scanning all the instruments he said, "Let's go."

Sitting in the jeep beside Colonel Gomez, Michael covered his ears with both hands as the large twelve-cylinder engines flexed their muscles. The aircraft slowly began moving alongside them. It turned to the right heading toward the center of the runway. A blast of wind followed, shaking the jeep. Dust, dirt, tiny pebbles, and sticks sandblasted the men. "Son of a bitch!" Michael spat, shaking sand out of his hair.

When the airplane reached the end of the airstrip, Captain Fisher eased the aircraft into a full circle. Using the tips of his toes, he brought the one-hundred forty-thousand-pound airplane to a complete stop.

"Let's run her up," he said and eased the throttles forward.

John watched the instruments dance about. The plane shook and expressed an urgency to be airborne. The massive brakes, gripping, held her captive in a foreign environment. His hand touched a panel, taking the pulse of the aircraft. He watched the manifold pressure steady itself at thirty inches on each of the four engines.

"Looks good." He smiled nervously, thinking of the relief he

184

would feel to be back in the air and away from this godforsaken place.

Captain Fisher saw the jeep parked alongside the runway. He looked over at Billy.

"All set?"

"Yes, Sir."

The captain looked back at John, nodded, and released the brakes.

She moved forward like a snail loose from the starting gate. As the aircraft moved faster, her struts started absorbing the shock of the crude surface. Swirling dust and debris from the prop wash felt like hurricane-force winds to those on the ground. The heavy airplane picked up speed. Parallel to the jeep, John noted the airspeed was at forty knots and increasing.

Captain Fisher held the rudder steady with his feet. At sixty knots, ailerons and stabilizers responded to his pressure on the yoke. Lift began to conquer gravity in a tug-of-war between those forces. Gradually, at one hundred ten knots, the nose gear lifted from the ground, free of resistance from the runway, slowly gaining speed and lift.

The air crew saw a wall of scrubby thorn trees growing larger as the plane approached the strip's end. "Come on, baby," Fisher mumbled, pulling back hard on the yoke.

The airspeed indicator approached one hundred twenty knots. They cleared the trees with ample space to spare. Continuing the maneuver, the captain kicked in some right rudder and aileron, dipping the right wing, causing the aircraft to make a graceful, climbing turn.

"Yeehaw!" Chemas shouted from the Bronco. A celebration was in order.

"Gear up," the co-pilot shouted above the deafening noise of the engines.

"Roger," Fisher answered, watching their instruments. The altimeter was reading two hundred feet.

"Flaps up."

Billy reached for a lever next to the landing gear mechanism and pulling it up, he raised the flaps.

"Flaps are up."

Fisher, glancing back at John said, "Give me the METO power."

John adjusted the throttles, holding the manifold pressure at forty-two inches and the RPMs at twenty-six hundred.

The big plane lumbered higher with her load. From the ground, she appeared to be fighting for every foot of altitude gained.

As the DC-7 passed one thousand feet, Captain Fisher called for climbing power and procedures. John began going down the checklist watching his instruments and flicking switches.

At fifteen hundred feet, the Captain leveled out and watched the airspeed indicator climb to one hundred and seventy knots.

"John, let's go to cruise power."

"Yes, Sir."

The power readings on engine number four caught his attention. *That's not right,* he thought, reaching over and tapping all the instruments.

"Captain! We're losing power and oil pressure on number four!"

Fisher and Billy scanned their gauges.

"Oil quantity is dropping rapidly!" John said.

"Damn!" Billy snapped.

Captain Fisher confirmed the problem.

"Feather number four."

John reached overhead and feathered number four. The Captain followed his motions to make sure the procedure was followed correctly. He looked at Billy.

"Is four feathered?"

Billy looked out the window. The propeller was slowly windmilling.

"Yes Sir. Four is feathered."

"John, let's go back to climb power."

"Roger."

The flight engineer adjusted the throttles.

"Stand by for an Emergency Engine-out Checklist on number four," Fisher said.

Billy reached for his flight manual, firing questions and confirmations back and forth to the flight engineer as Captain Fisher maintained control of the aircraft.

Fisher began to assess their situation. He thought of the two thousand miles lying ahead of them. He had no idea what the problem was with the number four engine. He did know that there was no way possible to repair the engine back at the landing strip. Turning back would be senseless. Quickly and carefully weighing the situation, he foresaw no difficulty in continuing the flight with three engines.

A red light blinked at him. For a split second, he thought his eyes were deceiving him. It appeared again, steady this time.

"Holy shit! We've got a fuel pressure warning light on number three!"

Billy and John abruptly stopped their checklist, staring at the light in disbelief.

The engine continued running smoothly.

"Think it's a faulty light?" Billy asked.

A fire warning bell went off, shattering the drone of the engines, in answer to the question.

"We've got a fire!" John shouted.

Billy looked out the window. Black smoke trailed the engine.

Captain Fisher turned in his seat, hammering orders to his flight engineer.

"Feather number three!"

John remembered the countless times he had practiced these procedures.

"Done."

"Mixture idle cut-off!"

"Roger."

"Switch firewall shut off on number three!"

John's hands moved swiftly across the panel.

"Switches off."

"Fire extinguisher discharge handle, right side – Pull!" John pulled the lever located on the right side of the panel.

"Extinguisher pulled."

Torque from the left engine was pulling that wing higher. The Captain fought back by applying the left aileron, keeping the right wing up. The fire warning bell fell silent, giving relief to the men's ears.

"Give me an Engine Fire check on number three."

Fisher looked at the instruments. Altitude and air speed were dropping. There was no alternative but to return to the strip. He estimated the distance to be about ten miles. He made a slow, banking turn to the left to counteract the torque. It was all he could do to maintain control of the aircraft. Slowly, he managed to get the craft trimmed. *Altitude is critical,* he thought. If they were going to make it to the runway, he would have to sacrifice air speed for altitude. The air speed indicator registered one hundred forty knots and dropping. Below ninety, the aircraft would stall, falling to its death. *Weight! That's it,* he thought, *or we'll never make it!*

"John, start dumping fuel!"

Reaching down, John put the Fuel Dump handles in the pump position. Avgas began pouring out of each wing. Four distinct vapor trails followed the aircraft as twenty-seven hundred pounds of fuel was released into the air each minute.

"Billy, give me a time check. We'll drop fuel as long as we can."

The copilot pushed a sequence button on his panel. "Time check – 0617 Zulu."

Fisher studied the runway in the distance. He wondered if they were going to make it. Looking at his instruments, he lowered the aircraft's nose to increase air speed.

"Start your Approach checklist."

Billy and John started their procedures. Their voices and movements remained calm and steady, the result of years of training and experience. But underneath this wrapping of expertise and qualification, the rank odor of fear blanketed the cockpit.

The Captain looked at the altimeter. *Seven hundred feet. The runway seems far away,* he thought.

"Put fuel dump chutes in drain position."

"Roger."

Fisher fought the controls as surface winds began to buffet the plane. *Two more miles,* his brain pounded. *Just two more miles!* His eyes found the altimeter. *Six hundred feet.* "Shit!" he groaned. He knew disaster was close.

"Approach flaps–20 degrees."

"John, retract the fuel dump chutes."

Colonel Gomez was reaching for the ignition switch in the jeep when they all heard the aircraft lumbering back toward them. Michael pointed her out as she passed over the shoreline. Silver streams of vapor were cascading from the trailing edges of her wings. They all knew she was in trouble. Empathy for the crew swept over Michael.

Fisher was gritting his teeth. *Maybe, just maybe,* he thought.

"Gear down," Fisher ordered.

Billy lowered the gear. A shaking "thump" confirmed they were locked into place. Resistance against the wind was taking its toll. Airspeed immediately dropped to one hundred ten knots. Fisher realized his order had been premature. He needed more air speed if they were to make it.

"Gear up! Max power!" he shouted.

John slammed the throttles forward.

A moment's confusion caused Billy to hesitate. Reaching for the landing gear lever, his hands blindly gripped the flaps control lever and pulled it up. The aircraft lost its cushion of lift. She shuddered for a moment in rebellion and then lost her angle of attack. Torque from her two left engines flipped her left wing up.

"Shit!" Billy said.

"Watch it!" John mumbled.

Fisher was the last to speak.

"Oh, Shit!"

Michael stood paralyzed on the edge of the runway. He felt faint from holding his breath. The ground shook. Black columns of smoke and flames mushroomed into the air; then they heard a continuous crackling sound as the scrub burned for a quarter mile.

A diesel motor fired up from somewhere within the bush. Moments later, a Caterpillar bulldozer slowly moved across the runway to the burial ground. The heat was unbearable. The driver sat and waited as he had done numerous times before.

A small tear of eulogy traced its way down Michael's dusty cheek as he remembered the sparks and cinders from the fire the night before.

Thiry-Three

The hurricane season is damn near in full force, Michael thought, as he listened to the weather forecaster amid the hum of conversation around him. Sonny had requested this meeting between the participants in the Cuban-sanctioned plan. This was going to be a big job, and Sonny wanted to be sure that there would be no glitches.

"On June 19, 1979," the forecaster was saying, "Tropical Storm Ana was born one thousand miles due east of Venezuela. Tracking a westerly course for four days, this tropical storm abruptly died south of Puerto Rico, never having reached hurricane force." The forecaster continued. "Tropical Storm Bob began brewing two hundred miles off the coast of Tampico, Mexico on July 9. At 7:00 p.m. on July 10, it was classified as a full hurricane. At 7:00 p.m. on July 11, it devastated the coast of Louisiana. After extensive damage, it finally dissipated on July 17, in the central part of Mississippi."

The forecaster kept on with the previous storms' locations and endings. "Tropical Storm Claudette followed Bob. Beginning on July 16, four hundred fifty miles east of the Virgin Islands, Claudette never reached hurricane force. However, this tropical depression, lasting for thirteen days, played havoc with shipping throughout the lower Caribbean, Puerto Rico, Haiti, Cuba, and the Gulf of Mexico.

The storm finally ran its course in the Hudson Bay area of Canada. Claudette was the longest traced storm so far this season."

"We now have a new disturbance," he said. "At 7:00 a.m. today, Tropical Storm David was spotted by reconnaissance planes two thousand sixty miles southeast of Miami. Although David is, at this time, considered a tropical depression, indications suggest that the intensity may increase. The National Hurricane Center here in Miami is continuing to monitor this depression. As added information is gathered, we'll keep you informed. For the latest weather updates, stay tuned to WQBA."

Sonny turned off the stereo. "All right, you guys," he announced, "Let's get down to business."

With heavy lids, Michael leaned back on the couch. He was tired. The trip to Colombia had been long and trying. He had arrived late the night before aboard a Lacsa Airlines flight from Costa Rica. Maria had kept him awake most of the night. They had made love for hours. She kept urging him on until he was totally exhausted. Now his body was sedate, but his mind kept drifting back to the DC-7. He kept remembering the stench of charred bodies as he and the Colombians had rummaged through the burned-out wreckage. That image would remain with him for a long time. He had not mentioned the incident to Maria, nor had he mentioned it to Sonny yet. *Anyway, what good would it do?*

Sonny made the introductions and spread a nautical chart over the coffee table as the group gathered around. Michael glanced at Howell, whom he had met the night before, and then at his partner, a man named Colgate. Michael had been surprised this morning to discover that two unfamiliar faces had been added to the group. Knowing Sonny, he was sure that he had taken the time to check both of them out. For some reason, though, he was leery of them. Something about them wasn't right.

Carlos dragged a chair across the carpet, taking a seat next to Sonny. *Carlos seems unusually quiet,* Michael thought. Manuel

Lopez sat beside Michael, puffing on his pipe. Sonny seated himself on the floor in front of the coffee table. He looked up and smiled.

"Gentlemen, we are going to Cuba," Sonny said. His words fell like a bomb.

"What did you say?" Colgate stared at Sonny with an incredulous look. "I mean, are you serious?"

Sonny nodded in the affirmative.

"Why Cuba?" Howell asked, almost as shocked as Colgate.

"Because that's where the stuff is. Lopez will explain that part."

Carlos, Howell, and Colgate listened with open mouths as Lopez brought them up to date on the operation. He explained to the group that the marijuana had been delivered by ship the night before to the Port of Cienfuegos on the southern side of the island. Through discussions with his contact at the Cuban Embassy in Mexico City, he had learned earlier this morning that the merchandise was currently in route by truck across the island. The destination was La Porto de Havana.

"Son of a bitch!" Howell grinned. "Chubby, you've really stuck your dick in it this time!"

Sonny smiled and then turned to Carlos. "You and Frank will take the forty-seven-footer."

Glancing at Michael, Sonny said, "You and Colgate will use the Cigarette. I'll man the communications center from the White House in the Keys."

"Tomorrow," he continued, pointing at the chart, "the two boats will leave the Keys just after dark. You have to enter Havana before daylight. Is that clear?"

Sonny looked directly at Carlos and then at Michael, stressing his point.

"The Air Force is overflying the island continually with U-2s. That means all daylight activities are out. I understand the resolution on their cameras is so good that they can tell the time on your wristwatch from ninety thousand feet."

Carlos turned to Lopez. "What assurance do we have that Castro's damn Navy won't blow us out of the water?"

"That has been taken care of; I assure you. The names and descriptions, in addition to the approximate arrival times of your boats, have been given to the Cuban Embassy in Mexico City. There are, however, several things you must remember."

"Yeah," Carlos grunted, "what's that?"

"When you enter the port, you are to follow their escort. Upon docking, under no circumstances are you to leave your boat. Otherwise, I cannot guarantee your safety."

Sonny again took control of the meeting.

"The Cubans will provide you with fuel and whatever mechanical needs you might have. Keep in mind that while you're in Cuban waters, all communications are banned. If, for any reason, I need to get information to you, Lopez here will go through the Embassy, and that information will be passed on to you through Havana. Once you're clear and in international waters, then and only then, can you use your radios. The Cubans are very touchy about this. The U.S. Navy has listening stations all along the Florida coast, and within seconds they can vector in on your transmissions. The Cubans want no allegations whatsoever of their involvement in this operation. Our discussion today, and any in the future, must be considered confidential. Is that clear?" His eyes darted from man to man as each acknowledged the warning. "Okay, we'll open the meeting for discussion."

Michael leaned forward, looking at the chart. "What's the return route, or should we play it by ear?"

Sonny placed his finger on Havana and then began tracing an invisible route to the east." Carlos will bring the Bertram in from the east, on the Atlantic side, into Marathon. Michael's approach will be from the west." His finger ran a line from Cuba, up between the Marquesas Islands and Dry Tortugas. "Once you're past Fort Jefferson, turn east and make your entrance into Marathon through

Big Spanish Channel. When you get to the Seven Mile Bridge, turn north and come in."

"What frequencies are we supposed to use?" Carlos asked.

"Channel twenty-two on the VHFs and channel fourteen on the CBs."

"Oh, before I forget," Sonny interjected, "the boats are ready to go. All necessary charts and everything you'll need are already on board. All you guys have to do is step aboard. The Cigarette's call sign will be Blanket One. The Bertram's will be Blanket Two. I'll be Sitting Duck."

Sonny stood up. "Any more questions?"

The men were silent. Bernie Colgate sat back, trying to hide the smug look on his face.

Thirty-Four

Bernie had to talk to his boss. There was nothing else he could do. With the importance of this case, a telephone call would not suffice.

Robert Cunningham appeared to be irritated as he walked into the back door of the Rancho Luna Restaurant on Southwest Twenty-Second and Southwest Third Street in Miami. It was obvious from Cunningham's expression that he did not like being rousted from bed at one-thirty in the morning.

Cunningham worked his way through the neighborhood restaurant. He stepped around a ladder, which had been used by a construction crew that had gone home hours earlier. The restaurant's facelift had been desperately needed. The restaurant now had an updated, modern look. Business was booming; the service was excellent, and the Cuban food was cheap and delicious.

"This had better be damn good," Cunningham grumbled, pulling out a chair, "and wipe that shit-eating grin off your face."

Bernie reached inside his pocket and took out a tape recorder. He set the compact machine on the table in front of Cunningham, pressed the "play" button, and turned down the volume as the voices came through the speaker.

Cunningham had been staring at Bernie with something close to contempt. A moment later his expression changed to one of astonishment. As the story unfolded from the tape, Bernie could see Cunningham imagining himself as the regional director. When the tape ended, Cunningham shut the machine off.

"Holy shit!" he whispered. "We'll have to have the Coast Guard in on this."

Thirty-Five

Aboard the Coast Guard cutter Cape Barnes, Chief Rogers looked down at the two messages in his hand. Neither was encouraging. He flung them on the mess table and then walked to the coffee urn for a refill. *When are they going to give us a break?,* he wondered. Of the last one hundred eighty days, one hundred sixty-four had been spent at sea. He could think of no logical reason for staying in the service this long. Twenty years was enough, yet he kept re-enlisting. A smile passed over his face and instantly vanished. *Maybe I should see a shrink,* he thought, and his smile returned. The day after tomorrow will be his twenty-fifth anniversary with the Coast Guard. The following week he would celebrate his forty-fourth birthday. *Next year I'll retire and have a life,* he thought. *Maybe…* Again, a slight smile tugged at the corners of his mouth. *Who am I kidding? I'll probably die an old man still sailing the seas for the Coast Guard.*

Rogers slumped down in the booth, absent-mindedly adding some cream to his coffee, and then he picked up and read the messages for the second time. The first message was an order. The Cape Barnes is to remain on station patrolling the waters from Alligator Light south to Key West. Her station distance was not to exceed fifteen miles offshore. Any forty-seven-foot Bertram or forty-two-foot Cigarette was to be inspected for contraband.

The second message was the clincher. It was in the form of a weather forecast. "At 7:00 a.m., August 31, 1979, Hurricane David was located 660 miles southeast of Miami, latitude 17.3 north and longitude 68.3 west. Wind speed 114 knots, expected to increase. David is traveling in a northerly direction, and forecasts indicate the storm will reach the Isle of Hispaniola by 1700 hours."

Chief Rogers dropped the two sheets of paper back on the table and sighed. Today, for some reason, he felt old. In the past, he had accepted orders as a challenge. Not anymore. Right now, it was just a job and a very tiring one most of the time. *Oh, well, maybe things will pick up on this run,* he thought.

First Class Boatswain Mate Herbert Williams entered the galley. Unmarried, he enjoyed the excitement of waking up each day to new experiences. He had almost married his long-time girlfriend Gianna, but, unfortunately, she had decided that she couldn't handle his being gone all the time and had broken off their engagement. A lifer, Williams now thought of the Coast Guard as his home. Around the Keys, the Cape Barnes was constantly searching for drug smugglers, and Williams liked trying to catch the bad guys. It got a little dicey at times, but it was all in a day's work.

"Morning, Chief."

"Keep that hat off your head while you're in the galley!" Rogers snapped. "Pass the word to rig the ship for heavy seas right away."

Snapping to attention, Williams said, "Aye, aye, Sir!" The chief's gruff manner didn't bother First Class Williams. He respected the chief and knew he was under a lot of pressure right now. Searching for drug smugglers with a strong hurricane in the vicinity had the entire crew on edge.

Thirty-Six

On the second morning, the boats were still empty of their cargo. The Cubans were quiet.

Strange, Michael thought. *It shouldn't take more than three days for the cargo to cross the island.* Michael was getting an uneasy feeling. Something just didn't feel right. He was onboard the Bertram with the rest of the men. He sat at a dinette booth drinking a Coke, while Carlos and Howell prepared breakfast. Colgate was in the main salon listening to the latest weather report. It didn't sound good. Hurricane David was bearing down on the Dominican Republic.

The weather in Havana had changed from sunny days and balmy nights to overcast skies, with precipitation falling in a foggy drizzle. A damp quietness lay about as if nature were telling the pelicans, seagulls, wharf rats, and other waterfront hangers-on to take refuge. Even the men had an uneasy awareness of the impending danger. The idea of waiting out a hurricane in Havana Harbor was unsettling to all of them.

Michael felt a slight movement of the boat and then heard footsteps along the main deck. He got up to investigate. Hector Rues entered the main salon as Michael left the galley. A captain in the Cuban Army, Hector was the liaison between the Cuban government and Sonny's crew. Colgate stood as the Cuban entered.

"Buenos Dias," Hector said as his green, plastic raincoat dripped water on the plush carpet.

"Your shipment has arrived." Hector's announcement was

spoken as if he was awarding a prize. Short and stocky with black, wavy hair and clear brown eyes, Hector was intelligent, but most who met him thought the opposite because of his sometimes overly friendly manner. It was an act that had served him well in his position over the years.

"Tonight, you must leave."

Colgate stepped forward. "When will we be able to load?"

"Right away," Hector smiled. He breathed in the mouthwatering aroma and said, "What is that smell?"

"Bacon," Michael answered.

"Tocino," Carlos said, leaning up the ladder from the galley.

"Ah, tocino," Hector said. "That is good."

"You're welcome to join us," Michael invited.

"Gracias, I will be happy to eat the gringo's tocino," Hector said laughing.

He followed Colgate below. Michael seated himself on the inside section of the booth, with Hector sat to his right. Colgate squeezed in on the left. Howell pushed himself in on the end, leaving half of his bulk spilling out into the passageway. Standing at the stove, Carlos began serving the bacon and eggs. Hector looked at Carlos quizzically.

Carlos had anticipated the question. A faint smile crossed his pursed lips.

"No, I am Puerto Rican," he said evenly. He intuitively knew the military captain was trying to trap him.

"That is strange," Hector paused as he responded. "I would have guessed that your accent is Cuban." Hector sensed Carlos's concern. *He must be hiding something,* Hector thought. "Have you ever been to America?" Carlos asked.

"No, I am afraid not. There is still too much to do for the revolution here. Vacations are a luxury I cannot afford."

"Then," Michael pressed, waving a hand, "you have no way of knowing the difference between a Cuban and a Puerto Rican accent, do you?"

"I suppose you are correct," Hector conceded. "However, we do have a lot of foreigners as well as Puerto Ricans here. I can usually tell the difference. I know you lie, but what the hell difference does it make?" Hector said shrugging his shoulders.

"These boats," he said after several mouthfuls, nodding his head about between forkfuls of eggs, "are they owned by your government?"

Michael chuckled. "Hell no! They are just pleasure boats that any middle-class American can own."

Hector's fork clanked against his plate. His eyes narrowed and his mouth set tight as if Michael were telling a capitalist's lie. The affluence of which this Americano was telling him was beyond his comprehension. The conflict resulting from the bombardment of communist indoctrination and the matter-of-fact conviction of Michael's statement was puzzling to him. This was the first time in seventeen years his thought processes had challenged the actual communist concepts of state versus the individual.

Colgate interrupted Hector's thoughts. "I said, do you think the hurricane will hit Havana?"

Bringing himself back to the present, Hector's response was slow in coming. "Havana radio is warning the coastal areas to take precautions. Presently, that is all I know."

Howell placed his elbow on the table, cradling his double chin in his oversized hand.

"Well, if it means anything to anybody, I'm against sitting out this storm in Havana Harbor."

"Let's not start making any hasty decisions," Carlos grumbled. "There's no telling which direction this storm is going." He paused when they heard a loud thump on deck.

The Bertram rocked lightly in its moorings. The group heard the sounds of hurried footsteps crossing overhead and then moving astern.

Carlos stepped back from the stove into the hallway, which provided him a clear view of the aft cabin door.

A soldier opened the portal and stepped through it. Dripping wet, he saw Carlos standing below holding a spatula in his hand.

Directing his attention to Hector, his words were high-pitched and rapid. Before the militiaman had completed his statement, Hector was pushing his way out of the booth. "Your shipment is here," he said.

Howell heaved himself aside, letting the Captain out. In the narrow passageway, Hector squeezed past Carlos to make his way topside. The men swept in behind him and up to the deck as if suctioned by Hector's rapid departure.

Soldiers carrying carbines stood watch along the dock, while other militiamen carried bales of marijuana from the trucks parked under the hangar to the boats. Stacks of bales were already forming on the dock as the two crews moved from the boat onto the dock to inspect their load.

Michael felt even more uneasy and had an inner sense of urgency to leave. He was not sure which was more forceful. Shivers ran down the back of his neck. *Must be this weather,* he thought. The stillness seemed as if the black ghost of death was hanging unrepentantly in the pre-storm air.

Thirty-Seven

Key West was a ghost town, deserted except for a few die-hard conchs determined to remain, along with a group of long-haired hippies waiting to begin their acid-tripped hurricane party, and the occasional patrol car prowling the rain-swept streets.

During the afternoon, Lindsey Lumber, as well as all other lumber companies and boatyards from Key West to Palm Beach, had depleted their stocks of plywood and candles. Doors and windows had been nailed shut on homes and businesses that had been recently abandoned in anticipation of Hurricane David.

In the darkening conditions, vehicles of all types made their way north. The forced gaiety of the occupants was a way of disguising their anxieties and fears. A pilot looking down would have seen a line of headlights that looked like joints on a luminescent caterpillar crawling mile upon mile as they headed for higher and safer ground.

Thirty-Eight

Chief Rogers held his ear close to the AM radio. Static overpowered the voice of the reporter. Hurricane David had devastated Haiti. Utilities and roads were out. Black, rain-soaked survivors, crawling on hands and knees beneath the debris, finally stood, swaying in a zombie-like stance, wailing and chanting. These poor, ragged, pitiful beings were crying loudly in grief for their lost loved ones and giving thanks to their Voodoo gods for their deliverance from the hellish disaster. The death toll had not been determined, but estimates ranged in the high hundreds. It had also been reported that David's winds were so strong that a four-engine aircraft was lifted from the ground and flipped onto the roof of a building. David had left the Isle of Hispaniola; its winds regenerated over the warm waters of the Caribbean and headed straight for South Florida.

At 1900 hours on September 1, Coast Guard cutter Cape Barnes was due east of Sugarloaf Key. She struggled to stay on station ten miles out from American Shoals Light. Her bow rose in the quartering swells, dropped into a twenty-foot trough, pitched to port thirty degrees, and sliced into the blue-green water. As she surfaced, gale-force winds caught the flying water and shrouded the vessel in a vaporous spray.

Chief Rogers sat stiffly in his captain's chair. He gripped the armrests as the ship slid into another trough. He couldn't relax. Concern for the safety of his ship and her crew was foremost in his mind. Not since early that morning had he thought about it being his twenty-fifth anniversary with the Coast Guard.

"Watch your helm, young man!" he barked at Seaman Stokes. A wall of salt water sprayed against the bridge windows. The ship shuttered.

"Yes Sir," Seaman Stokes answered, spinning the wheel. "She's hard to manage in this weather, Sir."

Softening, Chief Rogers reassured the young man, "You'll get the hang of it after a while."

Rogers balanced a cup of coffee in his hand. *Stokes is a good sailor,* he thought. The lad reminded him of himself when he was a seaman; confident, gung-ho, and by the book. Rogers allowed himself a moment to reminisce back through the years of his career to the days of exotic ports of call, unpolluted harbors, and fabulous whore houses. His mind slipped back in time when he could buy a piece of ass and a case of the clap for the bargain price of two dollars. There had been an indescribable closeness with his old shipmates, drinking buddies, and fighting partners. Looking over at Stokes, he knew that this young man would never live the raptures of adventure that he had experienced. Stokes was a by-product of the new Coast Guard.

The watertight door leading to the bridge flung open. Rogers looked toward the noise. First Class Boatswain Mate Herbert Williams stood in the hatchway, precariously balancing a white cardboard box in one hand. A fleeting smile passed across his face. He stepped through the hatch followed by Fireman Parks, Seaman Avanger, Radioman Johnson, and Fireman Jaworski.

"You men do not have permission to be on the bridge!"

"Yes Sir!" Williams exclaimed. He was off balance and allowed his momentum to flow with the new role. Grabbing the edge of the chart table, he balanced himself. With the ease of a waiter and one available hand, he placed the box on the table. "We want to share this with you, Chief," Williams said, after a moment. Stokes spun the wheel, trying to watch the compass and the chief at the same time. He was unsuccessful at either task.

Rogers instinctively detected a change in the ship's rhythm.

"Mind your helm!" he admonished. He hoisted himself from his chair and staggered to the table as the men gathered around.

Williams opened the box, revealing a small coconut cake with a single candle stuck in the center. He smiled at Rogers.

"Happy anniversary, Chief."

The men began singing "Happy Anniversary" to the tune of "Happy Birthday."

The chief's eyes moistened. Stokes thought the chief might cry. Rogers checked himself. He stood there looking down at the cake, then at his men.

Williams had already pocketed his Zippo by the time the song was over.

"Thanks," the chief mumbled as he bent forward and quickly blew out the lone, flickering candle. A little embarrassed, he was touched that his men had remembered.

Thirty-Nine

Carlos Martinez could not remember seeing a darker night than the one he and Frank Howell were presently trying to penetrate. Frontal weather from Hurricane David blocked the stars and moon. A blanket of darkness like a black shroud covered the boat.

The radar had been performing well upon their departure from Cuban waters. Now, for some unknown reason, the sweep circled endlessly, leaving a blank picture. The only source of direction was from a compass and Loran C.

Carlos looked at his watch. Ten thirty-five. He made a time notation in his last plot. He placed the sharp point of the dividers on American Shoals Light, and with a sweeping arc of the lead tip, he adjusted the divider on the chart next to the plot. Moving the dividers to the left side of the Mercado's projection, he laid them along the north latitude scale and read the distance. *Twenty-two miles,* he whispered to himself as he dropped the dividers on the table.

"How does it look?" Howell asked. The spokes of the ship's wheel flapped across his huge stomach.

"We're all right. Just stay on this course."

Carlos staggered across the deck to stand beside Howell. For a moment, Carlos thought there was lightning near. His eyes burned from the blue-white arc, but there was no crashing of thunder. The flash became a blinding, relentless ray of light. "What the hell is that?" Carlos mumbled, shading his eyes with his hand.

Forty

The water was considerably calmer on the Gulf side of the Keys. The small chain of islands linking U.S. 1 through the Keys served as a windbreaker, of sorts, against David's frontal attack.

Michael and Bernie Colgate left the Straits of Florida and then passed the Marquesas Islands, turning toward a northeasterly heading. The wave crests were farther apart and became large rollers, which allowed the boat a smoother ride. Michael eased the throttle forward, increasing the Cigarette's speed to thirty-five knots.

Lights attached to radio towers, water tanks, and high-rise condominiums sporadically presented themselves as homing beacons to Michael. Numerous rain squalls moved all along the coast.

Earlier the previous day, and in anticipation of Hurricane David's wrath, employees of the South Florida Dredging Corporation dropped their tools, battened down their barge, and fled to the islands to begin their pilgrimage north.

The dredging project was in its infancy, having been underway for less than two weeks. Developers had pushed their political influence and acquired contracts with the dredging company to fill in the low-lying areas adjacent to the Seven Mile Bridge south of

Marathon. It was the perfect location for a multi-million-dollar marina and hotel.

For ten days, the dredge's ugly snout, two miles from shore, had been grinding into the shallow waters of Florida Bay. It had sucked up thousands of yards of sand, limestone, and muck, pumping it through a one-and-a-half-foot diameter steel hose supported on the surface by floats, and then dumping it ashore.

In his haste, an employee had forgotten to turn on the flashing markers on top of the pipes, leaving the entire rigging hidden in the dark. In the Cigarette, Michael and Bernie were unaware that they were going directly toward it.

Forty-One

Still partially blinded by the arc of light, Howell suddenly screamed, "It's a damn ship!" He quickly spun the ship's wheel to starboard.

The abrupt turn caused the Bertram to lurch into a roll, slamming Carlos against a built-in bar. Bottles shattered, pouring their contents on him. Groaning with pain, he heaved himself up from the carpet. Cursing, his face red with anger, he headed for the stern. "What the hell is going on?" Carlos mumbled to himself. "Howell had better have a damn good reason for the way he's handling this boat. Over the roar of the engines, Carlos had failed to hear Howell's warning.

———————————

Standing on the bridge of the Cape Barnes, Chief Rogers shouted, "Williams, mind your helm!" Then he added, "Stand off about fifty yards."

"Yes Sir," replied Williams. gale-force wind took his breath. Leaning over a guardrail, he shouted down to Avanger.

"Keep that light on her!"

On the Bertram, Carlos soon discovered the reason for Howell's sharp turn and the increasing speed of the boat. He ran back through the opening to the main salon. His eyes were glazed with anger as he ground his teeth. "It's the goddamn Coast Guard!" he bellowed. "Whatever happens, don't stop this son of a bitch!" He was almost hysterical. "I'll fix those bastards!" he screamed and stumbled below deck.

Standing in the howling wind on the Cape Barnes, Chief Rogers held a bullhorn. He had one leg twisted around a stanchion to keep from being washed or blown overboard.

"Ahoy there! This is the United States Coast Guard. Heave to!"

The Bertram presented a stark, white image in the bright, narrow beam of light. She was rolling excessively. Her course was parallel to the huge rollers. If the wind increased another ten knots, the wave crest would begin to break and cause the waves to tumble. That type of sea was the most dangerous for small craft. The Cape Barnes and the Bertram both fit that category.

Again, Rogers yelled into a bullhorn. "Heave to!"

The Bertram changed course trying to make a run for it, but the cutter was much faster. Williams was performing superbly at the helm.

Howell fought the wheel. His mind raced in jumbled thoughts. *What the hell am I doing here? Son of a bitch!* He said to himself. *I'm supposed to be on their side now!* If he stopped the boat, Carlos would kill him. If he ran, the cutter would sink them. Either way, he would lose. There was one thing Howell knew for sure; he did not want to die.

Carlos came scrambling back from below deck, carrying a suitcase. Balancing himself, he threw it on the sofa. Puzzled, Howell saw Carlos lifting the lid, and then he quickly returned his attention to the cutter.

"This is the last warning," Rogers said. "If you do not stop within ten seconds, I'll commence firing!"

Howell looked back at Carlos. Carlos was unfolding a green tubular object. Howell recognized it immediately. He had seen them in Vietnam. It was a LAW, a Light Antitank Weapon.

Howell's eyes bulged with comprehension of what was about to happen. He wanted to cry out, but his tongue was paralyzed. *This is absolute lunacy, he thought. Carlos has lost his mind!*

––––––––––––

Stokes clung to the handles of his fifty-caliber machine gun. He had been standing in that position for over five minutes. Drenched from the waves breaking over the bow, he ached from the cold, but he didn't even feel the saltwater stinging his eyes or his arms burning from the strain. His mind was totally occupied as he concentrated on the task before him.

"Fire!" the chief shouted above the wind.

Stokes heard the command.

He aimed toward the stern of the Bertram. He closed his eyes, gritted his teeth, and pulled the trigger. Concussion from the shells hammered his ears. His shoulders jerked fiercely from the recoil of the gun, but he did not let go.

Rogers watched a line of searing, red tracers walking across the water. The first burst was unsuccessful. The second volley tore into the target.

Carlos and Howell hit the deck at the same time. It was the most God-awful noise they had ever heard. Howell clamped his hands over his ears, screaming in fright. He squirmed about the deck as the boat shuddered with the impact of the tracers. Carlos rolled himself into a fetal position, trying to find protection from flying debris. Bullets were ricocheting about the engine room, tearing at wood, metal, and fiberglass as if the entire structure was made of paper mâché. Black smoke and fumes rushed from the exhausts, spreading throughout the cabins. Stokes ceased firing.

When Howell had let go of the ship's wheel, the Bertram turned to starboard, leaving a perfect target for a stern shot. Her damage was fatal. The engine room was quiet now except for the crackling of burning fiberglass resin.

Howell lay uninjured on the deck, paralyzed in fear, crying, his pants wet with urine. His bowels had loosed as well, causing a disgusting smell.

Carlos looked over at the fat man, who had been transformed into a sniveling heap of feces and urine. Sneering with disgust, the LAW still clutched in his hand, Carlos made his way through the choking smoke to the fantail. *I'll show those bastards!* Gasping for air, he crawled across the open deck and crouched against the transom. He stuck his head up for an instant to locate his adversary. The spotlight was blinding. *Fifty yards,* he thought, *maybe sixty.*

"You bastards!" he yelled defiantly. "If I'm going down, I'll take you sons-of-bitches with me!" His voice was carried away in the wind. He bent forward and flipped up the range finder. In a suicidal gesture, he stood upright, and straddle legged as he aimed for the light.

Chief Rogers saw but could not believe what was happening.

"Fire! Fire, dammit!" he screamed at Stokes.

It was too late. Rogers watched the three-foot back blast of the weapon as it left its tube.

Carlos heard a "swoosh" and the high-frequency sound of the projectile. He did not live to see or hear the explosion. A tracer from Stokes' gun tore into his chest. Blood, bone, and marrow exploded from his back, flipping him backward to the deck. He died before the missile reached its target, killed by the bullet of a teenage, pot-smoking seaman.

The explosion rocked the Cape Barnes through forty degrees. A five-foot fireball rose from the bridge and left seared metal grotesquely twisted in free form, giving the appearance of a burned-out hulk.

The saving factor for Stokes was the safety harness, which kept him from being blown overboard. His limp body was tangled in the lifelines encircling the main deck. Salt spray diluted the blood and plasma trickling from his mouth and ears. A wave washed over him. His eyes popped open. He began to sputter, slowly moving his head about.

Chief Rogers was not so fortunate. He landed forty feet from his ship. His left arm was severed at the shoulder.

Stokes saw Rogers thrashing in the water. In his pain-filled stupor, he was unable to get a lifeline to him.

Rogers regained consciousness, wondering what he was doing in the water. There was a numb feeling in his arm. He reached over and felt where his left arm had been. It was gone. *Strange,* he thought, that he felt no pain. He took a deep sigh of relief; seawater filled his lungs. He remembered his daughter's flailing arms on that fatal day screaming "Mommy! Mommy! Mommy!" His last thought was relief that the nightmare would finally be over.

He vanished into the depths of the murky water.

First Class Boatswain Mate Herbert Williams was never found. He had been standing behind the ship's wheel at the moment of the missile's impact.

It was later believed that Frank Howell burned to death. The last time the crew of the Cape Barnes saw the Bertram it was burning at the waterline. Of the cutter's crewmen, three were dead, two were seriously injured, and the remaining five were trying desperately to keep her afloat while making for port.

Forty-Two

Moments before the Cigarette and the dredge pipe came together; Michael caught a glimpse of the barge. Its silhouette blocked the lights from shore as the boat raced past at thirty-five knots. He had no time to react to the unfamiliar object and avoid crashing into the barrier.

The speedboat's needlepoint bow exploded into thousands of minute fragments. Momentum catapulted the screaming machine into the air as if launched from an aircraft carrier. A terrible rending noise ensued as the drive shafts and propellers raked across the pipe, tearing out the twin Caterpillar engines.

Michael could feel a jarring sensation as the transom and stern section separated from the hull slightly aft of his seat. The Cigarette was no longer a sleek ocean racer. It was a distorted mass of flying debris. Michael felt his knee shatter against the dashboard as his head hit the Plexiglas windshield. Pain exploded through his body. Half-conscious, he heard an inner voice saying, *"Get away! Get away from it!"* With all his strength, he pushed out and away from the cockpit. The fierce wind slammed against his body. The breath was sucked from his lungs, and his head began to spin. He realized his entire body was spinning.

I don't want to die like this, Michael thought. *Not this way. Stop the spin! Stop the spin,* he heard a voice say. Using an almost supernatural power that he had never known before, he managed to overcome the centrifugal force relentlessly turning him around. His arms extended from his body and his legs straightened and separated. Almost instantly, the spin was in check. Michael found himself floating downward on a cushion of air, almost peacefully, except for the painful throbbing in his leg. He heard a strange sound. Space age technology disintegrated all around him upon re-entry from a two-hundred sixty-five-foot flight.

Five minutes later, a U.S. Customs boat plucked Bernie Colgate from the water. The Customs crew thought it was a miracle he was still alive. He was suffering from a dislocated shoulder and a concussion. Hurricane winds had forced the Customs boat to find shelter after a half-hour search for Michael Jansen, which had proved futile.

Forty-Three

The houseboat was not designed for foul weather. The shallow draft and high superstructure were evidence of its instability. A course was virtually impossible to hold in these high winds.

A huge wave suddenly broke over the bow, washing rearward and stripping the UHF antennas from the roof, leaving only the radar operational. As images of rain squalls moved across the scope, Sonny noticed a small contact, presumably a boat, slowly moving in the area. Not knowing what it was or why it was there, Sonny was forced to stand off and wait. Standing helpless and watching the scope, he saw the Cigarette come into view. It moved rapidly across the screen. What Sonny had tried to prevent was now happening before his eyes.

When Michael and Colgate left Islamorada, the course to Havana had taken them down along the Atlantic side of the Keys. Their return route would bring them in along the Gulf side.

The day before, Sonny had been cruising aboard the White House and had unexpectedly passed the dredging operation. Upon checking his chart, he discovered that the out-of-date chart Michael had did not show the newly established operation. Realizing the serious implications of the situation, he contacted Lopez and had him pass this latest information via the Cuban Embassy in Mexico City to Michael. Sonny had no confirmation that his message had been received, and he didn't want to chance using the radio. Considering the deteriorating weather conditions, he had taken the White House out on the night of the movement in a last-minute attempt to intercept the Cigarette.

Sonny had the White House built about the same time he met Michael. It was custom-built to Sonny's exact specifications. A nondescript boat builder in Bradenton, Florida, not known to the public, manufactured high-tech boats for buyers around the world. The buyers were mostly countries that wanted to own an inconspicuous platform for electronic and offshore surveillance. Sonny concluded that a houseboat was the best type of boat suited for recreational boating in South Florida and the Keys. It would blend in perfectly with the local partiers. Bud 'n Mary's Marina in southern Islamorada has been her homeport.

Eighteen feet wide and eighty-seven feet long, she was propelled by twin V-6 Mercruiser 4.3 Liter, 220 horsepower engines. In calm seas, her maximum speed ran about forty-eight miles an hour. Today, fighting the wind and heavy seas, she had barely been able to maintain eight knots. Her saving grace was that she had automatic pilot and stern and forward bow thrusters to help stabilize and maintain her course.

If anyone ever had the opportunity to step aboard the White House, one would enter a different world, a breathtaking creation of luxury and comfort. Solid cherry floors shined like glass as one first entered the White House. On the right, a custom granite bar and a stainless-steel galley greeted visitors. Directly in front was a massive, solid mahogany table that comfortably seated twelve people. Indirect lighting throughout the ceiling conveyed a feeling of peace and serenity. Soft music flowed throughout the boat. On the stern sat an unusual-looking hot tub. If one looked long and hard enough, the hot tub might resemble a satellite dish. Three well-appointed staterooms welcomed guests, and the master stateroom was always reserved for VIP's.

Below the main deck was an entirely different world, one of electronics and surveillance equipment, all top secret.

Even Michael, Sonny's closest friend and ally, was unaware of it. Sonny was a man of many secrets.

A few months after Sonny had retired from the City of Miami Police Department, a casual friend of Sonny's approached him about joining the fight against drugs. Along with Sonny's police background and thorough knowledge of South Florida and the Keys, his friend believed Sonny was the perfect candidate for the job he had in mind. Sonny was shocked when his friend confessed that he worked for the National Security Agency. He promised Sonny that the Agency would give him carte blanche to all the resources he would need for the upcoming operation that was currently being planned. For security reasons, part of the plan was that Sonny had to recruit a novice and introduce him to the business of smuggling. The people in his operation had to be legitimate smugglers.

The moment Sonny had met Michael; he knew that Michael was the man with whom he could trust his life. Sonny was now out of position for an intercept.

His communications were dead. Hopelessly impotent, he saw the contacts blink. Within one sweep around the scope, Michael's boat disappeared.

Sonny watched the screen for the next half hour as another strange contact moved about the area.

With the precision of an experienced navigator Sonny hurriedly worked out a plot for set and drift. Allowing for the gale-force winds, he began working his way from downwind toward the site of the wreck. He could only hope the boat at the scene had rescued any survivors.

Minutes later, wreckage began drifting past the houseboat's powerful floodlights. An orange object reflected in the light. *Maybe, just maybe, it's a life jacket,* Sonny thought. Maneuvering closer he found that it was a life jacket, and floating in the life jacket was the severely battered body of Michael Jansen.

Forty-Four

Bernie Colgate eased himself up from the bed. The antiseptic odor of Marathon's Fisherman's Hospital no longer irritated him. He had become accustomed to it over a week ago. He swung his legs over the side of the bed and sat up. His head began to spin, forcing him to grip the edge of the mattress with his good hand for balance. A tinge of nausea rippled through him. The dizziness and nausea subsided after a few moments.

I'm ready, he thought to himself, *to get the hell out of this torture house.* For the past ten days, he had been gouged, poked, x-rayed, and monitored over every square inch of his body. *No more,* he thought. He had reached the point of saturation. He was fed up to his ass with this entire scene.

He sighed with relief as his bare feet touched the cold terrazzo floor. His equilibrium welcomed him back to the world of the mobile. He was ready to trade in this silly-looking gown, with half his ass hanging out, for a pair of jeans and a pullover.

Marlene and the children had brought his clothes from Fort Lauderdale the day before. "You're damn lucky to be alive," Bernie remembered her saying. "You just won't listen to a thing I say."

Deep down inside, Bernie knew that his and Marlene's separation had been the best thing for both of them. Yesterday, beneath her stare, he had slid further down under the sheets, hiding in weakness, waiting for her to ask for a divorce. He and Marlene loved each other, but she couldn't handle the dangers and separation of his job, and she knew he needed the freedom to achieve his goals. He was damn good at what he did, and he wanted to make sure everybody at the Agency knew it.

Weak and shaky, Bernie painfully moved to the narrow closet and opened the door. Grabbing the hangers holding his clothes, he threw them indifferently onto the bed. His pain was in part from his injuries, but the real pain was the failure of his marriage and losing Marlene. *Damn it! Why couldn't she understand?*

Not wanting to lower his head too much, he bent at the knees to a squatting position and picked up his shoes from the floor of the closet. He could not recall the details of the accident. He only remembered a slight jarring sensation upon impact with the barge pipe, then the horrible noise that followed. He did not remember hitting the water. His next awareness was in the emergency room here at the hospital and the agonizing pain he had been subjected to while in the X-ray room. The attendants had been unable to administer any painkillers because of his head injuries, and his shoulder still hurt like hell.

While recuperating over the past few days, Bernie's thoughts had shifted from his injuries to Sonny Mitchell. Just thinking of Mitchell temporarily blocked his mind of his broken marriage, giving him new purpose. Regardless of what was required, he was determined to find Mitchell. That son of a bitch was going to spend the rest of his life in prison. Bernie would see to that.

Bernie managed to pull his pants on, but his socks were more difficult. The sling restraining his left arm was a nuisance. Bending down and using one hand, he fumbled with a sock. After several attempts, his throbbing shoulder forced him to accept the fact that he needed help.

"Dammit!" he said aloud and pushed the call button.

Thinking back over the course of his conversations with Sonny and Michael, he had been unable to establish the location of the White House. Bernie had no way of knowing that the "White House" was not a house at all. It was a forty-nine-foot houseboat equipped with the latest electronic equipment available. It had radio scanners, radar, and even a Sat Nav tracking system. The DEA had exhausted all available resources trying to locate Mitchell. A low-profile search carried out by the Monroe County Sheriff's Department, starting at Key Largo and terminating at Key West, had proven negative. *Where the hell was he?*

Carlos, Michael, and Howell were dead; Sonny was on the run, leaving only Maria Jansen. She was under twenty-four-hour surveillance. Her telephone had been tapped; still, no contact had come from Mitchell.

Colgate knew he had no real case against the woman. All he could hope for was to try scaring or intimidating her into cooperating. He had gathered enough information to give the appearance of a solid case. At least he could lead her to believe he had a solid case. That, and probably her feeling of being abandoned by Michael, might be enough to sway her his way. Regardless, as soon as he could get dressed, he was going to Miami to force her into cooperating.

Forty-Five

Following Michael's memorial service, Maria, with her head high and her back straight, determinedly walked down the twenty-odd steps of the chapel. She stopped at the base of the walkway to enjoy the fragrances of jasmine and the lush foliage lingering in the air. Shimmers of sunlight filtered down through tall oak trees shading the chapel and surrounding grounds. Raindrops had sprinkled the lawn during the memorial services, casting brilliant colors about her feet as she made her way on the sidewalk toward the limousine. Friends and members of her and Michaels' families walked silently behind. They also sensed freshness in the air.

The past two weeks had been a living nightmare for Maria, yet somehow she had managed. She had an inherent strength of which few were aware. During the height of Hurricane David's fury, she had read a report on page five of the Miami Herald, of a shootout involving the Coast Guard Cutter Cape Barnes and another boat, which was allegedly smuggling marijuana. The smuggler's boat had been sunk. That same afternoon, the Miami News reported the accidental sinking of a speedboat, which had crashed into dredging equipment off Marathon. In either case, no survivors were listed. Those two articles were evidence enough. Maria knew she would never see Michael again. She waited expectantly for Sonny to call, but he never did. Using her own money and resources, she had initiated a private search for her husband. Five days and thousands of dollars later, the search was abandoned as hopeless.

She pondered the questions about which all widows are forced to face. Michael had left her financially secure. *What about my life?* she thought. *In what direction should I exert my energies?* She only had her mother and father. She and Michael had no other children since Jeffrey had died. *What am I supposed to do without Michael? Charity, maybe? There has to be more.* She was still young and needed to stay busy. She knew she couldn't let herself fall into a state of depression.

Earlier, her mother had suggested taking a trip to Hawaii. "Why don't you spend a few months traveling," she said, "and then you'll meet another nice young man like Michael." Her words of wisdom caused Maria to flee the apartment in a hysterical frenzy.

Maria was relieved to be out of the apartment and away from everyone. Her mother didn't understand the depth of her love for Michael. No one except Sonny had understood their feelings for each other. Although she had agreed and encouraged Michael in the pursuit of his business dealings, she had known it was wrong. Trapped between the love for her man and the immoral implications of his activities, she had no choice but to hold herself as accountable as Michael. The conflict had been there from the beginning, buried under the glitter of their lifestyle.

In the wake of the accident, guilt began to surface. Irrational or not, she felt responsible for Michael's premature death. Had she been honest with him, stating her position and standing firm on her principles and morals, Michael might still be alive. But now, however, as destiny would have it, she would never know.

As she slowly moved along the walkway, fond memories of Michael brought tears to her eyes. Through her tears, the blurred image of a man moved toward her. There was an oddness to his walk. His left arm was cradled in a sling. He stopped several yards in front of her, allowing her to move toward him.

"Mrs. Jansen?"

Maria paused. All she could think of was to get to the limousine and be left alone. Common courtesy prompted her to stop.

"Yes?"

"My name is Bernie Colgate," the man said, reaching into his pocket. Wincing slightly, he withdrew a folded paper.

"I'm sorry about your husband. I was on the boat with him."

"Boat?" she asked quizzically. He handed Maria the document. "That's a warrant for your arrest," Colgate said, looking straight into her eyes.

Maria stared blankly at the man. Her reaction was one of confusion.

"I ...I don't understand," she stammered.

Maria's mother stepped up beside her and took her elbow.

"Dear, do you know this ...Honey, are you all right?" Maria's face was flushed.

A policewoman stepped out from the group of mourners surrounding them. Maria suppressed the urge to run. Dazed, she felt her hands being lifted, then heard a series of clicks, followed by the pain of the handcuffs as they tightened about her wrists. She felt like she was in a fog. Vaguely, she thought, *this must be about Michael and Sonny's business.* She was faintly aware of being ushered into the back seat of a police car. Colgate sat beside her, twisted around in his seat, and looked at her.

"I'm prepared to make you a reasonable offer, Mrs. Jansen, one I'm sure you can live with."

Bernie was pleased with himself. His last-minute dramatics were seemingly yielding results. The policewoman and patrol car, obtained through his long-time association with Captain Watson of the Dade County Public Safety Department, were his props.

"I don't know what you are talking about," Maria snapped. "Please, why must you embarrass me in front of my friends and family? I just buried my husband," she sobbed. Her voice began to quiver from fear and uncertainty. "Can't you see this is a memorial service?"

Giving her a lopsided grin, Colgate said, "You're going to help me locate Sonny Mitchell." His voice took on a cold, hard edge. "Otherwise, Mrs. Jansen, I'll see to it that you get ten years in prison."

Maria's eyes cut into the man. Suddenly, her temper flared.

"You go to hell you son of a bitch!" she hissed and then slumped back in her seat.

The beefy-faced policewoman turned from behind the wheel, looking back at Bernie.

"Any place in particular you want to go, Mr. Colgate?" Her voice sounded crass and hoarse from smoking too many cigarettes.

"Just drive around for a while."

"I want a lawyer!" Maria spat, her eyes blazing at the insensitive, smirking jerk in the front seat.

Bernie Colgate glimpsed a limousine pulling alongside the cruiser, effectively blocking them.

"Damn it! I said I want a lawyer!"

"Wait a minute," Colgate motioned and then pushed his door open to step out. He turned in the seat and put one foot down on the asphalt when he noticed the limousine's windows were tinted, preventing anyone from seeing the occupants. Bernie sat staring at the man who was getting out.

Stepping from the limousine on the opposite side was Sonny Mitchell, who hiked up his pants and walked in front of the limousine toward Bernie.

Bernie was almost unable to speak; he was so stunned. "What the...?" he whispered. Confusion spread through him. *This doesn't make any sense,* he thought.

Maria sat forward in the seat to see to whom Bernie was staring. Seeing Sonny, her eyes instantly brightened. A sound of intense surprise and relief escaped her lips.

In one fluid motion, Sonny opened the front door of the cruiser and slid in beside the policewoman. Nonchalantly, he placed his left arm on the top of the seat and turned to face Colgate and Maria. He looked down and saw the handcuffs shackling Maria's hands. The calmness about him reached her.

Bernie could no longer restrain himself.

"You're under arrest, Mitchell," snapped Bernie confidently.

Sonny just smiled and then looked over at the policewoman.

"Lady, you mind stepping outside for a minute?" His quiet voice held command.

The woman paused, wondering what the hell he meant ordering her about, particularly if he was supposed to be under arrest.

Sonny glanced at Bernie. His piercing eyes were calm but intense.

The woman looked at Colgate for direction.

"Yeah, go ahead," he nodded. "Give him a minute."

The hefty woman pulled herself up from the car seat to her feet, slammed the door from behind, and then walked to the front of the cruiser. Perplexed, she leaned against the front fender.

"You okay?" Sonny asked Maria.

She dropped her eyes, swallowed deeply, and gave him a sullen nod.

Sonny's attention moved back to Colgate.

"Somehow, we got our wires crossed up." He withdrew a blue laminated card from his shirt pocket and handed it to Bernie Colgate.

"If you've got any questions, call Cunningham. Meanwhile, take the cuffs off her."

Maria's gaze was drawn to the blue card Colgate held in his hand. It was laminated in plastic, with a photograph of Sonny looking serious. At the top of the card, printed in bold, gold letters were three words that shocked both Maria and Colgate. National Security Agency.

Bernie Colgate's fingers began shaking, causing him to fumble the card and drop it on the floorboard. Picking it up, his mouth dropping open slightly, he slowly began shaking his head as if denying what he was seeing. He was having difficulty sorting out this new revelation. *This can't be true,* he thought.

"The cuffs," Sonny repeated firmly. "Now," he snapped, snatching his identification from Bernie's trembling fingers.

Somehow, through Bernie's bewilderment and anger, he managed to unlock and release Maria's shackled wrists.

Sonny got out of the cruiser, walked around the vehicle, and opened the door for Maria. Holding her arm tightly, he walked with her toward his waiting limousine.

Forty-Six

Maria could no longer contain her curiosity. She had to know what was going on. She couldn't believe it. *Sonny was with the National Security Agency? Had Michael known?* She wondered.

"Sonny, for God's sake, will you please tell me what's going on?"

"Hold on a second, Little Bit," he said quietly. "Wait until we're in the car, and then I'll fill you in completely." Taking her arm, he guided her around the limousine and opened the rear door.

Stunned beyond comprehension, Maria gasped at what she saw. A multitude of emotions simultaneously ran through her body. She felt her knees weaken and her heart begin to race. *Am I hallucinating? How could this be happening?*

"Oh, my God," she whispered. Her hands went to her face and tears poured freely from her eyes.

Michael was reclining in the back seat. His roguish grin drew Maria to him. Stepping into the vehicle, she fell into Michael's arms. With a small smile on his face, Sonny took a seat beside them and closed the door. As the limousine pulled away from the cruiser, Sonny glanced through the rear window and saw Bernie Colgate still sitting in his car. One leg still hung half out of the open door. An angry expression played across his dispirited face. For an instant,

Sonny felt sorry for the man. Secure in Michael's arms, Maria could not control her sobbing.

"It's all right, baby. Everything's all right now," he kept repeating.

The limousine rounded Cocoplum Circle and pulled out from the exclusive hub onto Old Cutler Road heading south.

Maria pulled away from Michael to look at him. Her eyes were red. Smudges of mascara gave her a clownish look.

"You okay sweetheart?" Michael asked her gently.

Maria sat anchored to her seat. She was experiencing mixed emotions and did not know whether to continue crying and laughing or if she should start raising hell with Michael. Instead, she collapsed back into his arms, her face wet with tears.

Michael smothered a groan as she hugged him. For the first time, she realized that her husband was hurt—seriously hurt. In the excitement of seeing him alive, she had failed to notice the cast on his leg.

"What in the world is going on?" she cried, looking at Michael, then over at Sonny. She had just left Michael's funeral, had almost been arrested by the DEA, had been rescued by Sonny, who just happened to be with the National Security Agency, and now she was sitting beside her "dead" husband. waving a hand. "He's playing on your sympathy, so you won't raise hell, that's all."

Maria twisted in her seat to look at Michael; her face was grim with concern.

Michael grinned and pulled her to him.

"Sweetheart, I'm okay. I promise."

Maria pushed him away. She moved to a neutral position between the two men.

"All right, damn it! I've had it! I'm not a mushroom, and I won't stand being left in the dark any longer. One of you has to tell me what's been going on, or you can stop this car right now and let me out!"

"Now, sweetheart, it's no big …"

"You hush up," she snapped as she turned to face Sonny with an accusing stare.

Sonny hesitated a moment. *She's been through a lot,* he thought. *She deserves to know the truth.* He had to decide exactly what to tell her.

"There's a lot I haven't been able to tell either of you," he began, "not until the accident, anyway."

"Come on, Chubby," Michael cut in, almost pleading. "I've heard this story half a dozen times since waking up on the houseboat. Don't make me listen to it again."

"Be quiet, Michael. I need to hear this," Maria admonished, gently pushing him back against the seat.

"Tell me what's going on, Chubby," she demanded.

Sonny sighed. "All right, but this information has to be confidential. You understand that don't you?"

Maria nodded her acceptance.

As the limousine turned off Southwest 104th Street onto U.S. 1, Sonny began telling Maria of the events leading up to their present situation.

"Six months before I retired from the police department, an old friend connected with National Security came to me with a proposal. I was to become a smuggler. The Agency's primary objective back then was to establish a rapport with the marijuana suppliers in Central and South America. The NSA's goal was that through this association, I could infiltrate some of their various social and political groups. Once established, I would be in a position to act as a barometer, so to speak, regarding communist subversive activities in the Americas."

Sonny continued, "Shit! Back in the early seventies, I hardly knew what marijuana was, much less what a communist was supposed to look and act like. Hell, I still haven't figured it out."

"Anyway, after thinking about it for a couple of weeks, I

decided—what the hell. So, I took the job."

Maria stared at Sonny. What she was hearing reminded her of a James Bond novel. *This is incredible,* she thought.

"Once I began the masquerade, I needed someone I could trust. When I met Michael that day at the hospital I somehow felt, don't ask me why, that Michael was that man. For some reason, I trusted him completely, and I don't trust easily."

Sonny lowered his eyes. "From that point on, it was just a matter of development." He twisted in his seat.

Maria was amazed at what Sonny had just told her.

"I can't believe that our government could permit tons of marijuana to come into this country, not for the sake of information."

"Hell girl, the tons of marijuana we've brought in has never hit the streets!"

Sonny paused and looked at Maria. He cocked his head to the side and grinned. "Well, maybe just a bit," Sonny said sheepishly. "We've got expenses too, you know. We have to go first class. That's the only way we can look convincing as drug smugglers. And you," Sonny barked at Michael, "wipe that shit-eating grin off your face."

"Anyway," Sonny continued, "almost our entire budget goes for the payment of those shipments to suppliers, crew expenses, hotels, boats, etc.. Besides, the value of information and the sources we've managed to develop far exceed any expenditure."

Maria considered Sonny's explanation.

"Why was I being hassled by the DEA?"

Sonny struggled for an answer. He didn't think Maria would like what he had to say. At least, not all of it.

"That was a mistake, damn it! Had communication between the DEA and our other American agencies not broken down, and it happens all too often, Bernie Colgate, or someone like him, could never have happened."

Sonny looked Maria squarely in the eye, pausing for a moment.

His voice became calculating. "Now we have to try to salvage what we can from this Cuban deal."

Maria instantly put her hand out in protest. "Now wait a minute, Sonny. I don't want to hear any more of this! You leave Michael out of it. We've both been through enough. Michael was almost killed."

Sonny's voice was cold as he interrupted her. "Those Cuban bastards are a thorn in Central America. We've recently discovered that Castro has been preparing an invasion force to send into El Salvador. Lucky for us, we managed to quash those efforts. We have no idea what's next on their agenda. That's why this Cuban deal is crucial. We're hoping that after several successful trips, they'll allow us to keep a permanent crew down there. If they do, infiltration of any sort becomes much easier."

Sonny was unconsciously twisting and turning his hands into odd, bizarre contortions. His voice softened.

"That's why I still need Michael's help, Little Bit."

Maria turned to Michael. She realized by his expression that further argument would be useless. Michael's face had a stubborn look, and when she saw that look, which wasn't very often, she knew Michael would have his way. Her shoulders dropped in silent resignation. She leaned forward and snuggled her head on Michael's shoulder. She would have to be thankful and content that her husband was still alive. *God, please, keep him alive,* Maria silently prayed.

Epilogue

Michael stood at the head of the operating room table watching, curiously fascinated at the highly skilled professionalism of the people in green scrubs, who were working behind the green drape at the foot of the table.

His gadget bag and camera equipment lay idle at his feet—forgotten. This moment was too private, too precious to share with anyone except Maria, and through necessity, with the people working so diligently in the sterile room.

A slight chill ran up his back and around his neck causing him to shiver. He folded his arms across his chest, wondering why the germ-free environment had to be kept so cold. *Maybe it's just me,* Michael thought. *Maybe it's just the anticipation after all the waiting and wondering if everything would be okay.*

He had heard it said that when people have a near-death experience, their last memory before unconsciousness is an instant replay of their life. Michael was undergoing a similar phenomenon, but he was not dying. His instant replay had begun eighteen months ago at the time of the speedboat accident. His life, and the direction it had taken, changed that night. He remembered the many agonizing nights that followed. Sonny had sat with him during those long hours of recuperation, talking, forcing him to understand why he had deceived Michael, and the importance and reason for the deception. Strangely, those painful moments alone with Sonny had drawn them closer. Michael had finally forgiven Sonny for his deception. Now he was able to see those past actions from an unfamiliar perspective.

After almost a month in the hospital and Sonny's new revelations, Michael eventually returned to work with Sonny. Their covert activities within the National Security Agency throughout the

Caribbean Basin were yielding tremendous results. The Cuban deal had taken so much of his time, forcing him to neglect Maria. She never complained, but he knew she wanted him out of that life. While he had been in the hospital, Maria hadn't brought it up, but he knew she was so afraid something else would happen to him, and the next time he wouldn't be so lucky.

Maria has changed, he thought. Their bond was stronger, and their relationship had taken on a new and different dimension. This was not to say that their marriage had not been strained for months after the accident. Maria had finally told Michael that she had been terrified of losing him every time he left for one of his and Sonny's ventures. All the money and the luxurious lifestyle Michael's work had given her would never have been worth it if he had been taken from her forever. He had been her soul mate since they had met, and she couldn't have imagined life without him.

Michael looked down at Maria lying on the operating table. She managed to smile at him. Her lower abdomen was stretched open while the doctors worked; yet she felt no pain. A spinal tap had blocked all sensations from her chest to her feet. She licked dry lips and then craned her neck in hopes of watching the procedure. Unfortunately, the green linen curtain draping her torso impeded her vision.

Michael knew Maria was genuinely happy now. His travels had been curtailed by Sonny's promotion to Regional Director for the National Security Agency. He had firmly insisted on Michael becoming his assistant. After Michael's background investigation had been completed, he had been appointed Sonny's special assistant, which delighted Maria. Their lives were finally on the right track, and she felt safe once again because she knew Michael would be safe.

Now that their lives were stable, and after several late-night discussions, they decided to open their hearts and lives to a child again. Losing Jeffrey had been devastating to both of them, and at the time neither thought they would ever want to have another child that could be so easily taken away from them. With the passage of time healing the wounds of their loss, they both realized they needed to be a family again, not just husband and wife.

Michael's vasectomy reversal had been successful, and Maria quickly became pregnant. Today, the moment had finally arrived. After nine months of waiting in anticipation, Michael saw the doctor lift a small, bawling bundle over the green drape, showing them a beautiful, healthy baby boy. Their life was complete once again

The End

Preview

Miracle at Indian Key

By J Thomas Stovall

Chapter 1

Three hundred feet over U.S.1, in the middle of Big Spanish Channel in the Florida Keys, the pelican rode the gentle thermals up and down over the bridge without flapping his wings. It was so quiet he could hear the fishermen on the bridge speaking with each other. Some spoke in English, most spoke in Spanish, but he couldn't understand what they were saying.

This view is spectacular, he thought, as he gazed into the pristine water below. He could see the bottom of the channel, which was at least thirty feet deep, if not more. Out in the distance, the water danced in different colors of emerald-green and turquoise, and finally out in deeper water, purple. To the north, he saw thousands of mangrove trees sprinkled about, which formed what is known as Florida Bay, his home where his friends call him Flapper.

Flapper made a steep right turn, then headed north by northeast along the Seven Mile Bridge. His keen eye spotted a school of mullet circling in a clockwise motion. Tighter and tighter, the school of mullet closed. This was his chance for a quick and easy dinner. He quickly slowed, reduced his altitude to about eighty feet above the fish, and began a slow circle, waiting for the right moment. *Now!* He decided. He lowered his head, folded back his wings, and made a high-speed plunge dive into the water. He caught two mullets in his pouch and headed for the surface. After bobbing up and down, he swallowed his dinner and gracefully took to the air. His belly full and content, he continued his course along the bridge, flying about ten inches above the clear water.

Skye Somers and CJ Jansen were fishing along the catwalk on the Seven Mile Bridge. They would rather have been out on CJ's fourteen-foot McKee Craft, but today the wind was blowing out of the south at about sixteen miles an hour, making the waves too high for CJ's little boat to handle. Reluctantly, they had to settle for fishing on the bridge.

Fifteen-year-old Skye was short and petite. Every year for the past five years, she left her home and parents in Connecticut to spend the summer months with her grandfather, George Hudson, whom she lovingly called Poppy.

She loved the summer vacations at his island home on the water next to Florida Bay on Islamorada. It had a long wide dock. At the end was a twenty-two-foot Seacraft boat hanging from its davits. Her grandfather occasionally allowed her and CJ to take it into deeper water to dive into the reefs.

CJ, on the other hand, lived the year round on Islamorada. He was a sixteen-year-old junior at Coral Shore High School, where he was first in his class. He was tall and gangly, with long skinny arms and legs. Most of his friends told him he should be playing basketball because he was about eight inches taller than most of them. CJ was not an athlete and had no interest in team sports. Sports didn't interest him unless they were on the water.

Skye stood next to her sixteen-year-old companion. She considered CJ her best friend, even though they only saw each other in the summer. Since Skye was so short, the difference in their height was a minor irritant to her, along with the fact that she had to take two steps to his one. Other than those two slight annoyances, she was happy to spend her days enjoying his company. They were a lot alike and enjoyed doing the same things, especially when it involved being on Florida Bay or the Atlantic.

Skye looked down and noticed the pelican. *How does he do that?* she wondered. Her small hands clutched her heavy rod as she leaned out over the bridge railing to get a better look at the bird. It amazed her how he could skim just inches above the water without crashing into a wave. She was envious of this prehistoric yet graceful creature.

Relaxed, satisfied, and enjoying the warm breeze, Flapper had not noticed the fishermen along the bridge railing casting their rods.

One fisherman drew back his rod and heaved with all his might. The heavily weighted hook flew through the air in a high graceful arc. The next moment, searing pain ripped through Flapper's body as the hook took purchase in his right wing.

Almost simultaneously, Skye felt an electric shock shoot up from the back of her neck and into her head. She felt like she was on the brink of passing out but somehow managed to stay on her feet. Something strange was happening to her, and it was frightening. Skye felt she could mentally hear the bird screaming in pain for some unknown reason. Terrified, she wondered, *What is happening to me? Am I dying?*

The fisherman was startled when he realized that he had hooked the bird, which was struggling to stay in the air. He had never caught a bird before. His first instinct was to pull on the line. He quickly realized his mistake and released the tension on the line so that the pelican could have some kind of flight control.

The heavy weight was just too much for Flapper to handle. He heard, and at the same time felt his right-wing snap. He knew it was broken. The only thing he could do was fall into the water. A fast-moving, incoming tide instantly grabbed him and began pushing him toward Florida Bay.

The fisherman panicked and put back the stop on his reel, causing the line to go tight. Flapper began painfully skipping like a pebble across the water as the line held him in the grips of the current.

Help me, please! Somebody, please help me!

Skye's ears were ringing with Flapper's words. *How can I hear the pelican?* she thought. *Am I going crazy?* "He's going to drown," she whispered aloud. She knew she had to do something.

The man holding his rod with the bird attached was less than ten feet to the left of Skye. Instantly she threw her rod on the catwalk and grabbed fishing pliers from the old bait and tackle box her grandfather had given her. Almost simultaneously, she sprang like a tiger toward the fisherman. In less than two seconds, she was next to the man, yanking the rod from his hands and cutting the line with her pliers, freeing the injured bird.

The man just stood there, paralyzed and in shock. *How dare this girl grab my fishing rod*! He thought. Not knowing why Skye had done it, he was enraged.

Skye could only stand there trembling, with adrenaline flowing through her body, staring at the fool who had nearly killed the poor pelican.

Deep in thought, CJ drew his eyes away from the slight tugging of his fishing line and saw Skye cutting the fisherman's line. *What in the world is she doing*? He hadn't noticed that the line was attached to the pelican floundering in the water. He dropped his rod and ran to her side.

"What's going on? What happened?" he questioned, looking into Skye's eyes. Suddenly, her eyes rolled back, and her knees buckled. CJ barely caught her before she hit the catwalk, and then he gently laid her down.

Just before Skye passed out, the last image she had of the pelican was of him being carried by the fast-moving current into the vastness of Florida Bay. He was flapping his good wing, trying to take to the air, but weakened and in terrible pain, his strength was waning. He was out of sight of the bridge within minutes.